OWNING DESTINY

Forsaken Sinners MC Series: Book Four

By Shelly Morgan

OWNING DESTINY

Copyright © 2016 by Shelly Morgan.
All rights reserved.
First Print Edition: September 2016

Limitless Publishing, LLC
Kailua, HI 96734
www.limitlesspublishing.com

Formatting: Limitless Publishing

ISBN-13: 978-1-68058-809-5
ISBN-10: 1-68058-809-5

DEDICATION

This book is for my dad—Roger.

Thank you for all the sacrifices you've made for me and my sisters. You worked yourself sometimes down to the bone. You barely ever took a day off, not even if you were sick or hurt. You rarely did anything for yourself or spent money on things you wanted, but on things me and my sisters needed. You always put your family before yourself, and though I appreciate everything you've done for me, it's my turn to take care of you now.

Mack's book is special to me because I think he's a lot like you; family is everything to him and he'd do anything for them, especially his daughters, even if they aren't blood. Just like you.

So this book is for you, Daddy. I may never become a millionaire off of this and you may not be able to retire, but if I *did*…I've got you.

Love you, Dad.

CHAPTER ONE

Mack

You may never walk again.

That's what the doctor told me almost a month ago, after I took a bullet to the back. Didn't matter that the surgery went well and they were able to get the lead out and fix some of the damage. It grazed my spine, causing irreparable damage. The doctors said there was nothing more they could do, that it was up to my body now to heal what was broken. But my body is being an uncooperative bitch.

There are days when I swear I feel tingling in my toes, only to feel like I'm sucker punched in the gut when I try—and *fail*—to move my legs. The physical therapist comes in daily to make sure I'm doing my exercises, says it will make me stronger, but it ain't doing shit except pissing me off even more.

Nothing is working; not the exercises, not the steroids the doctor put me on, and not the *positive thinking* that Dani and the rest of the girls keep saying I need to do. I'm fed up with all this bullshit. I wish that fucker that shot me was still alive so I could kill him myself. With one shot, he was able to take away everything I hold dear—the ability to ride with my brothers, to stand on my own two feet, and to chase my grandchildren around the fucking yard. The simplest fucking things that I took for granted are now gone in a blink of an eye.

The rage takes over, and I grab the nearest thing I can reach and hurl it across the room. I hear the vase of flowers that Harlow left me yesterday shatter against the door. Fuck those flowers and fuck this hospital. Neither are doing me any fucking good.

"What the—" I hear as the door to my room opens and in walks the only bright side to being laid up in this place, but even she can't seem to shed any light on my mood.

Nurse Rose looks down at the mess I just created on the floor. When she looks up at me, I expect to see pity or disappointment, so when I see fire within her crystal blue depths, I'm thrown off guard. And then she opens that beautiful mouth.

"What the hell is this?" she asks, anger not only evident in her eyes, but her voice as well.

"What does it fucking look like?" I shoot back, just as pissed, if not more so. She only has the mess of glass to pick up. Me? I've got my mess of a body and life to deal with. Somehow, I think what I'm dealing with is worse.

"It looks like you had a tantrum and threw those flowers that were given to you by your daughter," she says, stepping over the mess and crossing over to where I'm sitting up in bed, not even worried about cleaning the shards of glass or wiping up the water.

"A tantrum? You think I'm throwing a fucking tantrum? Let me tell you someth—"

"Yes, a tantrum. And let me tell you something else, Mr. DeVin," Nurse Rose yells, interrupting me. "I understand that you may be upset over what happened to you, and I don't even blame you for being discouraged by your progress. It's normal. But instead of being thankful for what you *do* have, you're throwing a tantrum like a two-year-old boy! You could have *died*. That bullet could have done so much more than it did. So no, you can't walk...*yet*. And you have to work harder than you thought you would to get better, but you still have things to be happy about. You have your life. You still have your family. And there is *still* hope that you *will* walk again. So quit acting like a little *bitch* and man the hell up."

I'm shocked, pissed, and turned on by the way she's speaking to me. Does she not know who the fuck I am?

"Now you listen, and you listen good, *Tiny Rose Chamberlain*. Yeah, I know who you are. And do you want to know *how* I know who you are? I'm the fucking president of the Forsaken Sinners MC. I'm the thing that nightmares are made of. So when you speak to me, you better watch your tone and address me with the respect I fucking deserve," I say in a deadly voice; the same voice I use on men twice her size when I need to get my point across. She may be hot as hell, and I may want to fuck the shit out of

3

her—and her sassy mouth—but she's not dealing with any regular patient. I'm Mack, president of a motorcycle club that's known near and far.

I expected to see fear written all over her face. Maybe confusion as to how I knew her whole name. But what I get is something else entirely.

Glaring at me, she crosses her arms. "Now it's *your* turn to listen, *Michael Scott DeVin*. Yeah, I know your full name too. Do you want to know how? Because I'm Nurse fucking Rose," she says, practically growling her name to show that she's pissed. "I am the head nurse at this hospital and in charge of your care. I deal with patients like you on a daily basis, so you don't scare me. I don't care that you're a part of some biker club. I don't even care that you're the president of said biker club. But if you want me to respect you for your title, then I highly suggest you take into account mine. I will not tolerate you speaking to me in any manner that is rude, threatening, or snide."

I'm speechless and even more turned on now than I was moments ago. Shit, I think I'm more turned on than I have ever been in my whole life. This woman is something else. She's sexy, smart, and has a mouth on her. I not only respect her for her job title, but I respect the hell out of her because she stood up to me. She didn't cower like most people do—men included. But I've never had a woman go toe to toe with me. I kind of like it…but hate it at the same time. I'm so used to people doing as I say…not questioning me or talking back.

"Good. Now that you've shut up for five seconds, do you want to hear why I came in here?"

she says.

Crossing my own arms to match her, I nod. Even though I like the fact she talked back to me and am no longer upset since this has taken my mind off of my problems, I don't want her to rest easy just yet. I want her guard to stay up because I love watching her like this. I never thought arguing with a woman would make me hot with want.

Letting her arms fall to her sides, her face loses a little of the tightness and anger, but not completely. "Like I said before, I know you're aggravated and disappointed with the way you've been progressing—or rather, lack thereof—I took it upon myself to look for other treatment options. And I think I may have found something that may work. At least, it's worth a try anyway."

She stares at me with patience and maybe a little bit of eagerness. When I still haven't answered, she starts getting irritated.

"Are you going to ignore me now? Did I hurt your feelings or wound your male complex a bit?" The words come out with attitude and mockery, but I also notice a little bit of disappointment and hurt. I wonder if it's because she doesn't think I'm interested in this new therapy or trust her knowledge. But she's way off.

When she huffs out a long sigh and turns around to leave, I finally reply, "What's the treatment consist of?"

At my question, she stops but doesn't turn around. She's probably contemplating whether or not she should tell me what she found or just leave. I wouldn't blame her if she did. I'm not the easiest person to get along with on a normal day. But with everything that's going on now, I'm probably not her favorite patient. If I was even her favorite in the first place.

After standing there silent with her back facing me, she finally turns around. She doesn't move to come closer again, but at least she didn't leave.

"Massage therapy. Some studies show that if you massage the area where the damage is, it may stimulate the nerves and muscles enough to allow feeling and movement back into the parts that are affected with possible paralysis. I have no idea if it will work or not, but I think it's definitely worth a shot."

I don't know what to think about what she just told me. Nothing else has worked, so why this? And if this was an option, why hasn't the doctor suggested it already? But she's right; it is worth a try. It's not like I have anything to lose. I'm not going to get my hopes up though; it probably won't work anyway.

"Okay. I'll try it. Where do I need to go and who should I call to make the appointment? I have no idea where there's a place that would do that, and it doesn't sound like something the hospital would do."

A small smile plays on her lips after I speak and I wonder why it's there. Is she just happy because I'm agreeing or is there something more?

"Actually, I'll be the one doing the massages for you. I majored in nursing, but I also have a license in massage therapy and medical massage," she says with pride.

The only thing I can do is stare at her. Everything that's happened in the last five minutes is enough to make me dizzy.

When her face falls from my lack of response, I snap out of it. I don't want her to feel even an ounce of regret or see any of that pride I saw in her eyes fade because of me. She has every right to be proud of her accomplishments. Some people can't even make it through nursing school. But she not only did that, but she added classes on top of her already heavy load. I'm finding that this woman is pretty fucking amazing.

"When do we start?" I ask, eager for her to touch me, eager for her to work her magic on my body.

With resolve and determination, she steps forward, rubbing her hands together. "Right now."

***

Over the next few weeks, Rose and I get in a routine. I can't say that it's a comfortable one, but I look forward to it every day. We're more comfortable with each other after our showdown. It's feels nice—*normal* even, considering the circumstances.

She comes into my room at two o'clock every day. She's never early and never late. One day I asked her if she stands outside my door waiting until the exact moment her watch hits two. She didn't laugh or blush or even shrug it off like I thought she would. Instead, she just said, "No, I'm just very good at timing things." I didn't question her or make fun of her because I have to admit it's a quality I like about her. It means she's dependable, and when you're in a position like mine, you want dependable.

When it's one-fifty-nine, I sit up in bed and stare at the door with a smile on my face, waiting for her to come walking in with a handful of oils and *special lotion*, as she likes to call it. But when the door opens and in walks my brothers Blaze, Louie, Toby, Skinner, Jax, and Tom Tom, I feel a pang of disappointment because it's not her. I don't think I've ever been disappointed when it comes to my brothers, and it pisses me off that she's made me feel this way now.

"How are ya, brother?" Blaze asks as he sits down beside my bed.

Louie takes a seat on my other side, Toby stands off behind him, Tom Tom is beside Blaze, Skinner has plopped down onto the small couch in the room, looking exhausted, and Jax stands in the distance beside the door.

Shaking the anger and disappointment off, I turn toward Blaze. "I'll be better once I can get out of this bed and walk around on my own two feet instead of being fucking wheeled around everywhere." Every time a nurse has to help me get in and out of bed, every time they have to help me do the basic everyday tasks that I can no longer do myself, or every time I see one of my brothers walk out of my room, a little piece of myself withers away. *Will I ever be able to walk out of this hospital, or will I be riding out of here on four little wheels?*

"We saw Nurse Rose outside your door before

we came in. She says you're progressing well. And it sounds like you'll be able to come home in a few days if all goes well. Maybe even as soon as tomorrow. We can hire someone to come to the clubhouse to continue your care." Louie is the one to speak this time.

My ears perk up at the sound of Rose's name. I barely even register what else he said. I can't stop thinking about her outside my door. A rush of anger washes over me. They got to see her before I did. And what's more, my brothers are preventing her from entering my room. I know it's irrational to be angry at them, especially when I'm sure the reason they're all here is for club business, but still. I need my dose of sunshine in this never-ending darkness.

But then the rest of Louie's words start to sink in. "Wait, what do you mean I'll be able to go home in a few days? I can't fuckin' walk! I can't even feel my goddamn legs," I yell, the anger from missing my daily dose of Rose now morphing into anger about my lack of ability.

"Mack, brother, I can understand that you are pissed. Shit, I'm pissed *for* you. But the progress you've made in the last couple of weeks is more than you made in the month since you've been shot. Being at home and continuing your physical therapy, you'll be walking in no time," Tom Tom says, and I know he's right. But fuck me, I still can't help but be angry. I just don't know if I'm angry because I still can't walk and may not be able to like I want to again, if I'm mad because I still haven't laid eyes on my sexy-as-fuck nurse, *or* maybe it's because I'll be leaving here soon and that means I'll be leaving the only thing that has brightened up my days since getting a bullet in the back. Well, besides my family, that is.

Ignoring Tom Tom's comment and words of wisdom, I turn my attention back to Blaze. "What are you all doing here? This doesn't seem like a tea and cookies type of visit. What's going on?" I ask, getting right down to business. And I know that this is exactly that; club business. Otherwise, they wouldn't all be here. Sure, they come to visit, but usually it's just one or two at a time. And even though my whole club isn't here, I can still tell this is more than a friendly visit.

Blaze straightens up in the chair he's sitting in, Louie leans forward with his hands clasped in front of him, and Jax moves away from the door to stand closer to my bed. "We've got a meeting set up tonight with the Kings. Gutter set it up, said he wants a truce." Blaze speaks with an edge in his voice, so I know there's more to it than that.

"You think it's a trick?" I ask, everything else I was feeling or thinking taking a backseat. I'm now in president mode, even though Blaze is acting president while I'm out of commission.

"We've heard chatter on the bug we left in their clubhouse from when Harlow was taken." This comes from Toby.

I look at each of my brothers, trying to decipher what it is they heard, but they give nothing away.

"And..." I prompt.

"And we heard enough to know this is a fluke. They have no real intention of calling a truce, but we can't figure out what it is they *are* trying to gain from this meeting," Louie answers. His voice would sound calm and collected to an outsider, but I can hear the undertone of his unease and rage.

Louie is still pissed about what happened to Harlow and the part the Kings played in it. I don't blame him one bit. Even though they weren't the ones specifically that took Harlow, they were a part of it even if they didn't know full on what was going on. Titus was a part of their club, doesn't matter if it was a different chapter. They would have backed him regardless of right or wrong, whether they got something out of it or not.

Letting out a long breath, I ask, "So what's the plan?" I'm not used to asking instead of telling, but I'm leaving this in the hands of Blaze. I know he won't steer this club in the wrong direction, and even though I appreciate they came to me with this, he is the president for the time being, so it's his decision.

A look of pride and determination overtakes Blaze's face. Me stepping back and allowing him to be in charge lets him know I trust him and realize that he's capable of leading this club. Fuck, I couldn't be prouder of him. He's come a long way since transferring years ago, but getting Dani back in his life and having the twins has changed him. He's more in control and has a leadership quality about him. He's a damn good kid and I feel comfort knowing he's stepping into my position completely—and he's doing a fine fucking job of it too.

"We're going, but we're going in hot and heavy. I want all the brothers in on this. I don't know if they have something up their sleeve for when we arrive or if they want us distracted, but either way, I want to be ready for anything. They actually wanted to set the meeting up for tomorrow, but I didn't want to give them even more time to set up a trap, if that's their intention. So we meet tonight."

Taking a few minutes to think about what he just said, I rub the scruff on my chin before I nod my head in agreement and add in my two cents. "I agree with you on that one, brother. The sooner, the better. But if you have every brother there with you, who will be with the girls? I wouldn't trust the prospects with them just yet. If someone comes after them while you and the rest of the brothers are at the meet, they'll need more than just the prospects there to protect them. We don't know if they'll crack under pressure."

It's not that I don't completely trust the prospects, but being that they're new, we haven't been able to test their commitment as well as I'd like. And I really don't want to do that with the safety of the girls and the twins. Plus, I'm still bitter about the fact that one of our prospects turned traitor a few years back and helped Sara's ex kidnap her and Dani. He blew up our clubhouse in the process, nearly killing Louie and succeeded in killing Lyle. So no, I don't trust them with my loved ones yet.

A smile breaks free from Blaze's serious expression. "Well, I'm glad you think that too, because they'll be here soon to stay with you while we're at the meet."

Now I understand the smile. Don't get me

wrong, I love those three girls and consider them my own flesh and blood, but having to babysit them while they know something is going on? Let's just say that tonight is going to be hell. I may have to have the boys chain them down to the chair before they leave.

"You think you're funny, huh, you little shit? You know damn well that this isn't going to fly well with them. And to leave a defenseless old crippled man alone with those three women all night? That's just cruel," I say, only half joking. I'm not old by any means at forty-four, though sometimes I feel like I'm in my sixties, and it has nothing to do with anything physical since I was in perfect shape and health before getting shot. But sometimes, the stress from being in charge of the club and everything riding on my shoulders makes me feel older than I actually am. Regardless of age or how I felt then or now, I know they will be safe here with me. Paralyzed or not, I wouldn't let anyone hurt them.

They all laugh at my words, but I'm not mad. It's the first time I've been able to joke around about my condition, and it actually feels good. Maybe I'm not doomed after all, even if I will never walk again.

"Actually, they were really happy when we told them what was going to happen. They didn't throw a fit like they usually do. It's like they *wanted* to come here, like it was their idea even," Louie says after he's able to stop laughing.

"Yeah, but you won't hear me complaining. We can figure out what they're up to after the meeting," Toby says, and I can see a hint of concern in his

13

eyes. He doesn't like not knowing what's going on with his woman.

"Well, somebody better bring me Betty. I'll need her in case shit goes south while the girls are here." I don't know how it will go over with the hospital when they bring me Betty—my favorite Berretta hand gun—but they'll just have to get over it. No way in hell I'm going to have my daughters here without some way to protect them. Ain't gonna fuckin' happen.

"We have a prospect bringing it up as we speak," Jax says finally. I almost forgot he was here. There's something going on with him that has him quieter and more guarded than usual. One thing's for sure…after this shit is taken care of and I'm out of this place, him and I are going to have a talk. It's time he comes clean about what's up with him.

A few seconds later, one of our prospects—Dusti—comes walking into the room with Betty concealed under his arm. Handing it over without a word and leaving the room as quietly as he came, I slip it into the drawer beside my bed with a hand towel thrown over top.

Then, pointing over to where my cut hangs on the door of the little closet, I wait for Blaze to bring it to me. I don't wear it much here even though I feel naked without it…but since anything could happen, I want it on.

Blaze hands it over and I put it on with little trouble. It's still a little difficult to maneuver and get things on, but it's easier now.

Turning toward my brothers, I say, "Come by after the meet. I want to know what's going on. It's killing me not to be there with my brothers," I say the last part through gritted teeth. I should be out there with them, *leading* them, not in this fucking hospital bed.

"That's the plan, brother. Plus, we want to pick the girls up to make sure they're protected after they leave here just in case the reason for the meet was to get us away from them," Blaze answers. Even though I don't like the sound of the girls being in danger one bit, I know that if they are ridin' with their men, they'll be safe. Or safer.

I nod in agreement, then shoo them out of the room.

"All right, now that that's all taken care of, get the fuck outta here so I can do my therapy session." I can't help the smile that overtakes my face knowing that Rose will be here soon, with her hands all over my body. Just not in the places I want her to be.

"Yeah, yeah, old man. We know what you're really wanting, but whatever it takes to get you better," Louie replies, but his words have me remembering something I wanted to talk to him about.

"Louie, why don't you hang back for a second? I want to have a word."

The rest of my brothers nod their goodbyes and promise to come back after the meet to talk about what happened. I tried to get Skinner's attention before he walked out the door, but he just slowly got up from the couch and walked out of the room with obvious strain. There's something going on with him but I don't know what. He seems sick or

15

something. Usually he's the first to put his two cents in since he's my VP, but today, he didn't even say a word about what is about to happen or what he thinks. Guess I'll have to wait to corner him once I get back home.

As soon as Louie and I are alone, I level him with a serious look.

"How's Harlow holding up?" I ask, worried about her. I know she'll be here soon, but I want a heads up before she gets here. I need to make sure she's doing all right. I hate that I haven't been there to help her through this after she was taken.

I've seen her quite a few times since everything went down because she visits me as often as she can, but I haven't wanted to bring up old hurts.

After she was released from the hospital and was on the road to recovery, Louie made a promise to her that the man who caused her brother and stepsister harm would pay for his sins. Harlow insisted that she be there. We all fought with her on it at first, but Louie finally decided it was her place to be there anyway. She was the one that suffered. I just hope it hasn't caused any adverse side effects to her already fragile mind.

She's been dealing with PTSD after her attack from Titus, and we don't need to see the man that caused so much damage to her causing any more problems.

Sighing, he takes a seat once more. "I was concerned at first. After the deed was done by her hand, I thought she'd break down or something, but there was nothing. She was quiet and closed off. I worried about pushing her too far after what had happened with Titus, but she surprised me. She never had one episode after we returned, even though she still didn't seem right."

Louie shakes his head, but when he looks back up at me, I see relief wash over his face. "We finally talked it through, and I think she's gonna be all right. Like, really all right, about everything. It's like this was a part of her healing process or something. It's allowed her to work everything out of her system—the fear, anger, and sadness—and now there's just Harlow left. She still seems a little different, she's harder, but I think that's good for her. But she doesn't appear to have any of the PTSD or anger. She's back to her old self—just stronger."

I see nothing but happiness in his eyes and I feel better knowing that after allowing her to go with him to kill her adoptive father, there will be no lasting side effects. If anything, it's made things better for her. I couldn't be happier about that. Harlow has been through so much in the past few years...Louie as well. They both deserve a break and to be truly happy for once.

"Glad to hear it, son. Damn glad to hear it," I say, then reach out my hand to the man I took in all those years ago. A man I think of like a son.

Seconds after Louie leaves my room, in walks Rose and I feel a smile tip my lips. "Damn, you're good. Timed it perfectly," I say.

"Like I said, I'm good at timing things." She winks before she gets me set up for my massage.

This woman is going to be the death of me, but fuck if I could even force myself to care. If what I feel when she comes near me and looks at me with that twinkle in her eye is what kills me, then I'll go willingly. Best way to fucking go, if you ask me.

CHAPTER TWO

Rose

Setting the oils down on the table beside Mack's bed, I head into the bathroom like I do every day when I come in here to do his massage. I've told him it's to wash my hands before we start—which is true—but it's also because I have to get myself into check and take a few moments to compose myself.

Every time I'm in his room, my heart rate picks up and my palms become sweaty. I don't know what it is that he does to me, but I don't like it. I wish I could say that it's fear that causes my reaction, or even dislike, but that would be a bold-faced lie. I'm attracted to him but I don't want to be.

Though I've only ever seen him lying in the bed and never standing, I know he's tall just by the fact that his feet practically hang over the end of the bed. He's muscular and looks fit, even after being bedridden for almost a month. I'm sure he's lost

19

some weight, but his build is still huge. His arms are what stand out the most to me and I think those have gotten bigger since the first time I saw him, which would make sense since he's having to use them all the time to lift his weight.

I like how he doesn't look like a body builder, though. He's big, but not *too* big. Like in an unnatural way. I've always hated how people look who do competitions and all that stuff. I mean, it's cool that they're dedicated and want to do it, but it just looks odd. On both male and female. But to each their own, I guess.

Then there's his strong jaw line with a little bit of hair that is barely gray. I know by looking at his chart he isn't really old—only six years older than me—but the gray works for him; makes him even sexier.

And his tattoos. I've always had a thing for tattoos, but the ones I've been able to see on the top part of his body are mesmerizing. It's like they tell the story of his life. I wish I had the time to really study them, but every time I try while I'm giving him his massage, I get too worked up and have to look away and think about something else.

But the thing that I keep coming back to is the fact that he's a part of a motorcycle club. And the president, to boot. I don't need to get mixed up with that. I've already been involved in one club against my wishes, I don't need to *willingly* associate with one.

No, Mack is my patient, and that's where it must stay. It doesn't matter if I'm attracted to him or if he seems different than any of the other bikers I've met before. It doesn't matter if every time I look into his deep green eyes, I feel like I was lost and now I've been found. He's bad news. I need to remember that.

After washing my hands, I take a deep breath before heading back into the room. Mack lies there and watches my every move, and damn it if that doesn't put me back to frustrated all over again. So much for getting myself together in the bathroom. I might as well not even do it anymore. It never works. The way I feel around him doesn't change, and, if anything, it just gets stronger with every passing day.

"Are you ready to get started?" I ask in a calm voice that belies my shaky interior.

"Whenever you are," he replies, then he grabs the remote for his bed and starts to lower it so he's lying flat.

I notice as he starts to roll over that he's already removed his shirt while I was in the bathroom. His stomach is completely visible to me now and I can see every ripple and ridge of his abdominal muscles and even a hint of the most defined oblique muscle line I've ever seen. His abs flex and grow hard as steel as he maneuvers himself on the bed.

My eyes then move toward his biceps that bulge from the movement to get himself turned over and situated. The tattoos on his huge arms move so it's like I'm watching a movie. My mouth waters and my panties are soaked by just watching him. It's as if I'm watching live porn, but without the sex.

It takes him a little longer to get completely turned over so he's lying on his stomach, but I never once moved to try and help him. Not because I literally couldn't force myself to move or get my eyes off of his body to make a coherent thought, but because this is something he needs—to do things on his own. There are so many tasks he can no longer do without help, so having this one thing he can accomplish by himself…it's a victory for him. And even though I hate to watch him struggle and want to help him—when I'm not drooling over him—I don't.

As soon as he's situated, he turns his head to look at me. He's sweating a little and out of breath with the exertion, but he has a look of pride in his eyes that I will never get tired of. It's there every time he does something, but my love of seeing it doesn't fade. And I hope it never does.

I make my way over to the table to grab some oil to start his massage. I always start with oil to loosen up his muscles and it makes it easier for my hands to slide over his body. *God, I wish my hands were sliding over a different part of his body right now.*

Shaking my head to try and dislodge the visual of his hard cock in my hand or filling my pussy, I think of everything but the man lying beneath my hands; my other patients, or the bills that I need to pay tonight when I get home. But it's the last one that really has the fantasies coming to a screeching halt—*my brother*. Yeah, thinking of him always does the trick.

I breathe out a sigh, irritated with myself for not being able to keep my thoughts and fantasies in check. *What the fuck is wrong with me?*

"Everything all right?" Mack asks.

Great, now I have to try and come up with an excuse. No way in hell I'm going to tell him I was just imagining my hand on his cock. Or anything about my brother.

"Yeah. Just had a long day is all," I reply, and it's not even a lie. Today has felt like it's dragged on forever.

Usually my days at the hospital go by fast; I come in around six in the morning, catch up on some paperwork, do my rounds, then come in here to do Mack's massage. Then I log any progress I see from our session before doing another quick round to see my patients before heading home. And today was no different, but everything just seemed to drag at a snail's pace. I'm ready to go home, take a long hot bath, and catch up on a few episodes of *The Vampire Diaries*.

A sad smile takes over his face before he asks, "Do you want to talk about it?"

I can't help the laugh that comes out of my mouth. It sounds harsh even to me, so when Mack seems to physically recoil from me, I want to slap myself.

"It may come as a shock to you, being a low-life biker and all, but I'm actually pretty fucking good at holding my own in a conversation." He's on the defensive now and I don't blame him one bit. I can be a real bitch sometimes, even when I don't try to be.

Look at what happened a few weeks ago when I came in to find the remnants of Mack's rage. And even though I knew he must be upset about what's happened and the fact that he still can't walk, I went right into bitch mode. I yelled at him and basically called him a brat. I've never been shy when it comes to voicing my opinion or being the stronger voice when it comes to my patients, or anyone else around me, but I've never been as bold and blunt as I was with Mack that day. It's just that it seems like he's the type that is so used to being in control that he'd need a heavier hand. And it worked, although we both were probably a littler harsher than we normally would be. Mack brings out the worst in me, it seems.

I still think back to that day and can't believe I wasn't scared. When he called me by my full name, I was shocked, but more pissed than anything. It's no secret I prefer to be called by Rose. Shit, most people don't even know my real first name, only my middle name. But he knew. He must have looked into me and done his research. It makes me angry and a little flattered he would do that, though I'm sure he does it for everyone he comes into contact with, not just me. I just hope when he looked into me he didn't find anything I don't want him to find. But that should be impossible after all the trouble I went through to erase everything that tied me to my brother.

Mack moving around on the bed has me snapping back to the present. He looks even more aggravated than I feel, though I can't tell if it's the course our conversation has taken or with the state of his condition. Either way, I feel bad and want to fix it. I don't want to leave when he's upset, no matter if it's at me or about something different.

"Hey, look, I didn't mean it in the way you took

it. I'm sure you are a great listener and—" I start but am cut off before I can explain further or make this better.

"Forget it," he growls, then grunts with effort to get himself turned over. "Why don't you just leave? I'm done with this shit."

His voice is angry and hard as steel, but I can't pay attention to that right now.

"Mack, did you—"

"I said get out!" he yells, interrupting me again.

Screw this. I'm done with his shit. I don't care if he's pissed at me or at himself, but he's going to fucking listen to me.

"Mack," I yell, getting his attention finally, though he doesn't seem happy about it. Tough shit. "Did you move your leg?" I ask in a calmer voice, hopefully relaying my excitement about what I think I just saw, but it doesn't work. The fog of his anger isn't allowing my words to get through to him the way they should. Either that, or he's just that much of a prick.

"What the fuck did you just ask me? Did I move my leg? For fuck's sake, listen to yourself! I've been trying to move my damn legs since I got here. For a nurse, you're sure dumb in the head."

I take a calming breath because I know he doesn't mean that. It's the anger and the disappointment talking, so I let it slide. This time.

"Try to move your right leg," I order him, moving my eyes from his face to his leg. Crossing my arms, I wait for him to obey, praying that my eyes weren't deceiving me moments ago.

Huffing and mumbling under his breath things

that I should probably be glad I can't hear, Mack does as he's told.

At first, I don't see anything—not even a shake of movement. But it's when he's given up and beginning to tell me off again I'm sure I see it. It's the smallest of movements, but it's there.

"Did you see that?" I question, excitement in my voice. This is great news for him!

He doesn't answer me, but when I chance a look up at him, I see confusion and even a little bit of wonder on his face. Then determination takes over, and I look back down to his legs, and this time, the movement is bigger.

"Oh my God, Michael! You did it. You're moving your leg," I say, then rush over to take his hand. I don't know what came over me, but I'm so ecstatic with this new development that I need to be near him, I need to touch him. I need to break him out of the shock he's in from the realization that he's moving his leg on his own. The massage sessions have been working, along with the medicine and physical therapy. He's getting better.

Moving his head toward me, his stunned silence now broken, he smiles at me. I thought it was because of his progress, but his words confuse me. "Say that again."

I don't understand. He just saw it with his own eyes. But if that's what it takes for him to fully get it, then I'll say it a hundred times. "You did it. You moved your leg. This is great news. It shows tha—"

"No, not that. The other part," Mack says, interrupting me, leaving me even more confused.

But then it hits me. It's not what I told him, it's

what I *called* him. I used his real name and not his nickname. That has to be what he's talking about. "Oh my God, I'm so sorry, Mack. I didn't even realize I said that," I say, upset with myself for letting his given name slip past my lips. There is a reason he doesn't go by that name anymore and I need to respect that. After all, I'd want the same respect, since I don't like my given name either.

"Say it again," he repeats, but there's something about his tone and the way he's smiling at me. He doesn't seem mad like I thought he'd be.

Sighing, I give in to his wishes. "Michael," I breathe out quietly, still a little unsure about calling him that even though he pretty much demanded it.

His smile gets even bigger and I can't help it when my heartbeat picks up and my own mood soars. When this man smiles, it lights up a whole room to the point you can't help but smile back.

"I haven't been called that in so long I almost forgot that's my real name. I always hated that name, but hearing you say it…I kind of like it," he says, squeezing the hand I forgot was still holding his.

I'm speechless. What do you say to something like that? Um, thanks? You're welcome?

Thinking it better to just not say anything at all, I return his smile a little shyly. I still can't believe I slipped and called him that. At least he's not mad about it. And now that I think of it, I do like calling him by his real name. It's different than what everyone else calls him. I like that no one else calls him Michael. Only me. I just hope it stays that way and he doesn't decide to start having everyone call him that now, even though I have no right to hope for that. He's not mine and never will be. And I don't want him to be mine, either. Not now, not ever. He's a biker. I need to remember that.

Suddenly, there's a knock on the door and a woman says, "Knock, knock," before the door starts to open. Realizing I'm still holding Mack's hand— or rather he seems to be holding mine—I pull my hand out of his grasp and take a quick step back.

I hear tiny, loud footsteps running before I see them. Two little kids—one boy and one girl—race into the room and yell, "Papa," simultaneously. Once their little feet bring them to Mack's bed, they jump at the same time, but each on a different side. Mack reaches out both hands and seems to be able to grab a hold of both children without too much trouble. His arms are long and strong enough that really the only trouble he had was trying to sit up in time to catch them.

I knew Mack had grandkids and I could see just by the way he spoke of them when I was around that he loves them dearly. But seeing him firsthand with them is a sight to behold. Here's this big, tough, and rough-looking man who's the president of a motorcycle club being gentle and loving to these children. I guess I just never imagined him being this way. Loving them and protecting them, yes. Talking about them and even playing with them a bit, yeah, I could even see that. But this— what I'm seeing now—is more than I thought possible.

The boy and girl have climbed completely on the bed and are now each sitting on his lap. At least he's big enough that they can both fit, though there's the bed beneath him, so it's not like they would be at risk of falling or not having enough room.

Mack starts to tickle them and laughter and giggles fill the room. It brings a big smile to my face. I love the sound of children laughing. I've always loved kids, though I wasn't sure if I'd have any. Or even want a child. Plus, you have to have a man to do that, and I could never find a man that was to my liking. I'd get bored before things got too serious, but I guess that's a good thing.

"Shocking, isn't it?" a woman's voice asks, making me jump. I was so caught up watching Mack with the kids that I didn't even pay attention to who came in with them.

Turning around to face the woman talking to me, I notice two more standing beside her. Three women, who are Mack's daughters, are standing there looking at Mack like I was moments ago.

The woman closest to me is Dani. She's the mother of the kids still giggling from Mack's tickles. I've seen her the most around here, visiting and checking in with me and the doctors on the progress of Mack's condition. Dani is beautiful in a badass biker chick sort of way, but it fits her like a second skin. She's so confident and bold.

The woman next to her is Harlow. She's the one who brought the flowers Mack threw across the room a few weeks ago. She seems to be younger than the other two, but I can't be one hundred percent sure. Harlow is both quiet and outspoken at the same time. It's strange really that she can be

29

both, but, like Dani, it fits her.

And then there is Sara. I don't see her like I do the others but I know she stops by as much as the other two do...I'm just never around when she does. I think she mainly comes at night after I've left for the day. I heard around the hospital that she works at a gym that helps battered women and children. What she does is amazing. Maybe on one of my days off I'll go down and see what I can do to help.

I nod to Dani's question even though she isn't looking at me, but I think it was more a rhetorical question anyway. Fuck, maybe it even still shocks *her* seeing Mack with her kids.

All three of the women move further into the room; Dani moving to the right side of the bed, Harlow and Sara on the left.

"All right, children, that's enough. Leave Papa alone," Dani says sternly, but I can hear the happiness in her voice. She loves the sight before her. I have to say, so do I. It's such a contradiction of what you'd expect from someone like Mack. He's a rough biker. He's as big as a truck and could kill someone with just one finger I'm sure. But with these children, he's as soft as a flower. It's humbling to watch.

"But, Mama—" the little girl starts to argue.

"Don't talk back to your mother," Mack says. His face is cut in hard lines but there's still a twinkle in his eye as he addresses the little girl.

She pouts a little bit, but she doesn't try to argue any more, gently getting off the bed and running toward the window, already preoccupied with watching what's going on outside.

The little boy is silent as he gets off the bed too, though he doesn't look upset about the order from his mother. There's something strangely older about the boy even though he couldn't be older than three. He's quiet and watchful, guarded and thoughtful. Definitely not what you'd expect from a toddler.

"So," Dani says, setting a large bag I didn't notice down by the side table before taking out a baggy of Gold Fish, two sippy cups, and coloring books. "How have the massages been going? Any progress?"

I open my mouth, my excitement from earlier coming back, to tell her about what happened moments before they came in, but one look at Mack has me snapping my mouth shut again. He's looking at me pointedly, like he's trying to convey a message to me, but I have no idea what it could be. Does he not want me to tell them about his progress? Or does he want to be the one to tell them the good news?

"It's going well, but no progress yet," Mack replies, and I'm flabbergasted that he's not telling them he was able to move his leg. I thought for sure he'd be jumping for joy about it and even happier to tell his family about it, but he's not, and I can't figure it out.

The three women look from Mack to me, questions in their eyes. I feel put on the spot with their eyes drilling into mine. But if he doesn't want to tell them yet, then I won't say anything either.

"Yes, things have been going great. Mack's body seems to be responding well to the massages. I have a good feeling about this form of treatment and know that he'll be walking again soon," I say, happy with my words. I didn't lie, but I didn't break Mack's trust in me.

My words seem to put the women at ease. They all take a seat around Mack's bed and start talking to each other about him getting released soon and the welcome home party they want to throw.

Mack isn't paying any attention to them though, looking right at me with a look I can't decipher. It's strange and intense at the same time. I look toward the window where the children are quietly babbling to each other in what sounds like gibberish, but is probably twin talk.

Suddenly, I feel out of place, like I'm intruding. Here Mack is with his daughters and grandchildren and I'm standing in the back looking in. I shouldn't be here. I finished his massage and now it's time for me to go.

"Well, if you'll excuse me, I really should be going," I say to no one in particular before turning around and reaching for the door.

"I'll see you tomorrow, same time?" I hear Mack ask. Turning my head to look at him over my shoulder, I see him staring at me with a small smile gracing his lips.

Returning the smile, I reply, "I'll be here."

Opening the door, I hear him yell after me, "Don't be late." It makes me laugh. He and I both know I'm never late.

I don't answer him, but I can't help the smile that won't leave my face. Mack is getting better and I couldn't be happier for him. But when I remember what his daughters were talking about, my smile fades to a frown. He's getting released soon, which means he'll be gone and I'll probably never see him again. This man is everything I thought I'd never want in my life—patient or not—yet I can't help but feel the loss of his presence. Tomorrow very well could be the last day I have with him.

My mood takes a nosedive as I rush into the locker room to grab my things. I should stay and do my final rounds but I can't stand to be in this place any longer with the knowledge that soon he will no longer be here.

Slipping past the nurse's station without being noticed, I make my way to my car in a daze. Why can't I get it through my head that Mack is just a patient and nothing more? Everything about him should turn me off, so how come I can't stand the thought of going a day without seeing him, talking to him, *touching* him?

Something white on my windshield catches my attention as I round the hood of my old beat up Ford Taurus. It's a piece of paper, but I have no idea what it is or why it's here. I know for a fact it's not a parking ticket because I have my pass displayed on my windshield and I'm in the employee parking lot. But if not a parking ticket, what could it be?

Pulling it out from under my windshield wiper, I read the words that turn my stomach and have chills breaking out all over my body.

Sister Dearest—
I have a surprise for you...

CHAPTER THREE

Mack

It's been a few hours since Rose walked out of my room, but I can't help but to look at the door every few seconds. A part of me prays that she comes back in. Maybe she'd have an excuse like she left something here, but we'd both know that's a fuckin' lie.

"You seem happy," I hear Dani say.

Moving my eyes away from the door, I look at her. She has a big shit-eating grin on her face and looks smug as fuck. On any other day, I'd probably give her hell and deny what she thinks is going on between me and the sexy as hell nurse, but she's right about me being happy. Today was a good day. For reasons she probably thinks she knows and reasons she doesn't yet know. But that doesn't mean I'm going to play into her hand or make it easy on her.

"Well, yeah. I have three beautiful ladies in my room," I say with a wink.

"Phor beetful gores, Papa," Harley says from the window.

Laughing, I say, "Yes, Harley Bear, four beautiful girls. How could I forget about you?" She graces me with dazzling smile, then turns back around to look out the window. The girls laugh with me but they don't comment. Harley is like her mother in a lot of ways. She likes to know she's right and always has to have the last word.

I love all my daughters, though. They are more than beautiful, which is where my granddaughter gets her beauty. But Dani, Sara, and Harlow all have spunk, which they need when dealing with their men. They've all been through hell, but have risen above it and come out the other side stronger. And they all have this glow about them that lets me know how happy they are. I love these three women more than I ever thought I could love someone.

I never thought I'd have children of my own, didn't even want any, but the day they each walked into my life, I couldn't have been happier. I love them as if they were my own flesh and blood. I'd do anything for them. They are my daughters in every way that matters.

"Uh huh. So it has nothing to do with the fact that *Nurse Rose* was just here?" Harlow teases, then chuckles.

I have half a mind to tell them about the progress I made during my massage today just to get them off the subject of Rose, but I don't. I'm not ready to tell them yet. A part of me is worried it was only a fluke; that the movement I was able to make won't last. I don't want to tell them so they get their hopes

35

up for nothing.

And then the other part of me doesn't want to share the moment Rose and I seemed to have after I was able to move my leg. The way she said my real name with excitement, the smile on her face, and the way she took my hand in hers. It was like she really cared about the fact I was getting better—that she had hope for me when I had lost it for myself.

Needing to change the subject, I cross my arms and give each of the girls a pointed look. "Speaking of happy...what's going on with you three? It's usually like pulling teeth from a lion trying to get you to sit back while the men go out on club business. I actually thought I'd have to chain ya'll down."

I thought me turning the line of questioning back to them would have them dropping the smug smiles on their faces, but instead, their smiles just get bigger. Now I'm really worried.

"What the fuck is going on?" I say with more edge in my voice. I hate not being in the know. Before I got shot, I knew everything that went down in my club; who was fucking who, where everyone was at, and what needed to be done. Now, I feel like I don't know jack shit.

The smugness drops from their faces but they're still smiling. I wish I could find comfort in that, but I can't.

Sara is the first to speak. "Well, we thought that bringing you some good news might cheer you up. So there's something I'd like to tell you," she says, but doesn't elaborate. I try to not show my irritation, but I'm not sure if I succeed. If they can tell though, they don't comment.

"Well, are ya going to tell me or make me guess?" I say after she doesn't say anything further.

Sitting up straighter in her chair with the biggest smile I think I've ever seen, she says excitedly, "I'm pregnant."

I feel like a fish out of water, my mouth is opening and closing with words that won't come to me.

Shock was the first feeling to come because I was not expecting that to be what came out of her mouth at all. I was thinking maybe she got a new job, or their buying a car, or shit, even they are getting another dog so the one they have wouldn't be lonely when they are both gone. But pregnant? That was so far from my mind that it was in a different fucking timezone. But now that I've had a few seconds to let it sink in, happiness bathes my body in complete joy. She's pregnant! Which means I'm gonna be a grandfather again.

A huge smile takes over my face and I reach out my hand. "Congratulations," I practically yell as she takes my offered hand and I pull her into me for a big hug. I wish I was able to get out of this bed and hug her like I want to, but this will have to do for now.

"Thank you, Mack. I'm very excited, though I'm nervous to tell Toby. I know he'll be over the moon about it, but it wasn't something that we planned," Sara says quietly. She lays her head on my shoulder while I continue to hold her. I'm surprised as fuck that I'm the first person she told, though I assume the other girls know already...but still. She told me before her man. I may have to gloat about this fact after the shock and happiness wear off.

Pulling back enough that I can see her face, I look at her with a serious expression. "Honey, he's going to be thrilled. It doesn't matter if you were planning on it or not, he's going to love this little baby with everything he has. But if he's being a shithead about it, you come tell me and I'll whip some sense into him. Don't worry your pretty little head, okay?" I reassure her. I have no doubt that Toby is going to be so fucking happy he won't even know what to do with himself.

I hug her close once more before letting her go. She makes her way back to her seat, then looks at Harlow with a cashmere smile on her face. What the fuck now?

Looking at Harlow expectantly, I wait her out. Does she have something to tell me too? I can't even imagine what she could want to tell me, and since any of my guesses for Sara were completely out of range, I'm not even gonna try this time around.

"Mack, I want to thank you for everything you've done for me. I'll be forever in your debt." Harlow starts, and I feel a little of the tension from my shoulders drain a bit, though I am a little irritated she keeps bringing this up. I didn't do anything for her that demands thanks. She's my family and I protect my own.

"But I do have something to ask of you. I want you to know that I'd like it very much if you accepted, but I completely understand if it's too much to ask." This time when she speaks, there's nervousness in her voice. What could she have to ask me that would make her feel like this?

"Sweetheart, I don't know how many times I'm going to have to tell you this, but there is nothing I have done that needs repaid. You can ask me whatever you want and I'll happily oblige. I'd do anything for you. You should know that by now." I hate that she feels like she's in my debt and like she can't ask me for something. I care about her just as much as I care about Dani and Sara. She's like a daughter to me. I would do anything to make sure she's safe and happy—give anything for her just like the other two. I don't need anything in return.

"Well, I'm glad you feel that way because what I'm about to ask you is very important. It'll most likely be a lot of work, and make you aggravated beyond belief, but I hope you agree."

"Just ask already," I urge, needing to know what it is. Hopefully my tone doesn't come off mean because that's not the way I intend it. I only want her to ask whatever it is she needs already.

"Okay, here goes nothing," she says, leaving the sentence hanging a little before continuing. "Mack, you've been amazing to me and I see the way you are with little EJ and Harley. Would you do the honor of being the grandpa to the baby I'm now carrying as well?"

Again, I'm completely thrown off guard by her request. Well, the news in general. I didn't see it coming when Sara said she was pregnant, but there wasn't even a molecule in my body that thought Harlow would be pregnant as well. What a fucking day! A great and amazing day.

"Of course!" I shout, reaching out and dragging her closer so I can pull her in for a hug as well. Like she even had to fucking ask, but I kind of love that she did.

These girls have made me the happiest motherfucker in the world. I love my grandkids more than my own life, and knowing that I'll be adding more is the best feeling ever. Better than being president of my club and better than the feeling of riding on my bike.

My smile is firmly planted on my face to the point of pain, but I don't give a shit. I am so happy right now that if someone came in here to do any of these girl's harm, I would shoot them with this smile still on my face. Well, I'd probably do that anyway…but still.

When Harlow pulls away, I look to where Dani is still sitting silent. She has a smile on her face that could rival my own. Knowing her, she probably has something up her sleeve. Do I dare take a guess?

"Are you pregnant too?" I ask, though I think I already know the answer.

Her smile gets even bigger and I can't help but laugh. No fucking way! This has got to be the best damn day of my life.

"Are you shittin' me?" I have to ask, because she could very well just be fucking with me, but I hope like hell she's not.

Shaking her head, she finally gets up and takes the few steps to my bed. "Nope. We're all pregnant. We found out a few days ago. We thought it'd be perfect to tell you first to bring your spirits up a little, but I gotta tell ya, I can't wait to see the look on the guys' faces when they find out."

"Find out what?" Blaze says as he, Louie, and Toby walk through the door.

His tone is cautious but also almost angry. I'm sure because there's something he wasn't *in the know* about. Well, how does it feel, asshole? It's nice to have a one up on someone right now when I can't seem to get ahead anywhere else.

"Daddy," the twins both squeal as they jump down from the chair they were sitting on, coloring, and run toward Blaze.

Leaning down, he takes both kids in his arms, gives them a smile, and kisses their cheeks before putting them back down.

"Go on back over and play while the adults talk," Blaze says, before turning back toward Dani. I don't know if something happened at the meet or if they are just waiting for the girls to reveal their secrets. I'm going crazy not knowing now that I remember why they're here, though finding out about the pregnancies still gives me a high like no other.

Looking each guy over for any signs of injury, my body visibly sags with relief when I see none. They're pissed and maybe a little rough looking, but no one is hurt. At least nothing physical seemed to have happened at the meet. Or if it did, our guys came out on top. Thank fuck for that.

The first hour after they left, I swear my whole body was buzzing with adrenaline, going crazy not being with my brothers to back them up and knowing what the hell was going on. But after the girls laid their news on me, I lost track of time and what was going down. They're here now though, so

41

I'll know soon enough what happened. But first…

My eyes move from Sara, to Harlow, and finally land on Dani. Now it's my turn to have a smug smile. Looking at Dani now, you never would have guessed minutes ago she was smiling like the fat kid who got the last piece of cake. Nope, now she looks like the fat kid that ate too *much* cake and is about to be sick. She has no reason to be nervous or scared, but I'm thinking it's because she was caught with her hand in the cookie jar. She wasn't ready to reveal their surprise just yet, but it's too late. The guys knew something was going on, but now it's confirmed. And they won't stop until they know what it is.

"Someone better start talking before I lose my shit," Blaze growls, but his bark is worse than his bite. He's more irritated and antsy than pissed.

When the girls told me about their news, Sara was the first to go, but this time around, it's Harlow.

"Louie, I wanted to wait and tell you tonight while we were alone, but I guess now will have to do," she says, taking a big breath.

"Whatever it is, babe, just tell me. We'll get through it. I promise." Louie's voice is calm but you can see he's nervous. He has no idea what's coming. Not a fucking clue! He's probably worried and thinking it has something to do with what happened to her, but it's so far from that subject. It's going to blow his mind.

"I'm pregnant," Harlow says quietly as a tear slips down her face, but I can tell by the tone of her voice they're happy tears. She may be scared to death to be a mother and a little unsure about what

Louie will say, but she's happy. And I know she'll make a great mother.

Louie looks like he's made of stone. This news completely shocked him, but it only takes seconds for it all to sink in and the look I knew would grace his face to appear. Smiling from ear to ear, he rushes toward Harlow, picking her up and swinging her around.

"Are you serious, babe? I'm going to be a dad?" he asks once he sets her back on her feet.

She nods. Louie then drops down to his knees, kissing her stomach before looking up at her. "I'm gonna be a father," he says, then stands back up, kissing her lips. Whipping around with one arm around Harlow's shoulders and the other planted lovingly on her stomach, he shouts to Toby and Blaze, "I'm gonna be a father!"

"Yeah, we heard, fucker," Toby says with a smile on his face, happy for his brother. Wait till he finds out he's about to be a father too.

He doesn't have to wait long. "Toby, I know it wasn't planned, but I'm pregnant too," Sara says.

Toby whips his head from Louie and Harlow to look at Sara. His smile turns bigger and he rushes over to Sara. Cradling her stomach, he says, "I fucking love you, doll." Then he takes her lips in a kiss that rivals all kisses. I look away, not wanting to eavesdrop on their moment.

Blaze starts laughing, though it's not cruel. He's happy for them all, but can't go without giving his brothers hell. "You fuckers just wait. You'll have shitty diapers, puke on your cuts, and blue balls before the year is up. But it'll all be worth it. You'll see. I can't wait to see you both take on the daddy role," he says, still laughing while he pulls each brother in for a man hug to congratulate them.

"I don't know why you're laughing. I'm pregnant too, motherfucker," Dani throws in there with her arms crossed. These two. I swear, they fight like cats and dogs. There is never a dull moment when you're around them. But even though they argue—all the time—you'd be blind if you couldn't see the love that shines in both their eyes, even when they are yelling at each other.

Blaze's laughter dies down and he levels Dani with a hard stare. Being around him long enough, I know it's not the fact that she just informed him she's pregnant. It was the way she told him. While everyone else got sweet issued surprises, Blaze did not.

"You carryin' my child, Baby Girl?" Blaze asks in a calm voice. I can just barely see the smile that is desperate to break free, but he holds it in. Fucker has balls of steel. Dani is going to rip him apart.

"Yeah, I'm carryin' your child. What the fuck you gonna do about it?"

Blaze takes a threatening step forward, then stops. "Oh, I'll tell you what I'm gonna do." He pauses for a few hard seconds, then engulfs Dani in his arms. "I'm gonna fuckin' take you home and fuck the shit outta ya cause I fuckin' love you and I'm so fuckin' happy that not only do I get you and the twins, but another baby to call my own." He kisses her hard on the lips and grabs her ass.

"Daddy, wat is *pucking*?" Little Harley asks, pronouncing *fucking* with a "p" instead of an "f."

44

Hearing her little voice, it brings us all back into the moment where we have little ears in the room.

Pulling away from Dani just enough that he can look at his daughter, Blaze replies with a serious tone. "It's something that will get any boy killed if he tries it with you, sweetie."

Slapping Blaze on the chest, Dani pushes away from him and scoops up her little girl. "It's nothing for you to worry about right now, honey." Kissing her on the cheek, she puts Harley down and grabs both her little hand and EJ's. "Come on, kids. Let's go down to the cafeteria to see what kind of goodies they have for us while Daddy and your uncles talk to Papa for a bit."

The men all watch as the women load the kids up and walk out of the room. After the door closes and we can no longer hear Harley's little voice asking why she can't know what *pucking* is, we get down to business.

"What happened at the meet?" I ask. I don't really know to expect. The meet was a setup, I know that, but I'm hoping they were at least able to gain some information. I just don't see what setting a meeting with us was going to do for them or what they were trying to do.

Sighing loudly, Blaze walks over to the chair Dani was sitting in earlier and takes a seat. "A truce," Blaze says.

"It's a fucking trap," Louie comments, spitting out the words like they taste foul. They probably do to him. Fuck, just hearing it leaves a shit taste in my mouth.

"A trap for what, though?" I ask, irritation and

confusion taking hold. It just doesn't make any damn sense. Why call us out for a meeting and dangle a truce out there if that's not what they intend? We *know* that's not what they want, so what is it they're trying to prove?

"I don't know, brother. Everything was too perfect, ya know? The way they talked to us, the way they backed down from any harsh comments we made about that shithead Titus like they were pussies. But I can't get a read on what their intention is. Fuck, if we hadn't heard it with our own fucking ears that they don't intend to ever call a truce with us from the bug in their clubhouse, then I might have even believed them." Blaze runs his hand through his hair stiffly. It's not sitting well with him not knowing what's going on. Shit, it doesn't sit well with me either, and if the looks of Toby and Louie are anything to go off of, they don't like it, either.

"Did they say anything else?" I ask. Even the smallest things that they didn't pick up on could tell us something. Maybe I'll be able to decipher them.

"Not much. We talked shit to see if they'd start anything, and they didn't. They threw the truce out there and we accepted," Blaze explains.

"I did notice they have a new VP," Toby adds in.

That's interesting.

"What happened to Rocket?" I ask.

"Not sure, but he wasn't there tonight. If I had to guess, I'd say he's six feet under because every other member seemed to be in attendance," Toby answers back.

Thinking that over, I figure he's probably right,

but how did he die? Was he murdered or did he die of natural causes? I may have Toby call our contact in the police department to get more information on that.

"Who's the new VP?"

"Brutus," Louie spits out through gritted teeth. Brutus doesn't have a good reputation and may actually be the worst of the group. Though we haven't caught him doing anything, he's got a record probably as tall as I am.

Something is up for sure, though. Fake truces and new leadership. But what does it have to do with us?

"What's the plan then?" I ask, leaving this up to Blaze since I wasn't at the meet and I wasn't there when they heard the hushed conversation from the bug.

"Only thing I can think of is to continue with the charade for now. We'll play along like we accept the truce, but we'll keep our eyes peeled and on alert at all times. We'll have someone on the girls, keeping them at the clubhouse as much as possible. And I want someone here too."

"What the fuck do I need someone here for? I've got Betty if any trouble comes knocking," I growl, pissed he's even suggesting I need protecting. I ain't no fucking pussy or invalid. I can take care of my damn self.

"Mack, I know you can take care of yourself, but you're still our president. I need to make sure you're guarded, especially after the comment the Kings made. It left a bad taste in my mouth," Blaze counters.

That part is news to me and has me curious. "What comment?"

"I can't be sure, but I think they know you're here. He said to give you his best and to get better soon."

Yeah, that would leave a bad taste in my mouth too if I were him. But it still doesn't mean I need a babysitter.

Opening my mouth to argue that fact further, Blaze holds up his hand. "Look. I know you got yourself covered and can handle any situation, but please. For my peace of mind? Let me place at least a prospect at your door. You're still our president and I need to make sure we have you covered."

Well, fuck me if that didn't shut me up real quick.

"Ugh, I guess if it gives you fuckers peace of mind, then what the fuck ever. But only one prospect and you better tell him that he answers to me, got it? If I tell him to do something, he better fuckin' jump and ask how high. You may be acting president but this show is still mine when I say so, and I'm saying fucking so on this one," I rant, pissed off. I guess I'm willing to do almost anything so these fuckers will sleep better tonight, but this shit is not going to last long, I can tell you that right the fuck now.

"Yeah, yeah, old man. We hear ya." Louie says, but I can hear the relief in his voice.

"All right, now get the heck outta here. It's been a long day and I have a big day tomorrow." A big day I'm looking forward to. I can't wait for Rose to walk into the room and hopefully have more progress with the feeling and movement in my legs. I'm even going to do those damn exercises before she gets here so hopefully I can surprise her with how well I'm doing now. And it'll all be thanks to her.

"Fucking right you do. Tomorrow you're getting released. Doc stopped us in the hall before we got to your door and confirmed it," Toby says, and it surprises me. I thought for sure I'd have a few more days here. But tomorrow?

I'm not sure if I'm ready to leave. Or maybe I'm just not ready to let Rose go yet.

***

After the boys left last night and the prospect came in to let me know he'd be right outside if I needed anything, I lay in bed counting sheep. I was too high off of the news Dani, Sara, and Harlow gave me earlier in the night. Too many thoughts rolling around in my head about what The Kings were up to. And lastly, and probably most importantly, I could not get Rose out of my mind.

The way she said my real name and the way she took my hand and praised me…I can't get it out of my head. It keeps playing over and over again like a broken record…one I don't want to fix or throw away.

It's crazy to think that in such a short amount of time, she's become like the air I breathe. I tried to think of every possible solution for what I was going to do today when I was released, but couldn't come up with anything short of either staying in the hospital or kidnapping her. And since kidnapping isn't something I'm fond of, unless it's a piece of shit man who needs to be taught a fucking lesson, I guess that left me with the former option. I'll just have to talk the doctor into keeping me just a bit longer.

Now, as I'm waiting for the clock to strike two, I go over my plan once more. When Rose comes in, I'm going to tell her I feel more comfortable continuing my care here. I'd be closer to the doctors in case I fell or had a setback. I know it sounds like a pussy's way out, but at this point in time, I'm willing to become the pussy if it means getting Rose for a few more days. Just till I can get her out of my system. That's all I need.

Looking at the clock again for the hundredth time in the last five minutes, I see it's one-fifty-nine. One more minute till my ray of sunshine walks through that door.

The minute passes and my smile fades. No Rose. Maybe there was an emergency and she was called in to help. Yeah, that's gotta be it. No way she'd be late for our session. She's never late or ever early. She's always on time.

Another minute passes, then five, then ten, and then fifteen. By now, I'm starting to get worried. Did she change her mind about doing the massages for me? Does she think that since I made progress yesterday that we're done? Or maybe she was told I get released today, so she doesn't think I need her here.

Two hours pass with no word from her. Just as I'm getting ready to pick up the phone to dial the nurses' station to see what the fuck is going on, my door flies open and in walks a haggard-looking Rose. Her clothes are wrinkled like she slept in them overnight, her eyes are bloodshot, with black marks underneath them. But it's the completely dead look on her face that has me really worried. There is no life in her eyes, none of her usual pep in her step.

"Where the *fuck* have you been?"

CHAPTER FOUR

Rose

After finding my brother's note on my windshield last night, I was a mess. Driving home, I was constantly looking over my shoulder, expecting Anthony to appear around every corner or to be hiding in the shadows just waiting to jump out at me.

Walking through my front door, I immediately locked it, using all four locks I had installed for this exact reason. I fear my brother Anthony more than anything else in this world. I know there's nothing he wouldn't do to get what he wants, so the fact he sought me out and left that note makes me believe whatever it is he wants with me isn't going to be good. Shit, what am I talking about? Nothing he wants from me is ever good.

I searched every nook and cranny in my apartment before I finally took a breath, but I still couldn't relax. Anthony was out there somewhere and God only knows what he wants. A *surprise*, he had said. What the fuck could it be? I know for damn sure it's not something I'll want.

My initial plans for the night were to take a long hot bath, maybe have a few glasses of wine, and binge on Netflix and Damon Salvatore on *The Vampire Diaries*. But that just wasn't going to happen now. I didn't even change out of my clothes. I went right into my closet, grabbed the hand gun I had purchased years ago, and sat ramrod straight on my bed, staring at my closed bedroom door. And I watched. And I waited. For my world to come crashing down in the form of my devil of a brother and his band of ruthless, fucked up followers.

The hours passed and no one showed, but I couldn't relax. My eyes were heavy and my body hurt with being so tense, but I never released my hold on my gun and I never took my eyes off the door. I worried that as soon as I closed my eyes, that's when Anthony would make his move. Like he could sense when my guard was down, and that's when he'd come.

No, I needed to be strong and stay awake.

As the morning light finally made its appearance, I finally started to relax a little. Sure, something could still happen or go wrong, but knowing my brother, he wouldn't risk it in the light of day. He'd wait till he had the cover of night or try to catch me unaware or alone outside my apartment. Maybe on the way to work or in a dark alley. Good thing I don't plan on taking any midnight strolls or even have time to wander around town during the day.

By nine in the morning, I finally allowed sleep to

take me. I knew I had to be in to work at noon, but I needed to at least get an hour of rest if I was going to be any use to the doctors or patients. Or if I was going to have any chance of keeping my brother at bay.

***

Rolling over, my body aches and my eyes burn without even opening them. I don't know how long I've been lying here but I don't think I got any restful sleep. Sure, I may have dozed off a time or two, but it didn't give me the reprieve I so desperately needed. I was restless and had nightmares of my brother doing unspeakable things. So much for getting any sleep.

As I lay here, I dread opening my eyes. I know I'm still in my room, but there's this fear that if I open my eyes, my room will be trashed.

Anthony did that once before; he broke into my apartment after I denied him money. He threatened and stalked me, along with his band of merry-fucking-men. I had just worked a triple shift and was tired as hell. I went straight home and crashed for twelve hours straight, but when I woke up, my whole apartment was torn apart. Every photo hanging on my wall was ripped down and broken. My couch was turned over and the cushions were slashed. My kitchen was trashed and every little thing that was worth anything was gone. I'm surprised I didn't wake up during the invasion, but I'm glad I didn't. I have no idea what I would have done or what *he* would have done if I'd walked out in the middle of their *fun*.

I knew my brother was behind it, there was no doubt in my mind, but there was no point in reporting it. There was no proof and there wouldn't be any. And the police wouldn't do a damn thing anyway because they feared him…maybe more than I did. So instead of turning him in, I called in sick and spent the rest of the day making order of my once peaceful home.

Taking a deep breath, I try to open my eyes, but find that it's nearly impossible. They feel gritty and burn like hell, but with a little extra effort, I'm able to crack one eyelid open. Everything looks in its in place, nothing trashed or showing any sign that anyone but me has been here, but I'm not breathing a sigh of relief yet.

Stepping out of bed, I tiptoe to my bedroom door with my gun still firmly planted in my hand. No way am I leaving it behind in case he's waiting for me outside my room.

Making my way quietly but swiftly down the hall, I pass the bathroom and spare bedroom before I enter the living room. Since I have an open floor plan, I can see everything; the living room, the kitchen, and the front door. All looks normal. Nothing out of its place, nothing broken. But that's not one hundred percent true. Nothing material may be broken inside my home, but I feel broken inside. Numb. Dead.

This is what my brother does to me. He's vile and poisonous. He always has been. Why can't he just let me be? I love my life. Sure, I don't have riches and fame or even someone to share what I do have, but I'm okay with that. I have what I *need*. I just want to live my life without having to worry about who is behind the next corner or when he's gonna show up again to take everything I hold dear away from me.

I *hate* him. I wish he were dead.

Once in my kitchen I start a pot of coffee. The clock reads two-forty-seven and I know I'm late for my shift, but I couldn't care less. Maybe I'll get fired and I can just move far away from here. Sure, I'd have to leave what few friends I have and a job I love, and a hospital that is amazing, but I'd be away from my brother. Hopefully in a place he can't find me.

With that last though in mind, I grab a traveler's mug filled with black coffee and my purse off the table. Not even bothering to change, I put my gun inside my bag and make my way out to my car, praying that Anthony will stay away for a few more hours. Just long enough for me to finish my last rotation at the hospital, tell my supervisor something came up and I have to leave. I think I'll take a vacation until I can find a place I feel is far enough away before telling them I'm not coming back. Sure, it's a shitty plan, and I'm sure I'll feel horrible about it when I'm in my car, driving God knows where alone. But that's just something I'm going to have to live with. For now, I'll embrace the numbness and do what needs to be done.

The drive to the hospital is all a blur. I walked out to my car, only paying attention to my windshield, looking for another note. There was none, but there was no relief either. Something was going on and it was coming for me in the shape of my brother; I just didn't know what it was. But I wasn't going to stick around to find out.

Stopping at the nurse's station, I look around for my boss. I know she's here somewhere, and I need to find her so I can get this over with. The sooner, the better. I figure if I get it out of the way now, I can leave as soon as my shift is over. Or shit, maybe she'll just tell me to leave now instead of waiting.

She's not going to be happy with me about the short notice and needing the time off, but I've never even taken one holiday. And I think in all the years I've worked at this hospital, I've taken a total of three days off, one of which was to clean up after my brother, and the other two were because I was so sick I couldn't even stand. And even then, I tried to work but they made me go home. So she'll have no choice but to give me what I ask for, even if it will leave them shorthanded.

"Rose, there you are. Everything okay?" Gloria asks.

Gloria is a nurse here and someone I've thought of as a friend these last few years. She's a little older than I am, but we have a lot in common. We both like to drink wine, we hate romance movies because we think they're over the top stupid and unreal, and we both came from shitty families. Mine is my brother and hers is her mother. Though I guess my parents weren't all that great either, but Anthony was by far the worst.

"Hey, Gloria. Sorry I'm late, but something's come up. Do you know where Monica is? I need to speak with her," I ask, noticing the dull note of my voice. I sound like a robot, but I'm afraid if I try to add feeling to my tone, then everything from the last twenty-four hours will come slamming into me and I'll freak out. I can't afford to do that right now, so the robot voice and act it is.

Looking at me with concern, she steps closer, like she wants to take me in her arms and tell me everything will be okay. But that's a lie. As long as I'm here, close enough for Anthony to find me, things will never be okay. *I* won't be okay.

"Yeah, of course. She's in surgery, but she'll be back in an hour or so."

I nod and pick up a file from the top of a pile. I don't even care whose file it is; I just need something to make me seem busy so Gloria will leave this alone. I can sense she wants to ask questions and try to comfort me, but I can't go there.

My distraction method works. Gloria stands there for a few more seconds before placing her hand on my arm as she walks by me. "Let me know if you need anything, honey." I don't acknowledge her statement, but it does thaw me a little. She cares about me and only wants to help. God, I wish there was something she could do, but she'd be powerless against my brother. Just like I am.

No, the only thing that can help me is to get as far away from here as possible.

After I see Gloria turn the corner, I let out the breath I didn't realize I was holding. Focusing on the file in my hand, I finally take in the words for the first time.

Michael DeVin
Patient # 001589
Discharge Notes: Releasing today with orders to continue therapy at home. Hire home care nurse and physical therapist to assist with recovery.

He's getting released today.

I feel a part of my brain try to pull at me. Or maybe it was my heart. But I don't let myself feel it. I can't let myself be sad or even happy that Mack is going home today and I won't ever see him again. With everything going on with my brother, it only solidifies the fact that I shouldn't get myself caught up with Mack. He's a biker. He probably doesn't care about right or wrong. Shit, he's in here because he was shot, which means he was probably in a gun fight. Sure, it could just be he was in the wrong place at the wrong time, but I highly doubt that.

Clearing my head of all thoughts of Mack, I pull out my phone. Checking my bank account, I see that I only have a few grand saved up. That's not going to last long, especially if I go as far from here as I want. Gas isn't cheap, plus hotel fees…I'm going to have to find work as soon as I get where I'm going. I doubt I'll be able to find a job as a nurse that fast—if ever since I'm leaving here in a hurry and will no doubt get a bad recommendation, plus that's probably the first place my brother would look for me—but maybe I can find something else. A bartender, waitress, or even working in an office. I could live with that. But doing that for the rest of my life?

Stashing my phone back in my purse, I stand to

go back to my locker to grab everything I don't want to leave behind. I'm hoping that after I talk to Monica, I can just go, and I don't want to have to make any extra stops if I can help it. Maybe I can be on the road within the hour and across the state line heading east by nightfall.

I'm halfway down the hallway when I see Dr. Yorkshire coming toward me. He's one of the attending physicians here at the hospital and is also the doctor that oversees Mack's care.

"Nurse Rose, I'm glad I was able to catch you before you went on your rounds. I need you to do a final visit with Mr. DeVin and sign off on his release orders before I'm able to discharge him," Dr. Yorkshire says as he reaches me.

Staring at him, I have no idea what to say. I can't really deny him his request, but I also don't want to go into Mack's room. Going in there will mean I have to see him, talk to him. I'm not sure if I can do that without feeling anything. Or knowing I'm never going to see him again.

"I really need to talk to Monica. I could have Gloria go check on things with him. She's well aware of his condition and progress," I try, but I know without even waiting for him to reply that he won't go for it. If I were in his shoes, I wouldn't either. I'm the one who was working with him and doing his treatment. It doesn't matter if anyone else knows about his progress. It *should* be me that signs off on everything.

Dr. Yorkshire crosses his arms and lets out a long sigh. "What's going on with you, Rose? Normally you wouldn't have any problem checking on your patients, *especially* if it's to discharge them and make sure they're set to go home. Personal issues aside, you always pick the patient."

He sounds disappointed, tinged with a bit of worry. I could *almost* stand one, but it's the other that really gets me.

Letting out a sigh of my own, I look down at my feet. I have so many thoughts going through my head right now, but he's right. Personal issues aside, my patients mean everything to me. It never mattered if I was sick or if there was a tragedy that struck close to home, I was always there for those that needed me.

But this time is different. I just can't tell if it's because this time my situation is worse or if it's because of Mack.

Out of the corner of my eye, I see him step closer. "Rose?" Dr. Yorkshire questions.

Looking up into his eyes, I try to detach myself even further. If I'm going to do this—see Mack—I need to cut my thoughts and feelings off more than ever. I need to be hard at stone, tough as steel.

"I'll sign off on his release papers and make sure everything is set for his release. But then I need to talk to Monica and leave for a while. I can't explain it all right now, but I need some time away," I say, then turn on my heel, heading down to Mack's room. I don't wait for Dr. Yorkshire to comment further or ask questions. I just want to get this over with.

Stopping in front of Mack's door, I take in a deep breath. Yesterday I was looking forward to continuing his care and seeing him make even more progress. But today…I'm in a fog of numbness. I don't know what's going to happen when I walk through this door, but I guess it's best to just get it over with. The faster I can sign off on his release and treatment, the faster I can talk to Monica and leave this place. And be far away from my brother.

Steeling myself, I hold my breath and open the door.

Catching Mack off guard, he swings his head around and looks at me first with concern, then anger.

"Where the fuck have you been?" he yells.

The breath I was holding whooshes out of me, but it's not from surprise or even from fear. With that one sentence he was able to break through my numbness and make me just as angry as he seems to be—if not more.

"None of your goddamn business," I say through gritted teeth as I walk over to the end of his bed where his file is hanging.

Grabbing it with angry movements, I flip to the last page, intending to just sign my name before leaving the room. I don't even care what it says or suggests for his treatment, I only want to get away from him. This man turns me inside out, makes me feel everything. I've never met a person who makes me feel every emotion at once; fear, anger, lust, happiness, compassion, and so much more. It's dizzying and annoying. I feel like a tornado has come crashing through my life, picking me up and spinning me around and around. And like a tornado, there will be nothing but mayhem and destruction in his wake.

I can't handle any more destruction in my life. Everything I've been through, it's enough to last two lifetimes.

Signing my name at the bottom of Mack's chart, I don't even bother to hang it back up again. Instead, I throw it down at his feet before turning on my heel to leave. I'm grateful for the fact that he can't walk right now so he can't stop me. He can yell and demand me to come back all he wants, but he can't stop me from leaving. Nothing will.

"What the hell happened to you?" I don't know if it's a rhetorical question, but it doesn't matter. I don't stop or falter in my retreat.

"I never pegged you as the type to run scared. Guess I was wrong," Mack says quietly, almost like he doesn't intend for me to hear. But I do, and those words make me stop. They make me question everything that's happened in the last few weeks and what I'm about to do now.

He's right. I've never been the type of girl to run away from things and I wasn't scared of much in my life. But my brother has always been the exception and probably always will be. With him around trying to interfere in my life, I'll never truly be free. I'll always be waiting for the next time he shows up, the next time he leaves me a cryptic message, or the next time he tries to hurt me.

Turning around to face Mack, I don't let my face show how much his words affect me. They hurt and make me feel like I'm giving up, but if he only knew what was going on, he'd see that this is me *fighting*. This is me taking control and not letting Anthony win. I'm not running scared…I'm running to take back my life; any way I can.

"You have no idea what you're talking about," I seethe, unable to hide the anger I feel. But I can't hold him completely responsible. The fact that I'm having to run because of my brother pisses me off too, both at myself and at him.

"Maybe not, but let me tell you what I *do* know," he shoots back. "I know that within the last month you have never once been late for an appointment you've set with me for treatment. I know that within the last month you have never once seemed weak or afraid. *Until today*."

I can literally feel the fuse he lit within me with his words and can only hold my breath and wait till the fuse burns all the way down to the bomb. I'm about to explode in three...two...one.

"You don't fucking know me. You don't know anything about what's going on or what I'm feeling! You think I'm scared? Maybe I am, but that's none of your fucking business," I yell, not even caring if the other patients, doctors, or nurses hear me. I've never been this mad before at anyone in my whole life.

"Then fucking tell me!" Mack yells back.

Just then, the door to the room opens and in walks Dr. Yorkshire. "Everything all right in here?" he questions, looking back and forth between Mack and I with a confused, yet demanding expression.

Taking a deep breath, I lie. "Yes. I was just explaining to Mr. DeVin that if he continues to work hard, he'll be walking in no time."

There's no need to get into what is really going on. Not with Dr. Yorkshire, anyway. It's none of his business and he wouldn't understand. Mack and I have grown into more than a nurse/patient role, though I'm not sure exactly what it is. We're not friends, that's for sure. But maybe in-between? I don't know how to explain it. But that doesn't mean he knows what he's talking about where I'm concerned, or even has a say in what I do.

"Good. That's good," Dr. Yorkshire says, moving closer to Mack's bed. "Now that Nurse Rose has signed off on your release and treatment plan, here is a list of home care nurses and physical therapists. Take a look and let me know if you need help contacting one to hire for the rest of your recovery."

I move backwards toward the door, intending to leave while Mack is distracted.

"That won't be necessary, Doc. I've already hired someone. She's perfect for both jobs," Mack answers, and even though I'm a little curious who it is, I don't stop. I *need* to get out of here.

"Oh, that's great news, Mr. DeVin. Who is it you chose to manage your care?"

"Nurse Rose."

CHAPTER FIVE

Mack

I caught her off guard. *Shit*, I caught myself off guard with that statement. What the hell was I thinking saying she was going to be my live-in nurse? I don't even know if she does that shit or if it's even a good idea. But fuck me, I need her to say yes. I need her to be the one to finish my care and treatment.

Dr. Yorkshire looks dumbfounded and then doubtful. I guess I'm not the only one who isn't sure if Rose will agree.

"I'll leave you two to hash out the details then," he says as he turns around to face Rose, who is frozen in front of the door, facing away from us. "Nurse Rose, please stop by my office before you speak with Monica."

Rose doesn't reply, but she nods like she's on auto-pilot. Dr. Yorkshire sidesteps her and walks out the door after a brief look at Rose. From where I'm at, I can only see half his face, but I can tell I don't like the look he gives her, no matter how short it is. It speaks volumes. It says, "Don't do it," and "He's not worth it."

I want to reach into my side table, pull Betty out, and point it at his fucking head. Tell him that he don't know me or what my intentions are. That he has no goddamn right to exert his opinion on Rose and what he thinks she should do. But I won't. Not because it's a bad idea that would most likely get me arrested, but because I don't think Rose would like it much.

Goddamn it! When did I start worrying about what bitches think?

The door closes and I wait for the storm to hit. If being around Rose every day for the past month has taught me anything, it's that she's going to come at me with guns blazin'. She'll yell and puff about me assuming she'd take the job or some shit like that. It's just a matter of time before it happens.

"I'm not going with you," Rose says calmly, with her back still turned to me. I'm surprised I didn't get more out of her than that, but it's not going to stop me.

"Yes, you are," I counter, trying to sound confident. "Look, I don't know what's going on with you, but at least hear me out." I need to be able to talk her into this. Not only because I don't think anyone else could treat me the way she can and I don't want to bring anyone else into the clubhouse, but because I need *her*. I barely understand it myself, but it's the truth. Maybe it's because she's hot as fuck and I'm not done with her yet, or maybe it's the fact that she stands her ground with me. She doesn't back down and I like that—respect it even. I just hope that once she hears what I have to offer she'll agree.

"I don't have time for this shit. I need to talk to Monica so I can get the hell out of here," Rose says but she doesn't make a move to leave. Her words say one thing but her body language says something completely different.

"Just give me five minutes. Please. I promise if you don't like what I have to offer, I won't stop you from leaving," I say. There's not much I could really do about her leaving. But you can bet your ass I'd raise some hell.

Letting out a long sigh, she finally turns around and gives me her eyes. It's then I notice how tired she looks. When she came in before, I knew something was wrong, but now looking at her, she almost looks sick.

Rose walks over to the chair that sits beside my bed and practically falls into it, like she could no longer hold herself up. "You have five minutes and then I'm leaving."

A slow grin starts taking over my face, which makes Rose scowl. "Just because I'm hearing you out doesn't mean I'm going to agree to whatever bullshit offer you have for me."

There's that sass and mouth I've been looking forward to all day. If she thought her words and attitude would have the smile slipping off my face in defeat, she was wrong.

Laughing to lighten the mood a little, I hold my hands up like I'm surrendering to her, but it's the exact opposite. I'm just going to fight that much harder to get what I want. And what I want is her.

"All right, babe. I hear ya loud and clear. I got five minutes to plead my case and then I'll be helpless and at your mercy," I say with a wink, which gets me a small smile in return, though she tries to hide it.

"You're now down to four minutes," she says, leaving the sentence sounding hard, but I would bet all my chips that she's not going anywhere. At least not until I'm done putting it all on the table.

Turning my body as best I can so I'm facing her head on, I jump right in. "When I was shot, I thought my life had ended. And then when I woke up here in the hospital, I had hope for about three seconds before the doctor told me that I may never walk again. I was angry, depressed, and at times I just wanted to let go of everything and be done with it. I hated what my life had turned into."

I didn't really know how I was going to start this conversation or get her to understand where I was coming from, but I never thought it'd be this. I can't believe I even spoke those words out loud. Yes, it's all the truth, but to admit that to *anyone*…let's just say I'm probably more surprised by what I just said than she might be.

"The doctors came and went, they shoved pills down my throat and medicine in my IV, and gave me looks of pity. They encouraged me, but I could tell they never thought in a million years that I'd get feeling back in my legs, let alone walk again. No one thought I'd get better…no one but *you*."

I can tell she wants to protest, but I hold my hands up, stopping her before she can say anything.

"You lit a fire under my ass, Rose. *You* are the one who started this, and I need *you* to be the one to finish it." It may not be worded that way, but I'm not going to give her a choice. She *will* be the one to finish my therapy and get me strong again. *She* will be the reason I walk again. Yeah, I'll have a huge part in it too, but I wouldn't even be here, having some feeling back in my limbs, without her.

"You can't just expect me to drop everything to cater to your every demand. Plus, I can't afford to not work for a few weeks. Shit, it could take months before you're back on your feet," Rose says, but it's with little venom. She's close to caving. We both know it. I just have to close the deal.

"I'm not expecting you to drop everything, Rose. Or to do this for free. I will make it worth your while. You'll be highly compensated. I'll pay you double what you make here," I tell her, setting the bait. "And you won't be catering to my every demand. I'll be the one catering to yours."

She's thoughtful for a few moments before she starts laughing. Even though I'm confused as to where her sense of humor is coming from, I love seeing her like this, even if it's at my expense.

It takes her a little while, but she finally settles down enough to talk. "I don't think you could afford my current salary, let alone double it." Again, she laughs. This time though, it's a cruel laugh, and I know exactly what she finds so hilarious. Me.

It pisses me off that she doesn't think I can afford to employ her and the fact that she's laughing makes me want to breathe fire, but I take a few deep breaths, trying to calm down. I don't want to say anything in the heat of the moment that will break this deal for me.

I wait until she's done laughing and my anger is down to a manageable level. I'm still raging on this inside, feeling like she unmanned me, but I think I'll be able to get what I need to say across without sounding like an insane asshole. Mostly.

"Since you don't think I can afford your salary, how about I show you just what I can afford by *tripling* it? I'll pay you three times what you make here, plus pay for everything else you need while working with me: housing, food, basic essentials, and anything else your heart desires," I say, ending with a smirk when I see her mouth drop open with the amount of money we're talking about here. I have no idea what she makes, but I know I can afford her, even if I have to quadruple her pay.

All the years being president of my club, and all the business we've had, I never had much to spend my money on until recently. I'm not hurting in the cash department one bit, and still won't be even after this transaction.

Minutes later, she's still speechless. "So what do you say, Rose? Will you be my live-in nurse for the duration of my recovery?"

Closing her mouth, she seems to actually ponder what I've offered, like it still might not be enough. But then she shakes her head, crosses her arms, and levels me with a look that is all business. "I'll agree to be your nurse. I'll continue your therapy and make sure you are well on your road to recovery, but, I have a few stipulations. If you can't accept those, then no deal."

Of course she does. But what she doesn't know is that I'd agree to pretty much anything if it means she'll take me on as her patient full-time. I'll have her full attention, her hands on me every day, and I won't have to share her with anyone else. Fuck yeah I'll agree to whatever she says.

I nod, letting her know to go on with her demands.

"First and foremost, I want my own living quarters. I don't know where you live exactly, whether it be at your clubhouse or home, but I want my own place. I want it stocked with everything I would need; fridge, microwave, TV, bed, and a couch. That way if I don't want to, I don't have to leave my room for anything," she says, then waits for me to answer.

"Done. What else?"

"I want to be able to come and go as I please. When I'm not doing something that isn't a part of your therapy, I want to be able to leave."

"I'll agree to that, but you'll have to take one of the brothers with. I don't know who will be watching, but if someone thinks they can hurt the club by hurting you, I need to make sure you're protected. I won't budge on this," I say without mercy, hoping she doesn't argue on this and that it won't break the deal for her. But I can't have her going off and getting kidnapped on my watch. I'd never forgive myself if she was hurt because of her affiliation with me or my club.

I thought it'd take a few minutes for her to decide on that one, or that she'd argue, but she doesn't. Instead, she answers right away. "Fine. But they will keep their distance, only interfering if they have to."

As shocked as I am, I don't waste a minute nodding my head, afraid she'll change her mind. "Done. Anything else you want?" I ask, wondering how many more demands she'll have, but so far, she hasn't thrown anything at me that I can't or won't do.

"Just a few more things, Mr. DeVin," she says with a genuine smile. "You may be my employer, but you will do what I say. If it has something to do with your treatment or even something that could affect your prognosis in anyway, you have listen to me. I won't have you jeopardizing all the hard work we both put into your recovery by doing something that will hinder your healing. This is a deal breaker for me, Mack."

I can tell she's serious, and even though it might be hard for me, I'll agree. "Fine. I'll be your little lapdog. If it's something to do with my treatment, I'll do whatever you say. You're the boss on that front. But outside of all of that, you need to understand that this is my club, and you will do as I say. Do you understand?" I ask with a demanding tone. My controlling nature has taken over.

"Fine."

And when I think she's not going to make any more demands, she adds, "And lastly, you aren't paying me triple my salary. I'll do it for a weekly base rate of what I'm currently making, plus all the extras you mentioned before."

Smiling, I say, "We'll see." No way in hell am I

going to pay her less than what I offered. Even if she doesn't want that much, I'll keep my word. So wanted or not, she's about to get a huge pay increase and there's no way she can stop me or give it back.

Shaking her head like she thinks I'm joking, I just let her believe that. Standing, she heads for the door. "We have a deal, Mr. DeVin, and you have a new nurse."

I'm so fucking happy I want to jump out of this bed and do a happy dance, but I don't. Half because I can't, but mostly because I don't want to make a fool of myself in front of Rose.

"Glad we could come to an understanding, *Nurse Rose*. I'm getting released within the hour. Leave me your contact details and I'll have one of my brothers meet you at your place to escort you to the clubhouse. You can stop and pick anything up that you need on the way. I'll make sure he has the money to pay for whatever you want," I say, finalizing the deal. I can't wait to get out of here and back to my own room...sleep in my own bed. But now, I'll know my sexy little nurse is just down the hall from me.

"I have a meeting to get to, but I'll be sure to stop by with my cell phone number and address before you leave," she says, then opens the door to leave, but I stop her.

"Oh, and one more thing. I'll need your bank account info so I can set everything up to send your payments to you. Unless you'd rather have cash?" I ask, but hope she'll want it to go into her account. That way I can deposit the full amount I want without her knowing right away.

"I'll get you my account information," she says right before she walks out the door.

As soon as I'm alone, I pump my fist in the air like a teenager who asked the most popular girl in school to prom and she said yes. Tonight can't come soon enough.

Shaking myself out of my schoolgirl celebration, I grab my phone off the bedside table and dial up someone who I know will help me with my next task.

"Aw, you just couldn't wait an hour to hear my voice, could you? You had to call. That's so sweet, Macky," Dani says over the phone with a baby voice that on any other day would piss me off, but right now, nothing can get to me. Nothing will break my good mood.

"Oh hush up and listen, would you? I need you to do something very important for me," I say without grief. Like I said, nothing can get me down now that I know I'll have my favorite nurse with me tonight.

"Sir, yes, sir!" she says crisply.

A laugh slips through because I can't help it. I love this side of Dani. When she first came into my shop, she had her walls up and she was hardened by the life destiny threw at her. But through the years, pieces of the girl I have no doubt she was before all that shit happened to her started to shine through. And even though she can get on my nerves like no one else, that's one of the things I love about my Dani girl. The woman I think of as my daughter.

"You think you're so cute, don't ya?" I ask. I'm

not expecting an answer, but in true Dani form, she answers anyway.

"I happen to *know* I'm cute, thank you very much," she says with cheer.

It's quiet for a few moments before she speaks again. "All right, old man. What is it you need me to do that is *sooo* important?"

"I need you to turn that spare office next to my room in the clubhouse into a bedroom. Grab a few of the prospects and take the truck down to the furniture store. I need you to buy everything there is to make that room into a home away from home. A refrigerator, nightstands, and maybe even one of those tiny couches," I say, thinking of everything I need her to get to make that room into something suitable for Rose.

"Okay...?" she asks, leaving the sentence hanging like she's not sure what I'm talking about.

"I hired an in-home nurse to help with my home recovery," I say, filling in the blanks for her.

My explanation gets the ball rolling and we're now on the same page. "Of course! Why didn't I think of that?"

I smile even though she can't see me. This girl is amazing; she really is. Always willing to help out and always trying to stay one step ahead of everyone.

"They got mini fridges there and I can pick up a twin-size bed with some sheets," she starts, but I interrupt her right away.

"No. I want a full-size fridge. And the bed needs to be queen size, if not king. Oh, and make sure it's one of those pillowy top ones too," I add in at the last minute. I'm sure Rose would love one of those. Maybe it will feel like she's sleeping on a cloud.

"Oh, um, sure. Yeah, I can do that," Dani replies, though I can tell she's confused, but I'm not explaining shit. Not yet anyway.

"Is there anything else I should pick up?" I think about that for a minute, but then realize I have no idea what a woman would want in her room. Aside from taking a bitch to bed, fucking her till she passes out, and then kicking her out before dawn, I have no idea what a woman would want aside from the necessities.

"Whatever else you think the room needs. I just want it to be comfortable and not look like a room that's inside a clubhouse." I know that may be impossible, but God dammit, I'm gonna try to hide that fact from her. At least visually inside that one room.

"Gotcha. I'll get right on this," she says, seeming to know exactly what I want even if I don't really know it myself.

"I need this done before I get home. I don't care what it costs, just get it done," I add. I want to be able to see it before Rose does. That way if I need to make any last minute changes or get anything else, I can before she arrives.

"Ten-four. Roger that," Dani says before hanging up the phone.

Placing my phone back on the nightstand beside the bed, I close my eyes and wait for the hour to end and I'll be able to finally go home. But mostly to make the time go faster before I see Rose again.

***

A half hour later, Rose steps into my room and hands me a single sheet of paper. She doesn't say anything, just hands it to me, and then walks back out the door saying she'll be ready and waiting at her place by nine tonight before she's gone again.

Opening the piece of paper, written on a prescription pad is what I assume is her address, her phone number, and what looks like her bank account number. It's all written in a feminine hand, but with a sense of urgency. I guess you'll have that when you're a nurse and having to do one hundred different things at once.

I'm actually a little surprised to see she wrote out her bank information though. She had no problem giving it to me or even worried that someone besides me would get a hold of it since it's all here on a single piece of paper. I'm going to have to talk to her about safety and not giving her information so freely to people. It pisses me off and I'm scared for her, but at the same time, it makes me feel like the king of the world knowing she trusts me with her sensitive information.

Ten minutes after that, in walks Dr. Yorkshire, followed by my brothers: Blaze, Toby, Jax, Louie, TomTom, and Tyke.

"Well, Mr. DeVin, it looks like you're all set to go. Do you have any questions for me?" Dr. Yorkshire asks, standing at the end of my bed.

Smiling almost giddily, I shake my head. "Nope," I say, popping the P at the end.

"Alrighty then. All your paperwork is done. I'll

have a nurse come in to help you get dressed and bring in your wheelchair. We'll bill your insurance for your stay and the wheelchair, so you don't have to worry about any of that." He hands Blaze the discharge papers.

"Everything is set up for Nurse Rose to continue your care for the next few weeks. I want to see you back in a month for a re-evaluation. We'll see how your progress is and decide what needs to happen moving forward. I've already made the appointment for you...it's all in your discharge papers." He points to the paperwork he handed to Blaze moments ago. "You're in good hands, Mr. DeVin. I have no doubt you'll be walking in no time with the help of Nurse Rose." He sounds encouraging, but the sneer on his face suggests otherwise. He's not happy that Rose will be coming with me, but I couldn't give two fucks what he thinks. There was no way I was leaving here without knowing she'd be the one taking care of me once I'm home.

"Thanks, Doc," I say as I reach out my hand to shake his.

He hesitates a second before he returns the gesture. "You're welcome."

Without another look, he walks out the door just as a nurse I've never seen before walks in.

"What do ya say we get you home, huh?" she says with a smile, and I couldn't agree with her more. I'm more than ready to get out of here.

It takes a little longer than I'd have liked to get dressed, pack all of my things, and get situated in the wheelchair. I already hate this thing with a passion and cannot wait until the day comes when I can throw it in a ditch. Shit, maybe I'll burn the fucker first. But finally we're on our way down to first floor and making our way to the front door.

I don't catch any glimpses of Rose, but that's for the best. If I saw her again, I'd probably demand she leave with me now instead of waiting till after her shift. And we all know how that would turn out—a pissed off nurse and a heated conversation most likely.

Finally, what feels like hours later, but is really probably only ten minutes, we are on the road heading home. Blaze is driving the van while I sit awkwardly in the front seat. In front of us, riding on their motorcycles, making me insanely jealous, is Toby and Louie. And behind us, riding on their bikes are Tyke, TomTom, and Jax.

"Dani was going to come with to bring you home, but she said you had her running around like a little bitch doing last-minute errands for you," Blaze says. I can hear the humor in his voice. He thinks it's funny.

Laughing, I say, "Yeah, she would say that."

We're both quiet for a few moments, then it's my turn to break the silence. "So, you're gonna be a daddy again, huh? How you feel about that, brother?" I have no doubt he's over the top thrilled, but I wonder how Dani feels this time around. Last time she found out she was pregnant, she took it a little hard. Not only because she was the last to find out, but because she was scared to be a mom. But now, she shouldn't have that worry.

"Yup. That's what I'm told."

"You're probably going to have twins again. Or

fuck, knowing your luck, triplets!" I say, laughing my ass off at the very real possibility that it could happen.

"No fucking way. If she has twins, I'm gonna be carted off to the loony bin. No way I can handle two sets of multiples," Blaze grumbles, though I have no doubt he'd be just fine if that *did* indeed happen. He's an amazing father and I'm so happy he's the one with Dani. No one else can handle her crazy ass, let alone hyperactive kids that take after their mom.

"You should probably start packing then, brother."

"Fuck off," he says, which has me laughing so hard, if I could feel my lower abdominal muscles fully, I'd probably be hurting.

We don't say anything else the rest of the way, but it's a comfortable silence. I hate being in a situation where I feel like every silent moment needs to be filled. Talking when nothing needs to be said is one of my pet peeves. It's annoying and pointless.

The van pulls into the clubhouse parking lot forty minutes later. Standing outside clapping and hollering obscenities and excited welcomes that I'm home are the rest of my brothers, their old ladies if they have one, and even a few club whores and hang arounds.

Blaze walks over to help me out of the van and into my wheelchair. I want to push him away and curse him to hell and back, but I know he's just trying to help. And to be honest, I need it, so I keep silent. He doesn't say anything either and doesn't make it seem like I'm a complete invalid. Thank fuck for that. I don't know how I'd be able to take having one of my brothers looking at me like I'm worthless.

As soon as I'm situated in the wheelchair, everyone meets us halfway to the clubhouse.

"Welcome home, Prez," my brothers say to me and clap me on the back as I wheel by.

"Glad to have you back, Mack," a few of the hang arounds say as I make my way inside.

When we pass through the doors, I take a look around and notice there's a banner hung crookedly above the bar. More people are inside, standing around, smiling and clapping. It's like a party in here. But I don't want a party. Not yet. We'll celebrate when I'm able to stand tall with my brothers by my side again.

"All right, fuckers. I'm home. Yes, it's good to be back, but there will be no party. If you want to sit around and drink, I'm okay with that. But that's all it will be," I say, maybe a little too harshly, but I can't help it. It pisses me off that they're ready to celebrate when I'm not at my best. *Yet*. But with Rose's help, I'll get there.

"Now, where the fuck is my daughter? Since I've been accused to making her my errand bitch, I figure I better put her to work more."

"I'm right here, asshole," Dani says from somewhere behind me. "And the work is all done. I'm confident everything will exceed your expectations, *sir*," she says in a mocking tone. "Now if you'll excuse me, I'll be at the bar. I wish I could say I'll be drinking something strong, but I'll have to settle for a bombass Shirley Temple. I think I deserve *something* after all the work you put me through."

I turn my head to look at her as she comes up behind me. She has a smile on her face, so I'm reassured she's not upset with me. And even though I want to give her shit about her giving *me* shit, I keep my mouth shut. I'll have plenty of time to fuck with her later.

"Yes, please go to the bar and get sugared up. That's just what we need," I throw back at her with a smile of my own.

Shaking her head, she gives me a hug and whispers in my ear, "It's so good to have you home. I missed you."

Her words make my eyes sting with unshed tears, but I won't let them fall. I've never been one to wear my emotions on my sleeve, and I've never been one to cry. I'm not going to start now. Shit, I'm already feeling lower than I'd like since I can't walk and have to have help doing the simplest of things. I don't need to add being a crying bitch on to that.

Releasing me, she turns away without showing her face. I'm sure it's because she's crying or close to crying as well, and she doesn't want to show that to me. Having emotions is still new to her, so always crying is something that pisses her off to no end. Though she'll blame it on the pregnancy, I'm sure.

Looking around the room, I see everyone doing their own thing, not even paying attention to me, which I'm thankful for. Everyone is here, including

Skinner. I should pull him aside now to figure out what's going on with him, but I have something else I need to do right now. He'll have to wait.

Wheeling myself down the hallway toward my room, I stop at the door before mine. The room that will be occupied by Rose for the next few weeks.

Opening the door, I'm shocked at what I find. It's like I'm no longer in the clubhouse. Dani has turned this whole room into something you'd find in a top of the line penthouse. The bed is a queen, with simple black and white bedding. It looks shiny, so it could be silk. The bedframe is solid oak and is covered in frilly shit that looks like curtains.

Beside the bed is a nightstand with a remote to a brand new flat-screen TV that's mounted on the wall right across from the bed.

Next is a full-size refrigerator that I have no doubt is filled to the max. Then there's a small sofa with pillows and a lap blanket.

This room has everything I asked for and then some, but there are a few things extra I want to pick up for Rose. I don't know what she has or what she's bringing, but I want to make sure she has everything she'd ever want or need here. My hope is that she won't want to leave for much when she gets here, even just to get away. This will be a perfect home away from home.

Dani did a great job making this room into a suite. It's more than I asked for, but I can only hope Rose likes it and will be comfortable here.

I know she probably wasn't thrilled with staying here, or even wanting to take this job, but hopefully after seeing this, it'll make the decision seem better.

Dani did an amazing job. I can't think of anything else that could make this room more comfortable or homey. I just hope Rose feels the same way.

CHAPTER SIX

Rose

By the time my shift is over, I'm exhausted. Actually, that's a lie; I've been dead on my feet since last night, but the adrenaline and coffee kept me going until this point. At least I know that by the end of tonight, I'll be on my way to getting out of here for good. I'll be safe somewhere Anthony will no longer be able to find me. At least, I hope.

The deal I made with Mack wasn't something I ever thought I would agree to, but I can't deny it will help me out immensely. I knew my money was low before I went to sign his release papers and I was unsure how I would survive or make more money to live off of once I got to where I was going. Now, I won't have to worry about that. Not for a while, anyway.

He's promised to pay me triple my salary, but that's way more than I can or will accept. Even if he paid me what I usually make in the next month, that will be enough. I won't have to pay for anything while I'm there, so I can put everything into my savings and not touch it until I leave.

Though I told him I would only agree under a few conditions, I probably would have taken the deal anyway. There's something between us, and even though I wanted to just leave and never look back as soon as possible, I have to admit I'm not sure I would have been able to go through with it. Mack has entered my heart and my head, and I want to be there while he recovers. I want to be the one to help him get back on his feet—literally.

He said he would provide me my own room, that was something I absolutely need. I want my own space and have a place I can get away when needed. And I know I'm going to need it around Mack. He gets in my head and makes my body do crazy things. I can't afford to be caught up in him right now or allow my body to give in to its urges. It's been a long time, longer than I'd like to admit, since I've had sex, but what my mind knows that my body does not is that I don't need sex. It's unneeded attention and opening the door to be hurt. I don't need that shit.

The condition he set out about having someone follow me around whenever I leave his house would normally be something I'd fight to the end about. But this time it's different. I have my brother to worry about now, and any extra protection is greatly appreciated. That's why I agreed to that demand.

I know I should probably fill Mack in about what's going on so he's aware of the possible threat, but I can't. I don't want him to know where I came from, who I'm related to, or think poorly of me because of it. I've gone this far being able to keep that part of my life away from who I am today, and I'll do whatever it takes to keep it that way.

And the last condition we both agreed to was something I knew Mack would have no problem with. Everything I know of him and the way our conversations have gone so far, I knew how that one would turn out. Yes, he'd listen to me and let me be the boss when it came to his care and medical condition. I'm the nurse and he is the patient, so he will listen to me. But I also know that I'm walking into *his* home, his territory…so anything outside of his treatment is his game, not mine. And if he respects my title, which he has thus far, then I will respect his. That doesn't mean when push comes to shove and something happens I don't agree with that I won't put my two cents in, but I know who will have the final say. And I'm okay with that. Or as okay with that as I can be.

Heading into the locker room, I grab my purse. I talked with Monica right before I finished my final rounds, but I never said I would be leaving after finishing with Mack. I just told her when I was done, I'd call her to let her know what was going on. No need to tell her yet anyway.

Who knows how long I'll be with Mack helping him get better, and honestly, I'm good with that, even if it's for a few months. That will just give me more time to save money. And spend time with him to hopefully get him out of my head, but I won't tell anyone else that. I barely want to admit it to myself, let alone someone else. Plus, it's not like I have a lot of friends I would want to talk about Mack to. I only have a few co-workers I talk to at work and maybe go out to eat or have a quick drink with. Not talk about men or even hopes and dreams. They might, but I don't. That shit is just for me. No one else needs to know my business.

Once I have everything out of my locker, I head toward the elevator.

"We'll see you in a few weeks," one of the nurses I work with yells out, but I don't answer back. I don't need to explain to her that I probably won't be back, and if I am, it will be longer than a few weeks anyway. I just nod, smile, and step into the elevator, keeping my eyes averted so no one else will try to talk to me.

A few seconds later, I'm on the bottom floor and heading out toward my vehicle. I feel jumpy and my eyes scan all around, aware of everything surrounding me. Last time I walked out of the hospital to my car, a nasty surprise was waiting for me. I just pray the same thing isn't waiting for me tonight. Or worse.

So far, I don't see anything out of the ordinary; no letters on my windshield and no one lurking nearby that could be my brother or one of his goons.

Making it all the way to my car, I finally breathe a sigh of relief that there is nothing here that I've been dreading all day. But that relief is short-lived.

I barely get my key in my car door when someone comes up behind me, grabbing my shoulder. I let out a scream and whip around, ready to defend myself by any means necessary, when I see someone familiar yet welcome standing there.

"Whoa, babe. It's just me." It's Jax, one of

Mack's brothers in the MC.

I feel stupid, but I don't let it show that I'm embarrassed of what just happened. I'm a woman, walking to her car at night. I have every reason to be jumpy when someone sneaks up on me.

"Sorry. You scared me. I thought Mack said you'd meet me at my place?" I question, though I don't really care if he answers or not. I'm actually kind of grateful he's here. Maybe he's the reason I don't have an unwanted visitor waiting for me or a note on my car.

Jax smiles sheepishly before answering, "Yeah, well, I was early so I thought I'd come here instead. Hope that's not a problem."

"No, of course not. It's not needed, but I appreciate it all the same," I half-lie. It shouldn't be needed but at this point, I think it is, at least for me and my peace of mind.

Jax doesn't say anything else, he just walks over to a motorcycle I didn't notice before, then waits for me to get in my car. Pulling out of the parking lot, I look in my rearview mirror. A small smile takes over my face. I never thought it would make me happy to be escorted back to my apartment. And by a biker to boot. But I think these guys are different than any biker I've seen before. At least, I hope they are.

Ten minutes later we're pulling up to my apartment and the happy feeling I had when leaving the hospital fades away just as quickly as it came. Now I feel like I'm back in a war zone and wondering when the enemy will strike. Will my brother be here? Is he outside watching me or is he inside my apartment waiting pounce?

Stepping out of my car, my eyes dart all around like a nervous junky who needs their next fix but still concerned that a cop will bust them. Paranoia is a bitch, but I guess it can't be helped at this point in my life. I just hope that after leaving here and finding a place far away will make it better. I don't want to have to look over my shoulder all the time and wonder when the other shoe will drop.

Jax parks behind me and gets off his bike. "I'll wait here for you," he says. I hate that his words strike fear inside me, but I try my best to not show it.

"Actually, could you come up with me? I may need help carrying some things down." I don't plan on bringing much, but I'll pack up my whole apartment if that's what it takes to make sure he follows me up and has my back if someone is waiting for me inside.

He looks at me with a confused look, but it fades quickly. Nodding, he holds out his arm as if to say, *Lead the way*.

I try to not seem fidgety and keep my eyes ahead of me, but I'm not sure if I succeed. If I don't, Jax doesn't comment though, for which I'm grateful. I don't want to explain my behavior, and even if he does ask, I won't tell him. I'll just play it off like this is normal for me; I'm a woman walking to her house at dark. It's a natural reaction, right?

We make it to my door slowly, but it gives me time to calm myself. Putting the key in the door, I open it in almost slow motion, waiting for a hand to reach out and grab me. But it doesn't come. Thank

God.

"Go grab what you need. I'm going to make a few calls and take a look around," Jax says.

I look at him with a questioning look. Why would he want to look around? Was I wrong? Did I not hide my fear good enough?

"Habit, I guess; always like to survey my surroundings and know every way in and out in case shit hits the fan," he explains. I'm not sure if he's just brushing it off as nothing or if he's telling the truth, but I go with it, hoping shit doesn't hit the fan while we're here.

Making my way back into my room, the low sound of his voice talking to someone gives me comfort as I grab a bag and start throwing stuff in there. I grab panties, bras, and a few pair of socks. Then I head into my closet to grab my clothes. One downfall to being a nurse and working all the time is I don't have a lot of regular clothes. I can count the number of shorts and pairs of jeans I have on one hand.

That's really sad, but what do you expect? I barely have time for myself and even if I did, it's not like I go out much. I go to work in my scrubs, then come home with just enough energy to take a bath and maybe watch a few episodes on Netflix. And that doesn't require pants.

Once I have my clothes packed, I go into the bathroom to grab all the necessities I'll need while I'm away. Again, it's not much. Just my shampoo and conditioner, body wash, razor, lotion, and the little bit of makeup I have. I usually don't do my makeup to go to work, and I doubt I'll need it where

I'm going because I couldn't care less what I look like, but I'm bringing it anyway. Some days you just need to wear makeup to make you feel better.

Tossing my bag over my shoulder, I make my way back out to the front of my apartment. As I'm turning the corner that leads into the living room slash kitchen, I overhear Jax on his phone. "I'll take care of it, Prez. I got this. We'll see you soon."

Hanging up his phone, he turns to see me standing there. He doesn't seem mad that I listened in or afraid I heard something I shouldn't. Which I really didn't. He just gave an affirmative to something that I have no idea about and that he'd see him later. That's it. Nothing to write home about or chastise me for overhearing.

"All ready," I say, wanting to get out of here. I don't want to leave it to chance that we're here too long and my brother decides to show up. I don't know what would happen if he saw me with Jax, but I know it wouldn't be pretty. I'd never forgive myself if Jax got hurt, or worse, because of me.

Jax motions to the bag over my shoulder. "Do you want me to take that so you can grab the rest of your stuff?" he asks.

"Oh, uh, no. I guess I didn't have much to bring after all. I'm sorry I made you come up here for nothing."

"No worries," he says, then takes a step toward the door. "Shall we?"

A laugh bubbles up and breaks past my lips as he folds his arm across his stomach, then bows like he's the driver awaiting the Princess to enter her limousine.

Moving forward, I take a step to walk in front of him, but before I can he holds out his hand, stopping my exit.

I look at him questioningly, not sure why he's not letting me pass, but he answers my unspoken question with a smile. "I'll carry your bag."

I pause for minute, but decide there's no harm in him taking my bag for me. It's not needed, but if it makes him feel better, than who am I to say no?

"Thank you," I say, then finally step out of my apartment, locking up after he closes the door.

"I'll follow you out of town. Make your way onto I-34 North. Once we get out of town, I'll pull out in front of you for you to follow me to the clubhouse," Jax says as we make our way down the steps.

"Okay," I simply say, not going to argue with him. I have no idea where this clubhouse is or even what town it's in. I should have looked at Mack's paperwork before he was released, but I never saw a need to. I could be following this guy into the gates of Hell, but I highly doubt it. I may not know this guy, but I do think I know Mack. Or enough to know that he wouldn't lead me to my death or trust Jax as my escort if he was bad news.

"Do you need to stop anywhere to get anything else before we head out of town?" Jax asks, interrupting my thoughts.

Thinking about that for a minute, I wonder if I should try to stop somewhere to see if they have a computer or even a tablet to keep me busy when I'm not working with Mack, but quickly shut that idea down. I'm tired and just want to fall into a bed or any soft surface and sleep for a week. I can see if someone can take me to a Best Buy or something tomorrow.

"No, that won't be necessary. I have all that I need right now. Thank you though," I answer.

"Not a problem, babe. Mack told me to make sure you got to the clubhouse safely, but also to be sure you had everything you want and need for your stay. I think he gave me enough money to put a down payment on a mansion to cover anything you wanted to buy." He laughs at that last part.

I smile even though Jax can't see me. It's not for him, anyway. The fact that Mack not only tasked this man with my safety, but to also take me anywhere I wanted to go and buy anything I needed is sweet. I've never had anyone care about my safety or if I had even the bare essentials before, so this is a nice change.

Getting in my car, I wait until I see Jax ready on his bike before I start my car. Pulling out of the parking lot, I don't even bother to look around the lot trying to spot ghosts from my past. For better or worse, things are about to change. I can feel it in the air, in my blood, down in my soul. I just hope that it doesn't end up killing me.

***

It took us a little under an hour before we pass the sign that said **'Welcome to Dixon—Home of the Few.'** I have no idea what the saying on the sign means, but I'm making a note to ask Mack or someone else about it later.

95

Jax gives me some hand signal just past the city limits. I wish I knew biker hand signs, but since I don't, I'll just have to suffice with following him. Hopefully that's what his little hand motion was.

We start to slow down and I think we are getting close to the clubhouse, but we continue to drive for what feels like hours. Or maybe it's just me and my over-tired brain.

Finally, I spot a huge building that looks like it could be Fort Knox's twin. The lot in front of it is filled with bikes and a few cars, so I'm going to go out on a limb and say this is the clubhouse. Jax doesn't disappoint as he pulls into said parking lot and stops right in front of the doors.

I'm not sure if I should follow him or choose one of the few parking spots left, but I go with the former. Someone else can move my car if it's in the way. I'm too fucking tired to care right now.

Jax unmounts from his bike, then walks the few feet over to my car. "Home sweet home," he says as he opens my door.

"Yeah, thanks," I say, not really sure what else to say. Yes, this will be the place I lay my head down for the next few weeks or so, but home? I don't think I've ever really had a place I'd consider home. Definitely not the place I was raised. That was more of a purgatory than home. And my dorm during college was just a place I rested my head between classes and clinicals. And my apartment after that? That was—*is*—my place, but I don't think I've ever referred to it as a home.

I follow Jax toward the front door and notice he still has my bag. It's slung over his shoulder like it's his. I should take it back or at least thank him for carrying it for me even though it probably would have been easier for me to just put in my backseat, but I let him carry it. I'm not even sure my tired body could carry the damn thing.

Right before we make it to the door, it opens and out walks one of the women I've seen at the hospital visiting Mack. It's Dani—Mack's daughter.

"Hey Jax, how was the ride here?" she asks my escort, before looking past him and right at me. I see a look of surprise cross her face before she covers it up with a smile. "Nurse Rose. I didn't know you were the one Mack hired to oversee the rest of his care." There's no malice in her voice. She's truly surprised I'm here. Does she not think I'm capable of taking care of her father? Or did she just not think I'd agree?

"Yeah, well, your father drives a hard bargain." No sense in asking what she meant. I highly doubt she'd tell me even if I did ask, and frankly, I don't really care about her answer. All she needs to know is that Mack needed an in-home nurse and here I am. Simple as that.

Dani laughs, then links her arm through mine, leading me into the building. "That he does, girl. That he does," she says.

We clear the door and walk into a big common room that looks like a full-on bar. There are tables and chairs scattered all over, and there are a few booths around the edges of the room. I can see at least two pool tables, a few couches, and even a stage on one end equipped with a stripper pool. Holy shit! What the hell am I walking into?

The bar is long and tall. I think it's made from mahogany, or something similar. It's very nice. Just looking at the bar, you'd think you were in some fancy restaurant, not inside an outlaw MC's clubhouse.

Looking around the bar, I see a lot of people. Some are drinking beer, some have something stronger, and some are walking around with soda cans. But the one thing that is the same; they all have smiles on their faces. They all look happy, like they've each won the lottery or something. It's so strange, but it's also amazing.

I've seen people who are happy before. Maybe about getting a promotion or they were proposed to by their boyfriend. But it doesn't last and in a way, it always seems fake. This right here? This isn't fake. I don't know if this is the way they all are all the time, or if this is because Mack is home, but it's nice to see. It makes me feel happy just witnessing it.

Doing another glance around, I don't see Mack among the dozens of faces. If this is a party for him, which I would assume it is because there's a small banner hung haphazardly above the bar, he should be here. But he's not. Maybe he's going to the bathroom or trying to change? I wonder if he's okay or if he needs help. Or maybe he's in pain and needs some meds. Shit, I should go find him to make sure everything is all right.

Leaning in toward Dani, I ask, "Where's Mack?" I'm not sure if she can hear the concern in my voice, but I'm too worried to try to hide it.

"Oh, he's in the back. Let me show you back

there and to your room," Dani says. She leads me away from the party and down a quiet hallway.

There are more doors down here than I thought possible. From seeing the place outside and even looking through the bar, you wouldn't think it was this big, but this place is huge...although I don't know what the rooms are for or how big they are. For all I know they could be small closets, but that seems unlikely. They have to either be bedrooms or offices or *something* more than just a closet. Maybe one leads to a bathroom or the kitchen? But still, that would mean this place is big. I could even get lost in here if I'm not careful.

We seem to walk on forever, but we finally stop at the second to last door at the end of the long hallway. These are the only doors this far down, like they were meant to be separated from the others.

Looking over my shoulder, I see no one else has followed us. I'm starting to get a little nervous. Being back here by myself—even with Dani by my side—it's kind of scary. I'm so used to being scared all the time and always looking over my shoulder, waiting for the monsters of my past to jump out and try to grab me. But here, I'm surrounded by people I barely know. Who's to say they aren't the same as my brother? Or worse.

"This is your room. Mack had me get some things for you, but if you think of anything else you may want or need, just let me know. Maybe you'll let me take you shopping. I'm sure Harlow and Sara would even like that. We're due for a good ol' shopping trip where we spend the guys' money anyway." She laughs and winks at me, which has me smiling back at her. It's so easy to be happy around Dani. It's weird, but welcome. I could see us becoming good friends, and staying friends even after all of this is said and done. If I stick around, that is.

"Anyway, I'll let you get situated. I'll have Jax bring your bag by soon. Let me know if you need anything, okay?"

Turning so I'm facing her fully, I say, "Thank you, Dani. I really appreciate it. And I may take you up on that shopping trip."

Dani pulls me in for a hug and whispers, "You're welcome, babe. Just be careful with him. He's a good man and hasn't had things easy. He deserves something good in his life and I know he's taken a liking to you." Pulling back, she casts a serious, almost angry look toward me. "But if you hurt him, we'll have problems." Then, as if she didn't just threaten me, she smiles. "And I'm always game for a shopping trip, now more than ever." Then she's turning on her heel, heading back to the bar area.

Well, that was weird, but I get what she's saying. Mack is an amazing man as far as I can tell, and he's her father. She's just looking out for him the only way she knows how.

I wait until she's out of sight, then take a deep breath. I have no idea what I'm about to walk into and I'm nervous. I almost want to wait until I see Mack before I step inside these walls, but Dani is already gone and I'm not about to go wander around by myself, opening random doors, looking for him. When Jax comes by with my bag, I'll just have to ask him where Mack is.

Blowing out a long breath, I harden my resolve and open the door. *It's now or never.*

Turning the knob, I slowly open the door, and what I see on the other side blows my mind.

The first thing I notice is Mack inside, sitting in his wheelchair beside a huge bed. It looks like he was setting something down, but I can't pay attention to that. Mack is taking up all my attention. He may be in a wheelchair, but he's the sexiest person I have ever seen. Wearing faded jeans, a black shirt, and his Forsaken Sinners MC cut, he is the definition of rough. And gorgeous. And orgasmic. Just looking at him now I feel like my panties are going to combust.

Needing to look away before I either say or do something that wouldn't be good for either of us, I glance around the room and notice for the first time that this room is amazing. Better than the one inside my apartment. The bed is huge with a comforter set that looks expensive. And comfy.

There's a huge TV on the wall, a big enough dresser that could hold my whole wardrobe at my apartment, a bedside table, and I can now make out what Mack was placing on top of it. A computer. A brand new computer. I don't know if it's his and he was just researching something and didn't want to take it back to his room, but knowing what I know of Mack and seeing what he's done for me with this room, I'm going to go with the answer that it's now my laptop.

"Wow," I whisper, continuing my visual around the room. They must have done a lot of work to

101

make this into what it is now. This must have taken forever and a lot of money. I'm just taking a guess here, but I don't think this room was like this before they knew I was coming. It irritates me that they went out of the way for me, but also it warms my heart that they wanted me to be comfortable here. Inside this room I can almost pretend I'm not in the clubhouse of a one percenter biker club. That my brother isn't out there looking for me for some unknown reason.

"What do you think?" Mack asks, with nervousness and hope in his voice.

Looking back at him, I can do nothing but smile at this man. He really is a good guy. "It's amazing."

CHAPTER SEVEN

Mack

I've been home for a little over two weeks and things are going great. I'm getting stronger and almost have full control of my movements in my legs. Rose and I spend the better part of the day doing the treatments and physical therapy. Plus, when she's not around, I work my ass off—probably more than I should—doing everything I can to make sure the progress continues. And so far, the outcome is more than I thought possible. Now, we just need to work on learning to walk all over again and getting my legs strong enough to hold my weight.

We're still doing the massage therapy, but instead of just focusing on my back, now we've moved to almost full body massages. And let me tell you—it takes all of my self-control and then some to not just grab Rose and pull her down on top of me before claiming her sinful lips. But that's a whole other battle.

Our routine has been perfected and I think she's even starting to like being here. Sure, it's still new for her and she's unsure about some of the guys—and some of the club whores—but she's smiling a lot more and talking more freely. It's a beautiful sight to behold.

Even though I'm getting stronger, I still haven't taken back my full title from Blaze. He's doing a fantastic job filling in for me…I almost don't want to take it away from him. I love my club and I love being their leader, but at some point in time, it's going to be time for me to step down. I don't want to be old and crippled when that time comes. But that's something we'll worry about after all the shit has settled with me and our rival club problem.

Hearing a knock on my door, I look at the clock to see it's too early for Rose. We've talked a lot more and things seem easier between us—minus the enormous sexual tension, that is—but she really only comes into my room for my treatments. Otherwise we meet out in the bar or we pass each other in the hallway.

"Yo, Prez. You got a minute?" Skinner says through the door, almost out of breath.

Sitting up more in my bed, I call him in. I never had the chance to pull him aside to talk to him after I first got back because I was too focused on getting better, but now that he's here, I'm going to see what's been going on with him.

He walks in and shuts the door before taking a seat on the small couch I have against the wall. "What's up, brother?" I ask, wondering what he's here about. We have church in twenty minutes, but that's basically just to go over anything new we've found out about the Street Kings and figuring out what we're going to do about them.

Skinner looks down at his feet and he looks completely lost. I don't think I've ever seen him like this and it has me really worried. I should have fuckin' pulled him aside as soon as I noticed something was off with him.

"I want you to put a call in to Elmo," is all he says, and now I'm even more concerned. Why the fuck does he want me to do that?

Elmo is our MC's national president. Even though we're one of the two founding chapters, Elmo was the best option for the job. He grew up in the life, and to be completely honest, I didn't *want* the title. Too much responsibility and a massive headache, if you ask me. My boys keep me busy and my mind going crazy enough. I don't need to add in *every* Forsaken Sinner chapter to that.

"And why is it I need to call our national Prez?" I ask, my voice hard. I'm not angry with Skinner, but the unknown is making me agitated. I'm more pissed at myself that I haven't tried harder to know more about what's been going on. He's my fuckin' VP, for fuck's sake! If something is going on with him, I should know about it—injured or not.

Blowing out a long breath, he finally looks at me and I see more than I care to see in his eyes—pain, anger, and detachment. "I want to retire my patch, Prez."

I'm completely blown the fuck away. Retirement? Why the hell would he want to do that? Skinner has been by my side since the very beginning. Decades worth of fighting beside each other, building this chapter up to where it is right now, and always having my back. He's been my level head and reason all these years. And he wants to retire?

Out of everything I could have guessed was going on, this was not one of them. Not many men retire their patch. It's almost unheard of.

Skinner sees the turmoil in my eyes, but before I can question him or make any sort of comment, he continues, "I've got stage four lung cancer, Mack. I've done all I can to keep it at bay, but it's starting to take a toll on me. So before it becomes a problem and I put one of my brothers in jeopardy, I've decided it's time. I know this isn't what you want to hear and I know this couldn't have come on at a worse time, but it can't wait. I'm a liability, brother."

I'm not only flabbergasted that he wants to retire, but now to add insult to injury, he's got cancer and I never knew. I'm not sure how long he's known, but for him to keep that from me? I don't understand it and I don't fucking accept it.

"How long?" I say through gritted teeth, trying like hell to not lose my shit right now. This has to be hard on him, but shit! He should have fucking told me.

"Eight months."

My eyes shoot fire toward him. "Eight fucking months! When the hell were you going to tell me, huh? When you dropped dead on a run?" I yell, throwing my arm out, needing to demolish something.

My arm makes contact with the first thing it comes up against and it just so happens to be my lamp. It comes crashing down, but it's not enough. Spotting my computer sitting on top of the table, I grab that and hurl it across the room, needing to destroy it, but I still don't feel better. Spotting my burner phone next, I hurl that too and watch it break into a hundred little pieces.

I thought destroying something, making it look like what I feel inside would make me feel better, but it doesn't. I still feel anger—at my friend, my *brother*—but mostly at the cancer that is taking him away from me. I feel pain and shame at my behavior, but not enough to apologize. I know he must be going through hell, and I'm not making matters better, but God-fucking-dammit! I'm barely getting back on my feet and almost ready to take back control of my club, and he goes and lays this bombshell on me. *Fuck!*

Skinner lets me throw my tantrum—Rose's words, not mine—and doesn't say anything. He knows I get like this when I get so angry I can't see straight. I have to exert the energy somehow before it swallows me whole.

I'm still breathing heavy and unable to look at him when he finally speaks again. "I know you're pissed off at me and won't believe me when I say this, but I *am* sorry, Prez. I just didn't know how to tell you—anyone for that matter. And then shit went south and it just wasn't the best time." He pauses for a minute, waiting until I can finally look at him.

"But I went to the doctor yesterday and they said it's time that I start putting all my ducks in a row and start preparing for the end. I can barely take a full breath and I'm hurting, Mack. *Fuck* am I hurtin'." Again, he pauses, but this time, it's for him to gather himself before continuing.

"I'm not sure if anyone has noticed or made a mention to you, but I'm not able to do my job anymore. I can barely keep up on rides and when we're not on our bikes. It's almost impossible. I hate to do this to you—now of all times—but it has to be done. The sooner, the better."

I have no more words for him, and honestly, he doesn't need them. So instead, I just nod and watch him walk toward the door. "I'll see you at church," he says quietly before slowly making his way out of my room and closing the door behind him.

Still needing an outlet for everything I'm feeling inside, I grab everything from my nightstand and throw it across the room. Then I throw the blankets off my bed before swinging my slightly limp legs over the side of the bed with angry movements.

Maneuvering myself into my wheelchair, I wheel myself into the bathroom and proceed to break everything in my reach.

By the time my anger is replaced with a numbing sadness, I'm breathing heavy, I have cuts on my hands and arms from flying shards of glass, and there's destruction and mayhem everywhere I look. I don't think I left anything untouched—it's either broken, overturned, or out of its place. But I do feel a little better. Well, not better as in I'm okay with what Skinner told me, but I'm not angry anymore. Just numb.

Blowing out a breath, I take one last look at the

mess I've made in the bathroom, grab a towel to wrap around my hand, then wheel myself back out into my room, trying my best to ignore the destruction here. Grabbing my cut off the desk chair, which is probably the only thing left untouched, I start to make my way to the door just as there's another knock.

Whipping the door open, I see a stunned Rose standing in front of me. She looks at me and opens her mouth, probably to ask if everything is all right, but then she sees what's behind me and her face falls even more.

Looking back to me, I can see a little bit of irritation in her deep blue depths, but there's also concern. "Everything all right?" she asks.

Completely ignoring her, I start to wheel forward, not even caring if she moves or not. I need to get the fuck out of this room and all the feelings I left there.

Rose moves out of the way, but just barely. "Whoa," she yells, but again, I choose to ignore her. It's not because I don't want to talk to her or because I'm angry with her. It's just that I can't talk about it. Not with her. Not yet.

I can hear her anger and agitation as I make my way down the hall toward the chapel, but I'll deal with her later. Right now, I just need to get inside the four sacred walls where I've led church for the past umpteen years. I know I'm early, but that's exactly what I want. I need the few minutes alone before everyone fills the chairs around the table and I have to tell them what's going to happen now.

***

Ten minutes later, I'm sitting at the head of the table and just hanging up the phone with Elmo when the doors to the chapel open and all of my brothers come walking in. Taking their assigned seats, I wait for everyone to quiet down before I look at them.

Looking first to my right, I lock eyes with Toby; my Sergeant at Arms. This man is the strength of the club and is always front and center through the craziest of shit.

Next to him is Blaze, my adoptive son-in-law and current stand-in president. I hate to pull that title away from him because he's done such a good job, but it's time I get back to business. It's time to get shit straight and figure out what we're doing.

After Blaze is Louie, Tom Tom, Slayer, and then there's Tyke. He's the Nomad who helped us out a few years ago and just never left. Not like I can complain. I love having his crazy ass around. I should probably talk to him about transferring and taking on our California bottom rocker. Make him our own.

Sitting beside Tyke is the newly voted in member Goose. I was still in the hospital when the vote went down, but from what I saw of him from his prospecting, he's going to make a great addition. That's why I gave a yea proxy for my vote.

And beside him is Thor, then finally, Skinner; my VP, who is sitting at my left. And speaking of him...

"Shut the fuck up so we can get on with the

110

meetin'," I say, even though everyone is mostly quiet, but I don't care. I'm in a shitty mood, and now everyone will know it. Heck, maybe now their moods will dampen too, and they'll match mine. Good. I shouldn't be the only one having a crap-fucking-tastic day.

I look all around the table once more, then I level a look that feels blank of all emotion at Skinner. "First things first. What's going on with our little friends?" I ask, then look to my other side where Toby is sitting.

Toby leans back in his chair and crosses his arms. "Nothing new, Prez. We've had our ears on them and have tried to follow them as much as possible, but we don't want them to catch on that we're on to them. So far though, they haven't even so much as mentioned our colors."

I don't know why, but I guess I figured with this being the first serious meeting I've been to since getting shot that there would be more than that. Shit, we've had the bug in their clubhouse for months. Surely they've mentioned something about a plan of attack or at the very least what they're hoping to gain.

We're both one percenters, but the Sinners have always been legit. Or mostly anyway. We may have dabbled in the occasional job that wasn't on the right side of the law, but we have our own law anyway, so it doesn't matter. But as far as businesses go, we're as legit as they come.

Now the Street Kings though, they're dirtier than your grandmother's panties. They've got their fingers in everything from drugs, slaves, and guns.

Maybe they're after our territory, but that's unlikely since we aren't really a threat. Sure, we pretty much own this state and the states surrounding, but why start a war when it's not needed? If they wanted to run their dirty business through our towns, we wouldn't have a problem with it. We'd only demand a percentage, which is par for the course. But I don't think that's what they're doing. It seems off and out of place.

Maybe it's retaliation from us killin' that sonofabitch Titus, though he had it fuckin' comin'. Shit, I wish that fucknut was still alive so I could skin him myself. So again, that doesn't seem like what they are after.

But if not a territory war and not retaliation, what?

"Anyone got any ideas for what our next move is? 'Cause I don't want to be standing around with my head in the clouds when shit comes piling down around us," I say, needing to have a plan of action, but am in no state to think of anything clearly. Not with my next order of business that I need to bring up.

"How do you feel about sending in one of the prospects? Let them get a feel for them and see if he can find anything?" Toby says, but I really don't want to have to resort to sending in a prospect. Yeah, they're committed, but that don't mean I fucking trust them. That's why they don't have a full patch, for Christ's sakes. I'd rather send my mother in before one of them.

"Nah, that's no good. If the Kings find out, they may be able to sway them to their side if we send in

112

a newbie," Blaze says and I almost want to smile. Boy fuckin' thinks like me. I like it.

Everyone is quiet again, hopefully thinking about something we could do to get the ball rolling on this little problem we have.

After a few quiet but tense moments, Louie speaks. "How confident are we that they haven't been tailing us or doing any research on us?"

I'm not sure where he's going with that question, but I don't have the answer. Thankfully, Toby is quick to speak up.

"I don't know about any research, but as far as putting eyes on most of us, I'm pretty certain there are only a select few they know about. At least, that they can put a face to the name. Why, what you thinkin', brother?"

"Well, if everyone is wanting to go the spy route, why don't we send the Nomad in? Yeah, he's been around for a few years, but he's not associated with our chapter. And let's be honest, it's not like you go out much." His last jab is directed at Tyke, but he doesn't seem to mind. Actually, he doesn't even look like he heard Louie if his facial features are anything to go off of.

I look around to the rest of my brothers to gauge what they think of the plan, then turn to Tyke. "What do you think about that, brother? Wanna go commando?" I ask, though it's our best bet right now, so even if he didn't like it, we may have to go against his wishes. I can only hope it doesn't go that route.

"I'm good with that, Prez. Whatever you need," he answers like the good solider he is. I swear, that boy lives and breathes the Marines even though he's been out for almost ten years.

"Good. Toby, bring Tyke up to speed and get him set up with everything he'll need to go dark. I want him in by tomorrow," I say.

All the brothers nod and then Tyke and Toby start discussing plans and supplies across the table, but I put a stop to that. We ain't done yet.

"Before ya'll go off and start talking wedding themes, I have one other thing to discuss." I pause and wait till I have every eye on me.

"We need to vote in a new VP." I let speculation and gasps of surprise float around before continuing. What can I say? My mama always said I was a drama queen. "Skinner here has been holding something back from us. It's come to a point where he no longer feels he can keep up his duties, but I'll let him tell you all about that later. What I *will* say is I spoke to Elmo and he's agreed to retire his patches, so as of right now, you are no longer VP of the Forsaken Sinners, Dixon Chapter."

Skinner nods sadly, but he keeps his head held high as he stands on shaky feet and pulls off his cut. Taking out his knife, he proceeds to stripe his patches from his cut, then hands them over to me before putting his cut back on. It all takes a matter of minutes, but it seems to drag on for hours. It's never a good moment when someone is stripped of their patches—of their free will or because they are a traitor.

Once I have his VP patch in my hand, I look around the room. "Skinner here has been on my right for as long as I've been sitting at the head of this table. I hate to see him go, but I do think I know the best person to pick up where he leaves off," I say, then look to my son-in-law. "I nominate Blaze to be my new VP. Let's vote." I don't drag it out. No sense in beating around the bush.

In order for the vote to go through and Blaze to be patched in as the new VP, it has to be a unanimous vote, but none of the brothers waste any time with their answers. "Yea's" and "Yes," ring out over and over until the vote is on me.

"Well, we all know what my vote is gonna be. Hell yes I want you as my VP, son," I say, then hold my arms out to welcome him into my arms. He doesn't hesitate and hugs me freely, without any quarrels that the men surrounding us would think any less of him. Shit, they'll be offering the same once I'm done anyway.

Blaze wraps his arms around me and whispers, "I won't let you down, Prez."

I just nod, then pull back. "I know you won't, son. I'm damn proud of all you've done for this club while I've been out, and I have no doubt of what you'll do while sitting on my left. I love you brother," I say.

"Love you too," Blaze says back, then stands up. He smiles briefly at me before he's engulfed in the arms of every other brother surrounding our table. Including his predecessor.

When things settle down, Skinner takes Blaze's old seat while Blaze takes the seat on my left. "Any other order of business we need to discuss?" I ask, then look down at my watch. It's almost time for my session with Rose, but I'm not sure I'm in the

115

mood for it today.

"Nope. We'll get Tyke put together and update you before he leaves," Toby says. And on that note, I pick up the gavel before slamming it down on the table, drawing our meeting to an end. Then, wheeling over to Skinner, I give him a hug and tell him we'll talk later before I head back down to my room. Fuck, I could really use a cold one right about now.

Opening my door, Rose is already waiting for me. Or maybe she never left since the mess I left behind is no longer visible.

"You shouldn't have done that," I say, not worried she won't know what I'm talking about. She cleaned up all of the remnants of destruction I left behind.

"Well, I did, so let's not discuss what is already done. Instead, why don't you tell me why you decided your room needed a makeover by the Tasmanian Devil."

I know what she wants from me and I probably even owe it to her to tell her, but right now, I'm not feeling very giving. "I think you need to just go on back to your room, Rose. I'm not feeling up to talking or even doing my PT tonight," I say in a monotone, trying not to let all the emotions that are trying to bubble to the surface come out. There are so many, but I fear that the one that will come out is anger, and if that happens, Rose will be caught in the crosshairs. There's a part of my mind that knows it's wrong, but the rational part of my brain is currently being overshadowed by something dark and uncaring.

I hear movement so I turn to make sure she's leaving, but instead, I find her plopped down on my bed with her arms crossed. Great, the sassy Rose is coming out now. Usually I love to do battle with that side of her, but not today. It'll be like a volcano and a tornado colliding. It may ruin us both to the point we won't walk out of it the same.

CHAPTER EIGHT

Rose

I don't know why I'm pushing him but it just comes out. I want him to talk to me, to confide in me. I want to push his limits and see how far he'll go. But mostly, I just want *him*. I can't deny it anymore.

Over the last few days, it's become abundantly clear I want this man more than my next breath. And I think he wants me too. He's just better at hiding it.

"Leave. *Now*. Before shit gets ugly, Rose. I'm warning you," Mack says, bringing me back to the present and what I need from him right now.

"Mack. I know something's going on and you can talk to me," I say in a soothing voice so he knows I'm being genuine. Is it so much to ask that I want to know him; know what is bothering him?

"I said fucking drop it!" he booms out, glaring at me with fire in his eyes.

There's a part of me that knows I should be

afraid of him, but I know deep in my soul that Mack would never hurt me. He'd go out of his way to make sure that never happened. I don't even know how I know this, but I do. I know it like I know my name or my date of birth. But I also know he's not ready to open up to me just yet, so I'll do as he demands and leave it be. For the time being at least.

"Fine. I'll drop the subject, but I'm serious. If you ever need to talk, maybe to run something by a person who isn't too close to the subject, I'm here. I *want* to be here for you, Mack," I tell him and I can see a little of the fire in his eyes ebb away, but not completely. He still has his guard up, but mine is completely gone. At least where he's concerned it is. I don't think I could put it back up if I tried.

"But we do need to do your physical therapy. You're so close to getting back on your feet, Mack." He needs to do this, but I would be lying if I told him I wasn't being selfish as well. I want my hands on him. I want to feel like I'm doing something to help.

Sighing, Mack wheels himself over to his bed. "You're not going to let me rest, are you?" he asks tiredly, and even though I don't think he actually wants an answer, he's going to get one.

"Do you remember our deal? You're the boss man when it comes to things outside of your treatment, and I accept that. But you promised me something too, Mack. Do you remember?" I ask. I know he remembers, but with the mood he's in, he may try to deny it or say he was lying about letting me be the boss with everything that includes his care. He promised he'd listen to me and do as I say.

But what would I do if he told me he lied? Tell him I'm leaving? I just don't think I'd actually be able to make myself follow through. I'd like to think I would because I try to always keep my word, but at this point, I'm not sure I could physically leave him.

Mack looks down at his feet and is silent for a few minutes. I don't know if he's thinking about our conversation from that day in the hospital or if it's something else plaguing him, but he seems really deep in thought; like he doesn't even remember I'm here with him. He looks lost and sad. Sure, I can tell he's still angry about something, but the pain and hurt I see goes deep. What the hell happened to make him feel this way? Fuck, I wish he'd talk to me. Open up about how he feels, but also about his life. What his hopes and dreams are. What does he see for himself in five years? I want to know everything about this man.

I've tried to deny it but we have a connection. I don't know what that connection is, but I feel it in my veins. The universe put us together, forced my life to intertwine with his. Like a force of nature, we are unpredictable, sometimes bad for each other, but at the same time, perfect for each other.

Moving so I'm standing in front of him, I drop down to my knees and wait until he looks me in the eyes. "I'm here, Mack. I'm not going anywhere. I know that something happened, and you don't want to share…that's fine. For now. But you also need to understand I'm here as your nurse too. And as your nurse, I'm telling you we *will* be doing your treatment today. Not because that's what you promised me, but because you know it's the best thing for you. So you can either sit there and pout while I force you to do them, or you can help me and we do them together."

Mack stares into my eyes for what feels like forever, but he finally breaks contact to reach out and grab my hand. "Any sane person would have left the moment they saw the chaos I left behind in a fit of rage and confusion. A smart person would have left as soon as I started yelling for you to leave. But you...you stayed. I'm not sure if that makes you the most amazing creature I've ever known, or the stupidest," Mack says without once looking up at me. He just holds my hand, playing with each of my fingers.

Reaching out my other hand, I grab his chin and force him to meet my eyes. "See, that's where you're wrong, Mack. A stupid person would have just left and never looked back. I may be crazy, but I'm crazy smart because I stayed when no one else would have."

I want to kiss him so bad it hurts. I want him to devour me, starting with my lips and ending with my pussy. I'm just afraid of what it will all mean. But I'm more afraid he'll reject me.

There's been times I think he's feeling what I'm feeling—this electric pull toward the other—but with my luck, it's probably wishful thinking or me projecting what I'm feeling and seeing it in him. What if it's not real but only what I want to see?

When the urge to pull him toward me and connect our lips is too great, I finally pull away. And with the loss of eye connection, I slowly feel the intense need to kiss him fade as well. It's still there—I have a feeling that will never go away—but it's manageable now, which is good because I don't think I could stand it if I leaned in and he pulled away.

Clearing my throat, I take a step back. "Let me just run to my room quick to grab everything we need for our session and I'll be right back. Why don't you get comfortable in bed and we'll get started as soon as I get back," I say, but I don't wait for him to agree or disagree. I just take off like a bat outta hell toward my room, needing the space to clear my head. If I don't, there's no way I'll get through Mack's massage and physical therapy without succumbing to my need for that man.

It takes me longer than I'd like to admit to cool myself down before going back to his room. I give myself about three pep talks and splash cool water on my face before counting to fifty. But finally, I'm ready to head back into the lion's den—or in this case, the sexy biker den.

Knocking before I open the door, I'm a little surprised to see that he followed my orders to get in bed. But he did one better, or worse depending on the way you look at it; he has the blankets thrown off the bed and is sitting up in only a pair of tight boxer briefs.

All the air whooshes out of my chest and my mouth hangs open. I wouldn't be surprised if my tongue was hanging out and I was panting like a bitch in heat. But holy shit this man was made from a sex god and cut with the finest body I have ever laid eyes on—both in person and on TV. Hell, he's better than my best fantasy.

Mack chuckles like he knows what has my panties on fire, which he probably does. Heck, he probably did this on purpose, but I can't be mad at him. I'm loving the view. I just hope I can keep my hormones in check and at least get through his treatment before I start acting like a teenage girl who gets to go backstage at her favorite rock concert. Somehow I think I'm getting the better deal though than those girls.

"Is there a problem, baby?" Mack asks with pure sex in his voice. I've heard him call me babe and even once heard him call me by my given name, but there's something about the way he calls me baby. I love it.

"No," I croak, then clear my throat. "No. Everything is fine."

Moving closer to the bed, my heart rate picks up speed and I feel sweat break out on my upper lip and forehead. I feel like I could pass out, but I'll be damned if I let that happen. No way in hell am I going to miss one second of viewing this amazing specimen of a man or feeling his enticing skin against mine.

"Could you, uh…could you lay down on the, uh, the bed," I stutter, but there's no way I can avoid it. I'm hot and bothered and don't even care at this point.

"How do you want me, baby?" Mack asks, but I don't think he means it in a medical fashion.

"I want you naked and your cock so deep inside my pussy while you make me scream your name," I blurt out before I can stop myself, but it's all the truth. And boy, do I want what I just said bad. Bad enough that I'll beg if I have to.

"Well then, what are we waitin' for?" he says. He reaches down to pull his boxers as far as he can down his legs. I don't even see where they stop because I'm too busy staring at the raging cock that's sprung free. And what a sight it is.

It's longer than any penis I've ever come into contact with and that's saying something. I'm not a whore—only having had slept with three men—but you'd be surprised the shit you'd see in the ER. I've had my fair share of being flashed by every type of penis there is, but Mack's takes the gold, silver, and bronze medals.

But that's not all. He's not only long—I'd guesstimate him measuring at about ten inches at least—but his girth is something out of a fairytale porno. I'm not even sure if I'd be able to fit both hands around his size, let alone take him inside my mouth or pussy. But goddammit, I'm going to try, even if he splits me in two.

The tip of his glorious cock is an angry red color. Almost like a juicy strawberry that you want to suck all of the juices out of. And that's exactly what I'm going to do.

Practically skipping the rest of the way to the bed, I take him in my hands; massaging the part of his body I've thought about handling since the moment I laid eyes on him. And the feel of him in my hands doesn't disappoint. If anything, it just gets me even more excited.

"Oh, fuck, baby," Mack groans, and the sound of him feeling pleasure from my hands alone makes my heart skip a beat.

Not able to take another second of not tasting him, I lean my head down and take him as far as I can go in one swallow.

"Shit," he yells, but at the same time, he grabs onto my head and forces me down even farther on his cock, pushing my limits and making me gag.

"Yes, just like that, baby. Take it all."

Enthused that he's enjoying this as much as I am, I suck harder and bob my head faster. I'm too eager to taste him, to swallow his cum that I don't care if I break my jaw taking him in or choke inhaling his dick. I want it so bad, I'm starved for it.

Humming my pleasure and eagerness, I start to use my hands; one stroking the parts of his cock I can't fit in my mouth and the other massaging his balls. They're heavy and pulsing already.

"Fuck, Rose. I'm gonna come if you keep that up," he moans. His words make it seem like he wants me to stop or the very least like he's giving me the option. But his actions are speaking louder than his words. He now has both hands tangled in my hair and his hips are working in tandem with his downward force on my head, and I'm loving every minute of it.

I've always been unsatisfied in the bedroom. I'm different than most girls. I don't know why, but there's never been anyone to give me exactly what I want—what I needed.

Every man I've brought home has been clean cut and polite, never taking what he wanted. And it's left me with a bad taste in my mouth. I want to be dominated in bed and fucked with force. I don't want hearts and flowers. I want whips and chains.

And Mack is giving me everything my heart and pussy desires right now.

Seconds later, I feel him stiffen even more, which makes it even harder for me to fit him in my mouth, but not impossible. I've got determination and will see this through till the end.

"Fuck, fuck, *fuck*," Mack chants over and over until finally he releases everything he has in my mouth and down my throat with a roar of completion.

I lessen my suction and slow my pace, but I don't release him from my mouth. I'm not ready to let him go just yet. But before he's even limp, he's starts to harden in my mouth again and I have to pull free. My jaw feels bruised and I fear I may need to go to the doctor to have them wire my mouth shut so it can heal. That thought has me almost bursting out in tears from laughter. *Almost.* But could you imagine that conversation with the doctor when I tell him what happened? Yeah, I can't either. Guess I'll just have to rest it the old-fashioned way.

"Holy shit, baby. That was the best fuckin' thing I think I've ever felt," Mack says breathlessly, which makes me smile with pride. *I* did that to him. I reduced him to a one-word vocabulary at the end and had him so out of breath you'd think he just ran a marathon. And to add to that, he said it was the best thing he'd ever experienced. *Ever.* Yeah, I'm proud, but also hornier than I think I've ever been. Having him in my mouth and hearing his pleasure spikes my own.

Crawling up on to the bed and placing my body

so I'm half on top of him and half not, I give him the most seductive look I can come up with. I don't think I have to try hard. With the way I'm feeling, I think I could come with just his command to do so. No contact needed. And I'd be happy to do it for him too. I wouldn't give a fuck, as long as that's what he wanted and I got to release this pressure that's building inside of me by the second.

"Think you got one more round in there, stud?" I ask. Not like I would be mad if he couldn't, but I'm pretty sure this man could go all night long if he wanted to. He didn't even get fully limp after he came the first time. No, he's got plenty more rounds to go and I'm happy to oblige.

"For you, baby, I'll go as long as you want me to." He reaches up and brings my lips down to his for our first kiss. Shit, to think that I had his cock in my mouth before I even kissed his lips is enough to make my grandmother turn over in her grave. It's a good thing I didn't like my grandmother.

The way his lips touch mine, it has so many emotions swirling around inside of me. It's more than I thought it would be, more than I fantasized about. His lips are soft but they move with authority and a hardness that I can't get enough of. He takes control of me with just the kiss. I can't wait to see what he'll do to my body once he takes my pussy.

Moaning into his mouth, I reach down to pull down my pants. I'm insanely happy I decided to wear a pair of my scrub pants today, though it's not as if I have much else.

Mack growls and pushes one hand into my hair, controlling the kiss as the other hand pushes my

127

shirt up. The feel of his hand on my stomach, then my side, and finally on my breast gives me a shiver all through my body. His touch brings fire to my veins, like a hit of the best fucking ecstasy on the streets would. Or so I've heard.

Hating to break the connection our lips have, but also having no other choice if I want to rid myself of my clothing, I pull away, but Mack doesn't stop kissing me. Instead of my lips, he moves his lips down my neck and suckles one of my breasts while his hand still works the other into a frenzy.

I can't get out of my clothes fast enough, but in my haste, I almost fall on top of him in a way that would probably end up hurting his manhood. Thankfully, I can correct myself before that happens and I'm able to rid my myself of my clothes, then I slam my mouth back onto his.

Kicking my leg up over his hips, I don't even hesitate to reach down in front of me, grab onto his huge cock, and guide him to my entrance. Before he penetrates me, Mack breaks the kiss once again. I pout, but I try not to sound or look like a brat. Good things come to those who wait, right?

"You ready for me, baby?" he asks. I almost give him a smart retort to that ridiculous question, but fearing he won't give me what I so desperately need, I just nod and beg.

"Please, Mack. I need your cock inside me."

Without any more delay, he grabs on to my hips and slams me down onto his cock.

"Oh, *fuck*!" I yell out. The pain is more than I expected, but the pleasure is even more intense. Mixed with the discomfort, it's probably the best thing I've ever felt. I could probably come right this second, but I do my best to hold off. I don't want this to end yet. I need more of him. I need him to slam into me over and over again until I can't feel my limbs. Until my throat is sore from screaming his name. And until I can no longer remember my own.

He doesn't waste even a second, nor does he give me time to adjust. He continues the rough pounding and fast pace, but I'd be lying if I said I wanted him to stop or slow down. Fuck no, I want him so far inside of me that I no longer have my own identity. I want it to be like we are one and the same, two pieces to a whole.

"Shit, you feel so fuckin' good, baby. So fuckin' tight," he growls and the sound of his rough voice brings me that much closer to the promised land.

"Oh God, I'm so close, Mack. Please," I beg, though I don't know what it is I need. Faster, harder? But even though I don't know, Mack does. He knows exactly what it is my body is craving.

He leaves one hand on my waist, but it slides around toward my ass. He grabs a handful of flesh so hard, I know I'll have a bruise in the shape of his fingertips by morning. With his other hand, he glides up my chest and grabs a fistful of hair.

Pulling hard, it forces me head to bend backwards to the point where it's almost uncomfortable. Almost. The little bite of pain excites me and makes me feel like I'm at his mercy.

I've never experimented with any sort of kink before—even the small stuff such as hair pulling—but what Mack's doing to me sets me on fire. It's intense and thrilling.

My toes start to tingle and the fire I felt burning in my veins hits a whole new level of heat.

"Let go, Rose. Give in to me and I'll give you the pleasure of a lifetime." His promise has me closing my eyes and giving everything I have to this man with no thought and no fear. It's freeing, giving up control and even giving into my orgasm. I've never felt this whole and peaceful before. I don't want to ever let this feeling go.

"That's it, baby. I got you," Mack coaxes in that sexy voice of his.

I'm a goner. I come so hard that it feels like I'm lifted off this plane of existence and into the land of pleasure. I fly so high and the pleasure is so great that I think I black out. But no, I'm still here. I'm just floating above the scene taking place and the visual of it all has me never wanting to come back down. I want to stay here forever and see how perfect I look in the arms of this man. And to watch the look of pure, unadulterated pleasure on Mack's face? That's something I will treasure and hold dear until the day I die.

A while later, I finally come back down from my high and I find myself sprawled out on Mack's chest, though he doesn't seem to mind. My body feels tingly and I can barely keep my eyes open.

Cracking one eyelid open, I look into his eyes.

"Hey," I croak, finding that it hurts to speak. I guess I was really screaming there at the end. Hopefully no one heard our little x-rated show we put on, but if they did, I hope they enjoyed it as much as I did.

"Hey, baby," Mack answers back, lifting my face up to capture my lips with his. It's a sweet kiss, nothing like the first one we shared, but I love it all the same.

Laying my head back down on his chest, I start to stroke over his heart as he makes long strokes up and down my back. It's pure heaven being here with him, especially after the mind-blowing orgasm he gave me. I don't even know if he came with me, but I can only hope he did. At least if he didn't, he's not fussing about it, which I appreciate. After not having sex for years, I'm going to need some time before I'm able to go at it again. I can already feel the soreness setting in.

I feel myself starting to drift off to sleep, but before I completely let oblivion take me, Mack speaks softly. "You know this changes everything between us, right?"

Thinking about his words and how I want to answer him, I stay quiet until I have the right thing to say. I know everything changes and I'm okay with that. But at the same time, I'm not some naïve little girl who thinks this means happily ever-afters or a diamond ring. Mack is still a biker and they do everything different. Am I okay with that? I think I am…for now.

I still think bikers are bad news, but I'm learning that not all of them are the same. There are good bikers, even outlaws. And I can only hope that Mack is one of them and this isn't just a front he's putting on.

"I know," I say, but it's not a sad confirmation or even a happy one. I'm just content to let this play out and see where this new road takes us. I'm still his nurse and he's still my patient. That won't change, nor do I want it to. But I also can't deny I want more of what he has to offer. I want him in-between the sheets and out of them. I want to know this man both physically, sexually, and intellectually. He intrigues me and it's been so long since something or someone has caught my interest. I can only hope he's okay with what I can offer right now as well. It's not much, but it's all I have right now.

As time continues, we can always re-evaluate where we're at, but right now, I just want to be what we are. No titles, no strings, or commitments. Just me and him. Mack and Rose.

"I'm not ready for anything concrete, but I like where we are right now. Can we just see where things go for now and not break everything down? We don't need to analyze it or overthink it, do we?" I ask, praying he won't be mad or demand more from me. I don't think I could handle losing him just as I'm finally starting to get him.

"Sure, baby. Whatever you want. But just so you know, while we're doing whatever we're doing, you're mine. I won't share you with anyone," Mack adds in a serious tone, and it makes me smile and feel warm inside. This man is truly something else. And I can't wait to see where this new road takes us.

"And you're mine. That means no club whores or whatever you call them. No random women or messing around while I'm not around. If you want me to just be yours, I expect the same thing from you," I demand, unwilling to budge on that note. Cheating is a deal breaker for me, whether we classify what we are to each other or not. If he's sleeping with me, he better be *only* sleeping with me.

Thankfully, Mack doesn't want to fight it either. "I don't think I could even if I wanted to, baby. You're all I can think about, and now that I've had you, I don't want anyone else."

CHAPTER NINE

Mack

Two Months Later

Waking up, I feel Rose's head on my chest, her arm wrapped around me, and her leg swung over mine. I've woken up this way for the past two months and I don't ever want there to come a day when I don't have this.

Meeting Rose was my light in a dark place. After getting shot, I didn't think I'd ever be the same again...and in some ways, I was right. I've had to work harder and in the end, I'm a different person. But on the other hand, I'd like to think I came out the other side a better person and in a better place. Sure, I had my club and my adoptive children and grandchildren, but there was still something missing.

Since I was a little boy and my father was killed, there has been a hole in my chest. It always ached and it never got better. My mother tried for the longest time to make things right, but the hole I was in was too deep. After a while, she just gave up; on me and on life itself. I wish I could say that losing her affected me like losing my dad did, but I was too numb to feel her loss. I didn't care about anything except trying to find something to make the pain go away.

But since meeting Rose, I can feel that hole inside my chest getting smaller and smaller. Now, I barely even notice it's there, if it even is anymore. And I have Rose to thank for that.

Feeling Rose start to stir, I tighten my grip around her waist before relaxing. Kissing the top of her head, I whisper, "Good morning, baby. How'd you sleep?"

Rose lifts her head just enough to look at me and smiles. "Great. You're actually quite a comfy pillow. Who would have thought a man as hard as a rock would be better than sleeping on feathers?"

"You think I'm hard as a rock?" I ask, amused with her morning banter. This woman still never ceases to amaze me.

"Well, most of you," she says with a wink as her gaze darts briefly down at my morning wood then back up to my eyes again.

Looks like someone wants to play this morning. Good thing I'm always ready for her. "I'll show you hard," I growl before flipping her over onto her back and lifting my body overtop hers. It's a little of a struggle, but much better than it would have been even a week ago. I just have to use my arm muscles a lot more when moving around, which I have no problem with.

"Hey now! What makes you think I want your morning breath all over me, huh?" If she wasn't laughing and already opening her legs so I can nestle myself right up against her sweet spot, I'd think she may actually be serious.

Staring hard into her eyes, I say in a demanding voice that she can't deny, "Because I say you do." I take her lips in a brutal kiss that may leave both of us bruised.

Moaning into my mouth, her sounds of pleasure completely contradict what her movements are showing. Struggling underneath me, she puts on the show that she doesn't want what she knows I can give her. But that's okay. It'll just make it that much sweeter when she finally submits to me—to what we both desire.

Grabbing both of her hands, I pull them above her head. Since we've started to sleep together, we've really gotten to know what the other likes when it comes to sex. Me, I like being in control because every aspect of my life demands that I have it. Plus, I'm used to being the one in charge. And Rose likes to be controlled, but only during sex. If you try to order her around otherwise, you better be prepared for a kick to the balls.

Holding her captive in one of my hands, my other travels down to her face, grabbing her chin to stop her from getting away from my kiss. "Stop fighting what we both know you want it, baby," I say against her lips and it makes all her playful struggling cease.

Giving in fully to my assault, my hand that was once on her chin now travels down to her wet

136

pussy. "Do you want me?" I ask in a rough voice, completely intoxicated by not only the smell of her pleasure, but from the knowledge that this woman is mine. She's at my mercy and willing to do anything I tell her to do. It's a heady feeling…one I would kill to keep.

"Yes, I want you," she says on a sigh.

"Do you need me?"

"Yes, Mack. I need you, please," she begs and I'm unable to put this off any longer. I need her more than she thinks she may need me.

Thrusting into her tight pussy in one go, I'm finally home. "Yes, please! Right there," Rose screams out and it's music to my ears. I love it when she begs for what only I can give her.

Wanting to tease her a bit, I stay seated deep inside her and don't move so she doesn't get any friction or pressure from my cock hitting deep inside her. "Tell me what you want, Rose."

I can tell she's getting frustrated but I don't care. I want her to work for it, to *beg* for it. "You know what I want, asshole. Just give it to me already," she spits out angrily.

Needing to punish her for her tone, I pull all the way out, only teasing the outside of her weeping pussy. "Tell. Me. What you. Want." I say through gritted teeth. It's almost as much torture on me as it is for her to withhold my cock from her, but if that's what it takes to get her to say it, then that's what I'll do.

"Jesus fucking Christ, Mack. Just fuck me already," she yells, the need taking over but her irritation still remaining.

I should make her beg more but honestly, I don't think I can hold out any longer. Thrusting into her hard and fast, we both moan at the feeling of being connected.

Keeping a fast rhythm, I don't slow down for anything. I'm racing for my finish, but I know she'll still come. It doesn't matter how fast or slow. I hit her so deep that nothing can stop her hitting that orgasm.

"Yes, Mack. Yes, please, don't stop," she begs, but I still need one more thing from her before I can allow either of us to fall off that cliff into oblivion. It's something I've never had before and something I only want from her.

"Say my name, Rose," I growl, pushing harder and faster yet into her.

"Mack, just fuck me, please."

"No, say my real name." I need her to say it. I know my given name coming from her lips will push me over the edge. I've dreamed of having her scream it since that first day in the hospital when she slipped and called me it by accident.

Rose's eyes focus on me fully, and instead of a look of confusion or irritation, I see a look that's close to love and devotion, but not fully. Either way, she obeys, and as soon as I hear my name from her sweet lips, I pull us both over the edge.

"Michael!"

***

A half an hour later, Rose comes walking into my room with a big smile on her face. "Are you ready to go, Michael?" she asks. Fuck, I love it when she calls me that. I've never heard sweeter words spoken.

After another round of sex, we lay around in bed quietly. I don't know what she was thinking about, but I was playing the scenes over and over in my mind when she would say my name. Needing to hear it more, I told her that when it's just me and her that I wanted her to refer to me as Michael. I liked the fact that she's the only person to call me that, or even know that it is my real name. Plus, hearing her sweet voice murmur those few syllables is like listening to your favorite song.

"Yeah, baby. I'll be ready in about five minutes. Why don't you head on out and I'll meet you at the truck?" I have a few things I need to do but I don't want her to see. It's not like it's anything bad like doing drugs or masturbating, but I still don't want her to witness it.

Truth is, our time spend rolling around in the sheets took a lot out of me. Usually I allow her to be on top because it's hot as hell, and frankly, I haven't been in the condition to take control as I'd normally like. But this morning, I had something to prove. To myself or maybe to her, I don't know, but it just felt right. I only wish I wasn't regretting it now.

I'm sore and shaky. I know she's going to notice as soon as we leave, or at the latest, when we get to where we're going, but if I can hold off on it, that's exactly what I'm going to do. I don't need her feeling bad or for her smart mouth to start spouting "I told you so's," or something of that nature. I'm fine and will continue to get better, but it takes a lot out of me sometimes. Usually I'm back on my feet and steady within a few hours, but no doubt after everything we have to do today, I'll most likely be wobbly for a while.

Maybe she wouldn't say anything about it, but I'm not going to take that chance. Not today; the day I go back to the doctor.

I've seen him a few times since I was released from the hospital for checkups, but this time I know it's different. I'm stronger now and can walk on my own. The only thing I need to work on is building my strength back in my legs and my stamina. I'm not completely certain what he's going to say today about how I'm doing or where we go from here, but I'm not worried about any of that. What does have me worried is what Rose is going to do. If they release me from needing an in-home nurse, will she leave? And if she does, will whatever we have between us go with her?

Not wanting to think about it just yet, I slowly make my way into the bathroom to brush my teeth and to shave. I usually don't care much about the way I look, but I care about what Rose thinks. I want her to want me and to want to stay with me even when the doctor says I don't need her to care for me anymore. I want her to stay for me.

I grab my cane—the other thing I can't wait to burn as soon as I'm able—and sit myself in my wheelchair. I hate that I'm going back to the doctor in this thing, but I figure it will give me time to rest my legs.

Wheeling myself out into the common area, I see Rose talking with Dani. None of the girls have said anything to anyone about their pregnancies. I've almost blurted it out a few times, but I'm going to honor their wishes. They want to wait until they're far enough along and they know for sure what they're having before telling everyone else.

That day just so happens to be today and I can't fuckin' wait. I wonder who's going to have a girl and who's going to have a boy or if they'll all have the same gender. And I wonder if Dani is having twins again. To me, it doesn't really matter, but I can't wait to find out. I want to brag that I'm going to be a grandpa again.

And yes, I'm excited about being a grandfather, even if it's not by blood. That shit don't matter anyway. It's the way you feel about those that you think of as family.

Most men wouldn't want to brag because they think people will consider them old. But news flash, assholes; age is just a number. If that's the way they think though, then they deserve to be called old. But not me. I love being a grandpa. It's the best feeling in the world. I think it even trumps the day I took on each of the girls as my daughters, the day I got my first bike, and even the day I helped start this club and took the gavel.

I never thought I'd get to be a grandpa because when I was at the ripe age of eighteen, I was told I would never have kids. It was impossible. I worked doing field work and we used lots of chemicals. I wore all the protective equipment necessary for such things, but it didn't matter. For whatever reason, I got sick and went to the doctor. I thought it was just a flu, but when I walked out of that office, I felt like half a man. I was sterile and would shoot blanks for the rest of my life. At eighteen, I didn't care that I couldn't have kids, but I did hate that I felt emasculated. I got over that fast though, because it made it easier for me to fuck whoever I wanted and only worried about wearing a condom so I didn't catch anything unsavory.

The other reason it didn't really bother me was because I never met anyone that I'd want to take on the sort of responsibility with or share a child with. Then, I joined the club, and it wasn't a place for children at that time. We were so busy getting ourselves established that there's no way I could have handled a kid.

I guess it was destiny's way of stepping in and making sure everything happened as it was supposed to. This is my road and I own it till the day I die.

Almost making it up to to the group before Rose spots me, I give her a smile and nod toward Blaze, where he stands off to the side with Louie and Toby. She smiles back at me and returns her attention to Dani just as Harley and EJ come barreling into the room with Jax hot on their tail.

"Morning, brother. You ready to get out of that chair for good?" Blaze asks, but he's not looking at me. His eyes are locked on Dani with a look of love and lust. Those two are crazy about each other and I couldn't be happier for them. They went through a lot of shit, but it brought them out the other side stronger and able to appreciate their feelings more. They still fight like hell, but it doesn't seem as hateful anymore. It's more playful now, though he still tries to tell her what to do and it pisses her off. She understands his need to protect her and the kids more, though.

"Fuck yeah I am, brother. Be ready for me with a big ass bonfire out back when I get home so I can burn this bitch," I say. Blaze finally breaks his gaze on Dani to look at me. He breaks out into a booming laugh and the other two men follow suit, laughing at what they think is a joke. They really should know better.

"I'm glad to see I can still surprise you assholes. But I wasn't kidding," I say, but then change the subject. There was a reason I wanted to come over here before leaving this morning.

"We heard anything from Tyke?" He's been undercover inside The Street King's clubhouse for the past few months. I don't like my boys going in dark, but we really didn't have many other options to try and figure out what they are up to. And frankly, Tyke was our best bet; not only because he's damn good at what he does and can take care of himself, but because he's the least likely to be made by the Kings.

"We haven't heard anything for a few days but that could just mean he hasn't had a safe opportunity to get in contact with us," Blaze informs me.

"Last time we heard from him though he said he thinks he's getting closer to being brought into the inner circle. Hopefully he'll have something for us soon so we can plan our next move." This comes from Toby.

The Kings don't do things the way a normal club

would, but we already knew that. They don't ride for the thrill of it and they aren't in the club for brotherhood. They want to rule wherever they land and they do that by striking fear into the eyes of the citizens.

This chapter hasn't made any wrong moves since they've moved in, but we've had our eye on them well before shit went down with Harlow and that piece of shit Titus. We've heard about the way they do things and we ain't gonna let them do that shit here. No fuckin' way.

They also don't keep every brother informed. They may hold church and discuss things like normal, but they hold a separate church for those in the inner circle. That's where they discuss what they're actually going to do or what they really want.

This is what my brothers are talking about when saying Tyke is close to being brought into that circle. Unfortunately, when we placed our bug in their clubhouse, we didn't know this. If we would have, we probably would have all the information we'd need right now and wouldn't have had to resort to sending a brother in.

Nodding, I look to where Rose is finishing up with Dani and looking at me, waiting. "All right. Keep me posted." I wheel myself over to Rose and smile at Dani as she walks over to where I just sat with the guys.

"I have to say, I'm surprised to see you actually in your wheelchair. I thought for sure you'd be a stubborn SOB and insist on walking," she says with humor in her voice but she doesn't mean it in a bitchy way. That much I know to be true. This is who Rose is; she's smart, witty, and sassy. But she's also one of the funniest people I've ever known. She just has her own form of humor sometimes and people can't understand it. It comes across as bitchy, but it's not.

"What can I say? I like to keep ya guessin'," I reply, then smile cheekily at her. "Onward, woman. This chair ain't gonna push itself."

Shaking her head, she walks behind me to push me out of the clubhouse and to the truck, which is parked not too far away. "You're lucky I like you, otherwise I'd smack you upside the head," she whispers in my ear before laughing softly to herself.

We make the hour drive to the hospital in a comfortable silence. I'm not sure what she's thinking, but I'm afraid to ask. What if she's planning her next move for when the doc says I no longer need her care? I'm not ready for her to leave yet. We have something here. I don't know if it's a forever type of something. I know I don't love her yet, but I could see that happening in the future. Maybe even the very *near* future.

I enjoy her company and look forward to spending time with her every day. I love that she's the last thing I see at night before I fall asleep, sated and worn out from our excessive amount of sex. And I love that she's the first thing I see in the morning. I've gotten so used to it, if she leaves, I'm not sure I could sleep at all with her gone.

Pulling into the hospital sooner than I'd like, I let out a silent sigh. *Here we go.*

Rose helps me out of the truck and into my

wheelchair. I don't comment or tell her I can do it myself. Shit, maybe if the doctor sees I still need help, he'll say I still need Rose to be my in-home nurse. I know it's a longshot and not probable being as I can now walk with very little help. I'll continue to get stronger the more I walk and build up my muscles again in my legs too. Plus, I'm sure Rose will tell the good doctor about my progress and there's no way I can lie about it. Not after everything she's done to help get me where I am today. Shit, without her, I may still be in this fuckin' hospital with no hope of ever walking again.

No, I'm just going to have to see how this plays out and hope Rose will stay on her own and not because she needs to take care of me for medical reasons.

Once we're up on the fourth floor and check in with the receptionist, we take our seat in the waiting room. Well, Rose does. I guess I brought my own today.

Rose is still quiet, though it's different now than it was in the car. Before, she seemed happy and comfortable to leave things unsaid or maybe she just didn't have anything that needed to be said. The same with me as well. I enjoy times like that when we don't have to speak and nothing needs to be said. It's simple. Sometimes in life those are the times that mean something.

But now, she's quiet but jittery. Like she's nervous or something. She looks like a junky right now jonesing for her next hit, but is fighting it as best she can. I hate to see her like this. I want to comfort her, take her into my arms, or better yet, take her away from the place making her like that.

"Mr. DeVin, we're ready for you," I hear called from behind me. I turn around. A nurse stands with a clipboard and a smile.

"Here were go," Rose says as she stands. There's a small smile on her face but it's not a happy smile; it's sad.

Nodding, I reach down to start to wheel toward the other nurse, but Rose places her hand on my shoulder. "I got you." Those words hit me in the gut. The way she said it, it's like she means more than just helping me down the hall and into the room. Like she means she has me in all things.

Neither of us says anything else while we make our way into one of the back rooms. The nurse doesn't talk to us either, she just reads something on her clipboard.

Once we're inside the room, the nurse motions toward the exam table. "If you want to get situated up here, the doctor will be in shortly." She leaves without offering any help—not like I'd accept anyway—then Rose and I are alone again.

"Are you okay?" I ask without moving. I know the nurse wanted me on that table, but I can't let this sad, quiet Rose continue. I need her to tell me what's going on, why she's upset, so I can help her. Fix it. *Do something*.

She looks at me with mock confusion on her beautiful face. "Of course. Why do you ask?" She thinks she's fooling me, but she forgets I've been with her for more than two months straight. I've watched her and know all of her expressions. I've been inside her and know what she tastes like. I know something is going on with her…she just doesn't want to tell me.

"You remember what you said to me that night when I didn't want to talk?" I ask, but before I can say anything else or before she can answer, the door opens and in walks Dr. Yorkshire.

"Good morning, Mr. DeVin. Nurse Rose," he greets us, then walks over to his chair in the corner of the room. "Now, let's take a look at how you're doing, shall we?"

Looking over to where I'm still seated in the wheelchair, he looks confused. "Do you need some help getting situated, Mr. DeVin?" he asks, but I shake my head no, never breaking eye contact with Rose. Our conversation may have been interrupted, but it's not over.

Standing from my chair, I show no weakness. I may be sore and not able to stand with all my strength, but I'm getting there.

Moving toward the table, I take a seat. Crossing my arms, I wait for the doctor to proceed with whatever it is he needs to do. Maybe he'll just talk, or maybe he'll have me show him my progress, but either way, I will not disprove Rose's time and expertise. She's the reason I'm here right now and I won't let her down.

Dr. Yorkshire does all sorts of tests over the next half an hour. He has me lift and hold my legs up to test my strength and movement. I move my legs side to side in the air to test range of motion. He has me walk to the door and back to the table three different times. He has me stand straight and then bend at the waist. I stand and lift one leg in the air to see how my balance is, then do it with the other. And finally, he checks both wounds and incision sites to make sure those healed properly.

"Well, Mr. DeVin. Everything looks like it's on the right track. I don't think we need to do the MRI after all. I'm not seeing any signs that there is any permanent damage. You still have a little way to go, but with what I see today, I don't think you need the wheelchair anymore. We'll have one of the physical therapists come in to give you some exercises you can do at home by yourself and we'll want to see you back every few weeks to check on things, but other than that, I think you're good to go."

Looking from me to Rose, he says, "And I don't think you'll need the in-home nurse anymore, either. I'll get the paperwork done and send in another nurse, and then you can be on your way. Nurse Rose, why don't you come see me in my office when we're done here so we can get you back on the schedule?" With those parting words, he leaves the room.

I stare at Rose, unsure what to do now. I feel panicked. I don't want her to go but how do I make her stay?

She's the first to speak. "I'm so happy for you, Michael. I knew you could do it." She doesn't look at me when she talks and that upsets me. She should always be able to look me in the eye without fear of me not understanding or angry.

Standing from the table on Jell-O legs, I make my way over to where she sits and kneel down in front of her. I'm hurting and this probably will only add to it later, but I need to see her. I need *her* to see *me.*

Lifting her face up with one of my hands, my other goes to caress her cheek. When she finally locks eyes with me, she gives me a watery smile with tears almost overflowing from her eyes. "Hey, don't cry, baby," I say quietly, wiping a stray tear that flows free from her eye.

She nods and tries to look away but I don't let her. "Talk to me, Rose. What's going on?" I ask, getting more concerned by the second. I've never seen her cry before and seeing it now breaks my fuckin' heart. I'll do whatever I have to do to make it better for her.

Pushing my hands aside, she stands up with jerky movements. She's angry now, but I'll take that over her crying.

Pacing the room, she speaks, but looks everywhere but at me. "I'm so fucking confused, Michael. When I agreed to help you, I figured I'd see you through this, help you get better, and then be on my way. And I *did* that. You're better and doing more than anyone's wildest expectations. You're so strong and you have determination to get better. You have a family who cares about you and will help see you through this. Me? I don't have that. And being there with you, I've gotten to know most of your brothers, your daughters, and even your grandchildren. I really like them," she says, pausing while shaking her head.

"They all like ya too, baby." I add in, not sure if she wanted to hear that or if she knew, but it seems like if she didn't, that she needed to know. She *should* know. My family thinks the world of her, and not just because she's helped me get better. Rose is a genuine person, nurse or not. And she's fun to be around, to talk to. She's fucking amazing.

Rose nods, but then shakes her head like she's having an internal argument with herself over something I'm not privy to.

Standing, I pull myself off the floor and sit in the seat she vacated. "Why does all that make you sad though, baby? Yes, you helped me and I can never repay you for that. You got to know my family and they got to know you in the process. They love you, baby. And to know that you like them as well makes my heart swell. They're not easy to get to know or like, but they let you in and you them. That's an amazing thing, baby, so why are you still upset?"

"Because you don't need me anymore, Michael! You're getting better and don't need me. My time with you is up and I'm not fucking ready for that, okay?" she cries out, but she's angry. At me or herself, I don't know, but her words make me so fuckin' happy. She doesn't want to leave.

Even though I've been through hell physically today, I stand and make my way to her. I need to hold her. I need to feel her in my arms.

When I wrap my arms around her, she cries into my chest and my heart breaks a little before it mends itself when I remember her words from earlier. *She wants to stay with me.*

"So don't go," I say simply, because it is as simple as that. I don't want her to go and she doesn't want to leave.

It takes her a minute to digest what I said and to

151

maybe think about what she's going to do, but a few moments later, I get her answer in the form of a nod; she's staying.

CHAPTER TEN

Rose

After making sure Michael was okay and had all his papers, I told him to wait for me in the waiting room. I just need to talk to Dr. Yorkshire and then we can leave. I'll give Monica a call when we get back home.

Home. That's what being at the clubhouse with Michael feels like to me. I've never had a place where I've felt like I can just be myself. Where I felt safe and wanted. When I'm at the Forsaken Sinners clubhouse, I finally have that. Even when Michael isn't in the same room with me, there are people there I care about. Dani, Sara, and Harlow have become my best friends. Sure, they're a little younger than me, but they don't make me feel like an older woman. I can be young and free with them and not worry about being judged. It's nice.

Standing in front of Dr. Yorkshire's office, I hesitate for a moment. I don't know what I'm going to tell him about why I'm not coming back, but I know it's the right thing to do. I just hope he understands.

Taking a deep breath and blowing it out slowly, I finally knock on his door. He answers right away for me to come in.

Once I'm inside, I close the door and take a seat across from him. "What can I do for you, Dr. Yorkshire?" I ask, though we both know what this is about.

"Well, first of all, I wanted to congratulate you on a job well done on Mr. DeVin. The way he's healed and the progress he's made, it's actually pretty amazing. A lot of us here never thought he'd walk again," he says, and it makes me angry. First of all, Michael's progress isn't because of me. Sure, I helped him along the way, but that was all him. If he didn't have the willpower to get better and the determination to see it through, it wouldn't matter what I did, he wouldn't be walking right now.

Secondly, it's disturbing to think the negative thoughts people at this hospital had about his recovery. I wonder, if I never would have done the extra research and found a new treatment for him, would we be where we are right now? It seems like the other physicians here pretty much just brushed him off as a lost cause. They didn't want to see what could be and do the extra work...they just wanted to diagnose him and let him deal with the damage alone. It's fucking wrong and I feel ashamed to say I worked with these people.

Trying not to show my irritation and anger, I nod slightly and say, "Thank you, but it was all Mr. DeVin. He was the one who did everything, not me.

I was just there to help him along the way." The man sitting in front of me should know it's the patient who does the work and us as caregivers are only there for support. Sure, sometimes we're the ones who save the lives of others and we do a lot more than just offer support to the patients, but in this case, it was all Michael. After the surgery was done and the orders were put in place, it's because of him that he's walking.

Dr. Yorkshire laughs and shakes his head. "Come on, Rose. You know that's nonsense. We both know that without you, someone like him wouldn't have progressed the way he has."

I'm completely flabbergasted and speechless right now. What the fuck just came out of this man's mouth? Did he really just say that? About Michael…or anyone for that matter.

"Someone like him?" I ask softly, afraid that if I speak any louder I'm going to start yelling and throwing things. I'm fucking pissed that we're even talking about this and he's acting like he's so much better. That we both are so much better than Michael.

"You know what I mean. Someone of his stature. He's in a gang, for goodness sake." I can't hold it in anymore. It was one thing to completely disregard Michael, but a whole other thing to put him down and think Michael is below him, but after the shit he's spewing, Dr. Yorkshire is no better than the mud on my boots.

Standing abruptly, I lean over and place my hands on his desk, staring right through this asshole. "Who the fuck do you think you are, talking about him like he's beneath you? He's your fucking patient, for Christ's sake. You swore an oath when you became a doctor to do everything you could to help your patients, to never give up, and to treat them fairly," I yell, pissed at what he's doing and wondering who else he's done this to. Probably to anyone he felt wasn't worth his fuckin' time; poor people, drug addicts, and bikers. "And it's called a *motorcycle club*, not a gang. They're not drug mules or gun dealers. This ain't *Sons of Anarchy*." I get more heated the more I talk. It's assholes like this that give guys like Michael a bad name.

And no, I'm not putting myself on a high horse, because I once judged him based on who he associated with and what he did, but I'll be the first to admit I was wrong. It's one of the reasons I will not let anyone else make that mistake or talk trash about him or anyone else in the Forsaken Sinners.

"Michael is a good man, a man who deserves to have the best treatment and doctors this world can offer. *And that's not you.* Someone of his stature…more like someone like *you* isn't worthy to be in *his* mere presence, let alone have you treat him. You're an asshole because you can't see the person he is behind his bike and the cut. I've had the pleasure of spending time with every single one of them and I'd take their company over yours any fucking day."

I want to say more, but he's not worth the energy and breath.

Standing to my full height, I shake my head in disgust and turn to leave, but before I open the door, I turn back to look at his stunned face. "You and this hospital can fuck off. I quit." With those last words, I walk out the door and slam it behind me so hard, staff members and patients stop what they're doing to look at what the commotion is.

Seeing the source of all the ruckus, they look at me like I've got two heads, but I don't care. I'm done with this place *and* the people in it. I don't even care if they send me my vacation pay that would be owed to me. Frankly, I don't even know if I'd cash the fucking check if they did send it. I'm done with this place and everything that goes along with it.

Michael is still waiting for me in the waiting room on the fourth floor and I almost wish he'd gone downstairs. Now he's going to see I'm upset and I have no idea what to tell him. And if I did tell him exactly what went down in that office, what would he do? Would I care? Probably not, to be honest. Craig would deserve anything Michael dishes out. I'd even happily sit and watch.

Shit, what is wrong with me? I'd never do something like that, let alone think it, and here I am almost wishing Michael would go into that office and do what? Not murder him, but I'd like to see him give him a good punch in the nose. Fuck it, yeah, I'm thinking it. There ain't nothing wrong with me. I think I'm finally seeing things clearly in the first time in forever. It's like I was wearing cherry colored goggles my whole life and being with Michael and the rest of the MC has finally lifted them off my face. I see everything for what it is and am able to think the way I should. I fuckin' love it, actually. I've been missing out.

As I expected, Michael sees right through me and knows there's something wrong. Instead of just wheeling himself over to me, or heck, waiting until I get to him, he gets out of the chair and walks over to me faster than he probably should after everything he just went through.

"Are you okay? What happened? Did that asshole do something to you?" he starts firing off in rapid succession, not even letting me answer one question before moving right along to the next.

Holding my hands up for him to wait, I walk over to his wheelchair and motion for him to take a seat. He looks at me with a hard look and crosses his arms. Stubborn man.

Flopping down into the chair next to his, I make him aware with just my look that I'm not going to answer any of his questions until he sits down.

It takes him a few moments, but he finally catches my drift, blows out an exasperated sigh, and sits down. "You better start fuckin' talking before I charge into that office and start throwing punches. It don't matter what he did, just that you're upset and he's the last person I know you were with. That alone makes him guilty," he says, getting louder and louder the longer I don't tell him what happened.

I wish we were out of this hospital before I told him, though. I don't want to cause any more of a scene than I already did, but I know he won't go for that. He's dead serious about shooting first and asking questions later. Not like I think he'd shoot Craig...well actually, I don't know if he would or not. I'm not sure if that makes me nervous or thrilled that he'd do that for me.

"Okay, okay. Calm down, Michael. I'll tell you," I say, hoping he'll relax a bit, but he doesn't. "I'm fine, I promise. Just a little heated about a discussion that happened, is all. He didn't do anything to me. You don't need to worry, I'm okay."

He sits there for a few moments, looking at me like he's waiting for me to go on, but that was it. I answered his questions. I just didn't give him extra details.

Not having any of that, he stands like he's going to go and do what he threatened, but I reach out and grab his hand, effectively stopping his retreat. Mission, more like it.

"Can you wait until we at least get out of the hospital before I tell you what the discussion was about?" I ask, but I already know the answer. He's not going anywhere until I give him what he wants, and he wants to know what was said and why it made me upset.

"No, it can't wait. You're going to tell me now, before we leave. That way I don't need to come back here if I need to make him pay for what he did or said. It's either that, or I'll just go beat it outta him. Your choice, though I won't promise I won't beat him anyway."

Well, I guess I'm telling him now. Not like he's giving me much choice.

"He congratulated me on the amazing job I did with you. He actually said that he and the rest of the staff had pretty much already written you off, thinking you'd never walk again. They weren't even going to try." It pisses me off all over again just

159

saying the words out loud. Michael didn't deserve any of this, yet he was subjected to Dr. Yorkshire being an uncaring ass.

"I'm just happy I was able to do what little I did to help you. Anyway, I thanked him, because I thought it was the polite thing to do, but then said it was all you. That I was only for support when you needed it. He laughed and said that someone *like you* wouldn't be walking right now after what you went through if it weren't for someone like me. I was pretty sure I knew what he meant, but I needed to hear him say it." I want to go back into that office and do what Michael wanted to do earlier. I want to give Craig *more* than a piece of my mind, I want to make him *feel* what I'm saying.

"He confirmed my suspicions; saying that because you were in a gang that you either weren't competent enough to get better without help or that you didn't deserve to. I don't know, I didn't let him elaborate. Instead, I told him that you're in a motorcycle club, not a gang, and that you were a better man than he is. I then told him to fuck off and that I quit before walking out. The end. Can we go now?" I ask at the end, eager to get out of here.

Standing up, I start walking away, but he stops me—whipping me completely around so that I'm now in his arms with him staring intently into my eyes. What gives me pause though is the lack of anger I see within his eyes. I thought for sure what I said would upset him, piss him off, or send him off on a rampage. I know if that was said about me, that's what I would do. But not Michael. He almost looks happy and amused.

Neither of us say anything for a minute. Me, because I don't know what to say right now and I'm literally speechless from looking at his handsome face and the way he's looking back at me. I don't know why he's not saying anything. Could he be feeling the same way that I am?

A smile starts to take over his whole face before he leans in and lightly kisses me on the lips for the world to see. If this would have happened even a few hours ago, I'm not sure if I would have been comfortable showing a public display of affection, especially at my place of employment. But now, I want him to deepen the kiss and take me right here on this damn floor. Just being around him gets me hot and bothered, but add in him kissing me…yeah, my panties are wet and I'm in need of more than his mouth on me.

"What was that for?" I ask quietly after he pulls away from the kiss.

Smiling even bigger, he says, "You quit your job for me." Then he kisses me again, this time longer.

"You stood up for me and my family without a second thought. And to your boss at that. What you did couldn't have been easy, baby." Now he talks with a hint of sadness, but I don't know why. I'm not sad or sorry.

"Well, he was wrong about you. I wasn't going to sit there and let him talk shit about you without saying anything. No one deserves that, especially not you," I tell him, then I decide to give him a little more.

"I don't know how to say this without it sounding bad, so I'm just going to say it and I hope you hear me out and know I was wrong," I start, a little nervous about telling me what I used to think about him—well, more the person I thought he was.

"When I first met you, I didn't like you. No, that's not true. Let me rephrase that better. I didn't *want* to like you. Not because you were sexy and I felt this connection to you, but because I was afraid of what it meant to be who you are. I've heard things about bikers, even seen some in action, but you aren't anything like them or the image people think up when they hear something about a biker. You're different, Michael. Your whole club is different."

I don't see any judgment or anger in his gaze, just understanding. I'm sure he's heard this before, or if not, he's suspected that people think this way about him.

"I feel ashamed I felt that way, but I'm so grateful for the time I've had with you and your family. It's shown me how wrong people can be about one another and why you should never judge someone by what they wear, who they associate with, or what they do. I'm so sorry I felt that way, but I promise you...I will never make that mistake again. I will not tolerate anyone doing the same thing I did while I'm around. Especially if the misconception is about you. I'm not sorry I spoke up to my boss and I'm definitely not sorry I quit my job. I don't want to work for someone who can't see past a persona or in your case, a cut. I sincerely hope you forgive me for the way I misjudged you, and believe me when I say I know I've seen the error of my ways."

I really hope he understands, though I'd get it if he couldn't. What I did, judging him before I even knew him—no matter if he doesn't know the full story behind why I felt that way about bikers—was wrong. I wouldn't wish what I did to Michael on anyone. I wouldn't like someone thinking I'm a goody two-shoes because I'm a nurse or that I think I'm smarter than everyone else. That's not what I think or how I want people to see me.

"Baby, I completely understand why you felt that way. I was once in the same boat you were when you met me. Bikers are kind of like the redheaded stepchild; no one understands us and are even afraid of us...even if they don't know why. And yeah, some bikers are exactly what people say; they're mean, don't take no for an answer, and rule through fear. But not us. I'm just glad you see that now because if you didn't, I would do everything in my power to get you to believe in us—in *me*. I would never do anything to hurt you, Tiny Rose Chamberlain. Never," he declares.

"What made you change your mind about bikers?" I ask, wanting to understand him more.

A dark look comes across his face, but he covers it up just as fast as it shows up. "I'll tell you about it another time. But right now, what do ya say we get out of here, huh? I want to see if we can catch Dani, Sara, and Harlow before they leave."

He squeezes my hand before slowly making his way back to his wheelchair. Falling into it, I notice for the first time since I came out of the office how shaky and almost pale he looks. I'm going to have to pamper him for the rest of the night so he gets his strength back.

"Are they waiting for you?" I ask, not sure why his daughters would be here.

"No, baby. But I don't want to spoil the surprise for you. Let's just get down there and hope we catch them," he says with a wink and now I'm even more confused. What surprise? I didn't even know there was one.

Deciding not to ask any more questions, I keep quiet and wheel him over to the elevator. When it opens, I'm happy to see no one else is inside. I hate being in an elevator when it's crowded. Makes me feel claustrophobic or something.

It only takes a few seconds before we reach the first floor and we're heading toward the door when we hear someone shout, "Mack!"

We both turn our heads at the same time to see all three of his girls smiling big and practically skipping over to us. I notice that Blaze, Toby, and Louie are here as well, though they're following at a more leisurely pace. But they too are smiling widely. I guess everyone knows the secret except me.

"Well?" Michael asks just as they reach us, rubbing his hands together in anticipation.

"Well, *what*, old man?" Dani replies back, which only has Michael seeming to bounce in his seat even more.

"What did the doctor say?" he tries again.

"Oh my goodness, are you okay? What were you being seen for? What doctor was it? If you need me to, I can refer you to someone else if you need a second opinion," I say, suddenly concerned. I know

I've barely begun to get to know her, but I care about her. If something is wrong, I want to help any way I can.

Michael and the rest of the guys laugh, but I don't pay them any attention, focusing solely on Dani.

"I'm fine, *Mom*," she says with mock attitude and a smile, but for some reason, her calling me Mom punches me right in the gut. I'm not one hundred percent sure if it was a good punch or not, but it got me right in the feelers.

"Yeah, they're fine. Now tell us what you found out," Michael tries again, but this time, I can tell Dani is going to give in and give him what he wants.

"Well," she starts, dragging it out in suspense.

Michael make a motion with his hands as if to say, "Spit it out."

"We're having a girl!" I hear Sara say happily before Dani can say anything else.

I look at her in surprise and almost don't understand what she just said, but then I look down to her stomach and notice there is a little baby bump there. How did I not notice that before?

"Another baby girl!" Michael booms, obviously happy with this news.

"Oh my gosh, congrats. I didn't know you were expecting," I throw in there, feeling a little odd that I seem to be the only one who didn't know.

"Thank you—" Sara says.

Michael interrupts, "And that ain't all."

He's looking between Harlow and Dani like he's waiting for them to say something. Are they pregnant too? No way. All three of them? That's highly unlikely.

"No, that ain't all," Dani says, then reaches down to rub her belly. Though she's not showing as much as Sara is, I can make out a little bit of a baby bump on her too. Wow, that's crazy!

"It's a boy!" Dani says excitedly. She's already got twins—a boy and a girl—but I can see how much she really wanted another boy. Though I have no doubt she'd be just as happy if this baby was a girl, she's over the moon that she gets another boy. I'm sure Blaze is as well if his smirk is anything to go by.

"Oh, look at that, brother. I guess destiny decided to give you a break after all and not give you more than one this go around," Michael says.

"It's about fuckin' time that bitch gave me a break. I have way more than I can handle with this one here," Blaze says, grabbing Dani around the waist from behind. She playful jabs him in the side with her elbow.

"Well, speaking of twins," Louie speaks for the first time, and everyone looks at him in surprise and disbelief.

"You're shittin' me," Michael yells.

"Nope. The doctor thought he heard two heartbeats the first time we were able to hear it, but the ultrasound confirmed it. We're having twins!" Louie says before Blaze and Toby clasp him on the back and give him a half man-hug, congratulating him while Dani and Sara hug Harlow full on.

"Oh wow, that's amazing, Harlow. I'm so happy for you. Happy for all of you," I say, standing off to the side, watching as the girls embrace and Michael laughs and talks with the guys. For the first time today, I feel out of place.

But the girls don't let that last long, because they close the few steps that separate us and engulf me into their arms, putting me smack dab in the middle of the three of them, creating a circle around me.

"Thank you, Rose. I'm so happy, but nervous," Harlow says. I'm pretty sure she's talking about the fact that she's having not one baby, but two, though it could be about having a baby in general. I know I'd be scared out of my fuckin' mind if I was pregnant.

I never really thought about kids except to say I didn't want any. I never wanted to bring a child up in the world we live in, thinking everything was bad and will hurt you because everything I'd ever experienced had. I'm not saying I'd be a shitty parent like I had growing up, or that if I had more than one kid that they'd turn out like me and my brother, but I didn't want to find out. Plus, when I decided I wanted to be a nurse, there was never any time to think about kids. And you need a man to have a baby and I never kept one long enough to even attempt to create one.

But I'm thankful for that because the life I live wouldn't suit a baby. I work long hours pretty much every single day, including every holiday. I'd never be home, so my kid wouldn't even know who I was. They'd grow up thinking the babysitter down the street was their mother.

"Oh, honey, you'll do just fine. Plus, I've been there before, babe. If you need any advice or help, you know you can come to me," Dani says. She would be the best person to go to. She has twins already, so what better person to ask advice from?

"Me too," Sara adds, and even though she doesn't currently have kids, I'm sure she'd be a great help as well.

Not sure if I should, but I just go with it. "And I'll help out with anything you need as well. I know you don't know me very well, but I'd be happy to do anything I can. Even if it's just answer medical questions or if you have concerns about health." Even though I didn't want to have a baby myself doesn't mean I don't like them. Heck, I was going to be a nurse in the NICU, but then I couldn't stand to see all those sick babies all the time and feel like I couldn't do anything. It's hard seeing a baby sick and struggling to live, even if they aren't yours. They shouldn't have to fight so hard for life that young.

"I'd really appreciate that...thank you, Rose. Though I may annoy you with all the medical questions I'll have." She laughs but I keep a straight face.

"Oh, nonsense, Harlow. You could never annoy me. Plus, talking medical is something I'll never tire of. Especially now that I don't have a job," I add that last part in there for my ears only, but they end up hearing anyway.

"You got fired? Why? Because you were helping Mack?" Sara asks, concern all over her face. Harlow's expression matches Sara's, but when I look at Dani, she looks exactly like Michael did before I told him what was wrong.

168

"No, no. I quit. I like spending time with you all and I wasn't ready to leave Mack just yet," I say, using his nick name because I know he only likes it when I call him Michael when it's just the two of us.

"Well, I'm not happy that you felt you needed to quit your job in order to still spend time with us, but I'm happy you're staying. You're such a great woman, and the way Mack is with you? He's like a whole new person. He's happy, and I like seeing him that way. He deserves it."

I couldn't agree more. He's what every man should strive to become; he's loving and loyal, but fierce and hard at the same time. It's a very lethal combination.

"So, are you going to make me guess or are you going to tell me what you're having? A boy and a girl like Dani? Two girls? Two boys?" Michael asks, ever the impatient one, but I don't blame him. This is exciting news.

Harlow looks at Louie first and they share a knowing smile. Then, turning back and facing all of us, she says, "We're having twin boys!"

169

CHAPTER ELEVEN

Mack

We've been in the truck on our way back to the clubhouse for thirty minutes and I still can't wipe this stupid smile off my face. I'm gonna be a grandpa again times four! Three more boys and a girl I get to spoil rotten. I'm over the moon fuckin' happy about it, but I gotta say, it's even more special that I got to share this with Rose.

She was in the dark about the pregnancies because the girls didn't want to tell anyone until they knew what they were having. They said they wanted to be able to tell everyone at the same time. I don't get that shit, but that was their decision to make, not mine, so I honored their wishes. Didn't mean it wasn't hard at times, especially when I saw Rose playing with EJ and Harley, or when I'd notice Dani or one of the other girls rubbing their stomachs when they thought no one was looking. But I'm always watching my girls; every single one of them. They mean more to me than my own life.

170

I know it was a huge shock for Rose to find out and to feel like she was the only one who didn't know, but as soon as we got in the car, I told her no one back at the clubhouse knows. She got a smile on her face when she heard that, thinking she's special. But even without all of that, she is very special. To me, to my girls, and even to all my brothers. They know something is going on with us, they just don't know how deep it runs. Shit, I don't even think we know how deep this runs, but we're gonna figure it out together.

Another thing that makes me insanely happy is that I know Rose isn't going anywhere. This morning, I dreaded going to the doctor. Not because I didn't think my condition was improving or that they would have bad news, but because I knew how well I was doing. Thanks to Rose. But that meant the doctor would say she'd done her job and I no longer needed her. And that may be true in the medical form, but in every other way, I still needed her. I was too used to going to bed with her in my arms and waking up next to her every morning. I don't think I could go a day without that, let alone forever.

"Hey smiley pants, did ya hear me?" Rose asks, breaking me out of my thoughts.

"Huh? No, sorry. What did ya say?" I ask. Judging by her playful tone, she's not mad, though.

"I was thinking out loud and wondering if I should plan a baby shower for Dani, Sara, and Harlow. Then I asked if you think they'd like that? I don't even know if Dani had one for the twins."

Thinking about what she said, it just makes me

171

like her even more. This woman is such a giver; always thinking about others and what she can do for them. I love that about her.

"No, Dani didn't have one when she was pregnant with the twins. Shit was kind of crazy during that time. We were having club problems and then her dad came into town wanting to see her, and Blaze and I were trying to take care of that and not upset her," I say, remembering all the shit that happened. The way Dani found out she was pregnant, Blaze acting funny, and her dad showing up, then the chaos and worry about how she delivered, the surprise about finding out she had twins, and then that fuckin' nurse trying to take EJ. Shit was crazy…it's no wonder we didn't have time to throw her a baby shower. Though, can't say that I'd plan that shit, or even be there for the party. Okay, that's a lie—if she would have wanted me there, I would have been.

"Whoa, wait a minute," Rose says, snapping her head toward me, then back to the road. "What do you mean her 'father'? I thought you were her dad." Ah, I can see how that would be confusing. I guess I'm just so used to people either knowing she's not my real daughter, or just not caring what they think on that subject because it's none of their business. It never even occurred to me to tell Rose. When she would call the girls my daughters, it didn't faze me because everyone calls them that.

"Shit, I'm sorry, baby. I guess I forgot to mention that because I'm so used to people knowing. No, I'm not her real dad. Her piece of shit birth father left her when she was three after her mother died. He signed his rights away to her grandmother—that's who raised her. She never even saw him until the day of her grandmother's funeral. Asshole," I say, wishing I would have thought to deck him one for that little number there. Oh well, I could always track him down and do it. Need to check up on him anyway. It's been a while since I've made sure he's kept to the agreement of staying far away.

"After some shit happened to her, she found her way here. I took her in and she became like a daughter to me. Same as the other two. They aren't my real daughters, but to me, they are. I love them like they were my own flesh and blood...the only thing missing is the adoption papers and name change. Though I think they're a little too old for that, huh?" I say with a laugh at the end, though I wonder what they would do if I did get those drawn up. Hmm, maybe I'll have to think about that.

"Wow, I never would have guessed. In a way, they look like you, act like you. Shit, Dani talks like you," Rose adds in last minute and chuckles, thinking she's funny. But she's right. Dani's been around me a long time...I guess my way of talking rubbed off on her.

"Yup, well, there's that too." I laugh with her, then get serious. "But they are my daughters in all the ways that matter, and that's good enough for me." They don't need to have my last name or even call me Dad. I know who they are and I'll always be there for them.

"Wow," she breathes out the word, like she didn't say it for me to hear, but I hear everything she says. I don't ever want to miss anything that comes out of that gorgeous mouth of hers.

"Back to what we were talking about though, and to answer your question, I think they'd really love if you did that for them. I think it's a great idea, baby." I love that she wants to do something so special and nice for them. I love it so much that I'd even help plan and prepare for this party. Well, only if she asks, that is. No need to torture myself unnecessarily.

Smiling big, she nods to herself. "All right then, it's settled. I'll talk to the girls and see about when they want to have it. Some moms like to have them before the baby is born, but others like to wait until after. Though, that's usually because they don't want to find out the sex of the baby, and Dani, Sara, and Harlow already know what they're having." She goes quiet, looking like she's in deep thought, then shakes her head before adding, "Well, I'll still ask them."

"You do that, baby. I'm sure either way, they'd love it."

The rest of the trip is quiet. I can't be sure, but I'd assume Rose is thinking and making plans for this baby shower she wants to do. Me? I'm thinking about lots of things, but the one that is the most important to me is getting Rose in bed and naked the moment we get back to the clubhouse.

***

The last few weeks have gone by amazingly. Everything seems to be perfect in my world. My

174

girls are starting to show more and they seem really happy with their men—my brothers. Rose and I are getting closer and it seems like she gets happier and more open with me every day that passes.

Things with the club have been okay, and the reason I say it's just okay is because there are still things that need to be done and things that are unfinished.

Tyke is still undercover inside the King's clubhouse. We hear from him less and less, but we're hoping that's because he's being brought into that inner circle. It still makes me nervous and twitchy, but I know he can handle himself if the shit hits the fan. He's a decorated Marine who served five tours overseas. For the last four years of his enlistment, he was a member of the Marine Corps Special Forces. So yeah, he can handle anything they throw at him. Doesn't mean I like it. I just won't risk putting him in danger by reaching out. He'll find a way to contact us if he needs to or if he finds something out.

So with no news from Tyke, we haven't done much on the front of preparing for what the Kings have planned. No need to start a war if one isn't needed, and no need to bring attention to ourselves when it's not the time to. We'll work it out once we have more intel.

But for right now, I think I'll stick to worrying about things I have control over. Like getting stronger.

I've been doing great with my recovery since my last doctor's appointment. The exercises they gave me to do at home seem to be helping, but Rose still helps me with a few more advanced exercises because she knows I can handle them. Plus, she knows I want to be at my best sooner rather than later.

She also still does those massages on me, but those usually turn into more. I can't help it though. Every time she touches me, no matter how professional she is, I'm instantly hard and can't stop myself from ripping her clothes off and sinking myself so deep inside her that you'd think we were the same person.

I haven't used the wheelchair since that day at the hospital. I've made it my mission to never use it again, but I do have to take things slow some days when I work particularly hard on my exercises and overdo it a bit. Rose gets on my ass, but I'm stronger than I look. Just because my body gets weak every now and then doesn't mean I'm down for the count. It's like I always say, "Life is like riding a bike—take it by the handlebars and own that shit." And boy do I own my shit like it ain't nobody's business.

I've been walking on my own and not getting as winded the past few days, so I think it's time for me to focus on the next thing on my 'to do list.' And that's riding.

"Blaze, meet me outside. Now," I yell across the bar to where he's sitting with Dani. I've probably interrupted something between them, but I don't care. He can get his dick sucked later. I need his help.

Making my way out to the garage, I feel confident in what I'm about to do. I'm nervous, but not because I don't think I can do it. It's only because it's been a long time since I've done this. But you never forget how to ride—

"Yo, Mack! What the hell was so important that you needed me out here right this second?" Blaze yells, a little irritated, but he's trying to hide it. I am his president, so he doesn't want to show any disrespect.

"Lose the fuckin' tone and I'll tell you," I growl, though it doesn't pack a punch like it usually would. I know Blaze isn't challenging me, so I'm letting it go. Unless he keeps it up.

"Sorry, Prez," he says sheepishly.

Turning back around, I continue what I had started before Blaze got here.

In the corner of the garage, there's a solid mass underneath an old sheet. It's something I haven't even dared look at since I got shot. My bike.

"It's time to jump back on the horse, brother," I say quietly.

Turning around, I see him looking at me with a concerned look. "You sure, Prez? What does Rose think about this?" he asks. It angers me a little, but I know he's not trying to make me feel like an invalid or like I need permission. He genuinely doesn't know if I'm ready for this, but it's not all in the physical when it comes to things like this. It's just as much mental, and I know that between the two, I'm more than ready.

"I didn't ask her, but it's time. I just need you to be close in case I need your help. Can you do that?" It's a huge thing for me to admit when I need help, but it's one thing I've learned to do more freely since all this happened. It doesn't make me any less of man or a horrible president to ask for assistance or admit defeat even if it's only for a short while. It means I'm human.

Blaze gives me an encouraging smile and nods his head. "Yeah, of course, Prez. Whatever you need."

For the next hour, Blaze helps me uncover my baby and we clean her up a bit, then check all her fluids. After that's all done, I try to lift my left over her and take a seat. It feels good to be back on her again after all this time. I feel at home...like a day hasn't gone by since I rode her, even though it's been months.

We practice getting on and off a few times to make sure my legs get used to the motions again before I kick the stand up and hold her up. I struggle at first, but once my legs steady, I start her up.

The rumble underneath me excites me and makes me long for the open road. I can't wait to take my baby out with my girl riding behind me. I wonder if Rose has ever been on a bike before. If not, I'll make it good for her. She'll never want to ride in a cage again.

On my first try to get the bike to take off, I almost fall off with her coming down with me, but Blaze jumped in just in time to catch both me and the bike.

"Thanks, brother," I say, out of breath. I don't remember this being so much work before getting shot. Either I'm that out of practice or it's my body giving me hell. Probably a little of both.

"I think we should call it a day. Give your legs

some rest. We can come back out tomorrow if you want," Blaze suggests. I think he'll fight me on it if I try to tell him I'm fine and want to continue, so I nod.

"Yeah. Tomorrow."

Covering the bike back up again, he helps me back into the clubhouse where Rose is sitting with all three of the girls talking. She, of course, sees me as I come in, and notices how unstable I am on my feet. Rushing over to me, she asks, "Are you okay?" The concern I hear in voice makes me happy because it means she cares, but I hate that she's worried.

"I'm fine, baby. Just had a long day," I say to ease her worries.

"Well then, what do ya say I take you back to our room and I'll give you a massage so you can relax?" she says, which has the guys whistling and the girls smiling big, wagging their eyebrows. They know as well as I do that a massage isn't all I'll be getting tonight.

"Yeah, I think that's exactly what I need, baby." I take her hand and almost run down the hallway with her right on my heels. Yeah, she wants it just as much as I do.

As soon as the door opens, I have her in my arms and my lips connect with hers in a desperate kiss. But Rose doesn't complain. Instead, she reaches up to wrap her arms around my neck and kicks the door shut behind us.

"I need you, Michael," she moans into my mouth before crushing her lips to mine again in a kiss that rivals the one I gave her seconds earlier.

Walking her backwards toward the bed, I spin us around so my back is to the mattress. Pulling away from the heated kiss, I smile wickedly at her. Sitting down, I lie back and pull my arms up and rest my head on them. "Strip," I order. I want dinner and a show tonight.

She doesn't hesitate, but instead of removing her clothes in haste, she surprises me. Taking a step back, she slowly lifts her shirt over her head. Twirling it around a few times, she tosses it at me. I don't try to catch it but let it hit me right in the face. Before I reach up and remove it, I inhale deeply. Fuck, I love the way she smells.

"Michael," she says in a singsong voice. "You don't want to miss the show, do you?"

Quickly removing the shirt from in front of my eyes, I grin at her. "Hell no, baby. That would be a fuckin' crime."

Next, she reaches down and pulls the drawstring to her pants. I've noticed that she wears her scrub pants a lot, so one day I looked in my closet to investigate. We'd moved all her stuff into my room since she was in here every night anyway. She only had one pair of jeans hanging there. The rest were scrubs. Not that I mind her in those because she's sexy as fuck in her nursing gear, but I wonder why she doesn't have more jeans. And even the one pair she does have, I don't think I've ever seen her wear them.

Maybe she's so used to wearing them for work that she just doesn't realize she's wearing them. Or maybe she's more comfortable in them. Who fucking cares though, because right now, she's

180

slowly pulling them down over her hips and letting them drop to the floor.

Standing in front of me, she's a vision of perfection. Her long brown hair is flowing down her shoulders, pieces hiding the view of her supple breasts. She's not very big, maybe a big B cup, but they're perfect for me. Just enough for me to fit in my whole hand. Anything more than that is just a waste, anyway.

The bra and panties she's wearing are a matching set. They're blue lace, which brings out the color of her eyes. I love the color of her eyes; they're deep blue. And when I stare into them, it's like I can see into her soul. I can see into my own soul. The way she stares back at me, like she needs me—it's the best feeling in the world.

Rose doesn't make a move to remove anything else just yet. She allows me to get my fill as she eyes me up and down. Her eyes lock onto my rock-hard cock that is currently straining the zipper of my jeans. My pants are going to have to go soon, otherwise my zipper will break from my dick punching its way out to get to our girl, who is now starting to reach behind her back to unclasp her bra.

Her bra straps fall down her shoulders, but her hands hold the front of her bra up, keeping the beautiful sight of her tits from me. I'll wait the few seconds for them to be revealed because I know they're worth the wait.

"Slowly," I say when she starts to lower her arms with the bra with them.

As she obeys my command, I watch in slow motion as her hands fall, followed by her bra, and then zero in on her erect nipples and breasts, that are heavy with want.

"Now your panties," I growl, needing this to move faster, but at the same time, I never want it to end.

Instead of obeying right away, she smirks at me, then turns around so her back is facing me. I start to protest and order her to turn around, angry that she's taking away the view of her tits, but then she starts to lower her panties in slow motion, and I want to kiss her feet.

From this view point, I'll be able to see everything. It doesn't take long before the little tease is bending over at the waist and flashing me an unobstructed view of her shaved pussy.

Not able to take any more, I jump to my feet and close the distance in one step. "I need to be inside you now, baby. I can't wait another second," I growl into her ear as I wrap my arms around her waist and lean my body over the back of hers.

She moans in approval, so I reach down to unbutton and unzip my pants, then as soon as my cock is free, I'm slamming into her wet heat in one thrust.

"Oh, fuck!" Rose yells, but I want to capture all her screams and pleas so no one else has the opportunity to hear her cry out in pleasure. I'm a greedy sonofabitch. I don't even want to share the sounds she makes as she takes my cock deep inside her.

Keeping one hand on her hip to steady her as I continue to pound into her from behind, I reach my other around her and clasp it over her mouth.

"Quiet, baby. You're mine, which means everything of yours is mine; your sweet pussy, this delectable ass," I say as I slap her hard once on her left ass cheek, "and that sassy fuckin' mouth."

She screams behind my hand, and I feel her cunt get tighter and tighter, letting me know she's close. Picking up my pace, I rock into her hard and fast, hitting her so deep and just right so I know she'll be coming all over my cock in no time.

Sure enough, not even four thrusts later, she screams and bites down on one of my fingers just as I feel her tighten her walls around my dick. It takes everything I have not to release inside of her and let her pussy milk every drop of cum I have, but I succeed.

Feeling her go lax in my arms, I walk us over to the bed and allow her to rest her body against it. "Want me to stop, baby?" I ask, rocking into her slowly.

"Yes, please don't stop, Michael," she pleads, and that's all I need.

I thrust into her hard but at a slower pace than I set before. My legs are starting to shake and I know it won't be long before my energy is completely depleted.

Lifting her right leg and setting it on the bed, I'm able to hit her deeper and her walls squeeze me just enough that she'll make me come before I can even say my own name.

"Fuck, yes. So goddamn good, baby," I groan, feeling the start of my orgasm taking hold. I am unable to stop it. Shit, not like I'd want to stop it anyway. It feels too fucking good.

Pumping into her two more times, I explode inside her just as she has another mini orgasm, but it's enough to set my own into overdrive. "Ah, fuck! Shit," I yell, unable to keep my voice down, but I don't care if the whole world hears me or not.

We stay like that—her half lying on the bed on her stomach with me on top of her—for a few seconds before every little bit of strength I have left starts to leave me. But before it does, I position us both so we're at least more stable on the bed with her lying on her side and me still behind her, with my cock still seated deeply inside her warmth.

"Shit, baby...you wore my ass out," I say in a soft voice, incapable of speaking any louder.

Rose laughs softly and it's music to my ears. Fuck, I love it when she laughs.

Minutes pass with nothing said between us and neither of us moving. Shit, we'll probably end up sleeping just like this.

Before I fall asleep and let the darkness take me, I hear her say my name and shake my arm a little. "Michael?"

"Hmmm," I murmur.

"I forgot to tell you before we came back to our room, but me and the girls are going shopping in the morning for the baby shower," she says softly like she too doesn't have the strength to speak louder.

I notice she doesn't ask for my permission or even what I think of the plan and I love that about her too. She's strong willed and not afraid to stand up to me when needed.

I'm starting to think that's not the only thing I love.

"Okay, baby. Just be careful with my precious cargo," I say.

"Don't worry. I won't let anything happen to your girls or the babies."

"No baby, not them...although I want you to look out for them too. But I meant you." She goes silent, but that's okay. I'll let that sink in for a day or two before I bring up what I've wanted to discuss with her for a few weeks now. I think it's time we made things official between us.

CHAPTER TWELVE

Rose

I wake to my alarm going off at six-thirty in the morning. Dani, Sara, and Harlow are going shopping with me today to get stuff for the baby shower, but also to just get out and have some girl time. I'm really excited for today but also nervous. This is the first time since I've been here that I'm leaving the clubhouse without Michael with me. It'll be strange not seeing him for most of the day, but I'm hoping that when I get back, things will be clearer about what we're doing.

Our relationship is fuzzy around the edges and smokin' hot on the inside. I really like Michael and I'm happy, probably for the first time in forever, but I'm still unsure about what our future holds. Even though I've gotten to know him and the others in the club, is this something I want to be a part of for the long haul?

I've had this deep hatred for MCs and the people in them, but now I know they aren't all the same. At least, not that I have seen yet, but will that change with time? Are the reason things are going so well because it's still new? I wonder if Michael will get mean and become uncaring and possibly abusive the longer we stay together and the more comfortable we get. I don't want to think that, but from what I've seen of my brother, that's all I know.

I'm trying so hard not to transfer everything I feel about the way my brother is onto Michael and the rest of his family. They have done nothing to deserve my mistrust and fear, so it's not fair to them to place them in the same category as Anthony and his gang, but that's easier said than done.

It's like being in a relationship with someone and you gave them everything. They were your world and you would do anything to make them happy. It didn't matter what they'd done or the things they would continue to do…you'd keep sacrificing yourself because you thought you could never be happy without them. Or maybe you didn't deserve or think you could do better than them. But once you finally get out of the relationship, and you're single for a while, you try your luck at love again. But your future starts paying for your past. That's kind of the way I'm feeling right now.

I hate being so caught up in my mind. It's a scary place in there and to be stuck in there alone? That's a disaster waiting to happen.

Needing to do something that will get my mind off these dark subjects, I carefully untangle myself from Michael's hold and quietly get out of bed.

Michael is still sleeping and hasn't even moved a

muscle, from the looks of it when I turn around to look at him. I'm not quite sure what he did yesterday, but I know what we did last night before we went to sleep. Damn, I'm getting wet just thinking about it. That seriously was probably the best sex of my life. The way he made me strip for him, and then not being able to hold himself back any longer so he rushed me and took be right then and there. He worked himself and me pretty hard last night, so yeah, I can see why he's still sleeping.

Jumping into the shower, I go through the motions of washing and drying myself, then walk out into the room to grab my clothes for the day.

I sneak a quick peek at Michael once more and find that he's still out like a light. Smiling to myself, I look in the closet for something to wear. I don't really want to wear my scrubs today, but they are comfy. I just don't think it's the best attire for a shopping excursion with the girls. No, I think I'll wear the only pair of jeans I have and I'll see if I can find a halfway decent t-shirt to go with it. I don't need to dress up, but I still want to look nice.

After getting my clothes of choice on, I put my long damp hair into a ponytail. I don't want to take the time to blow dry it, but I do want to put a little bit of makeup on. Once I'm finished, I head back out to the bedroom and find that Michael is finally starting to wake.

"Good morning, sleepy head," I say, smiling at him. Damn, he looks so sexy after he wakes up. Actually he looks sexy no matter what time of day it is or what he's doing, but there's something about his bedhead, sleepy eyes, and lazy smiles that get me.

"Well, it's a great morning now that I've laid eyes on you," he says and my heart melts. This man could say the cheesiest lines yet I know with every fiber of my being that he's speaking from his heart. That's one of the things that I really like about him; that no matter what or who he's talking to, he'll always speak the truth and say what's on his mind. That's one of the things we have in common, not being afraid to speak our mind. His comes from being a leader and mine comes from knowing what I want.

Laughing, I make my way over to the bed and sit down, but he's got other ideas. Grabbing me and pulling me on top of him, he looks satisfied. "So, you're a man of many talents, huh? Talking dirty and spankings at night and sweet words and smiles in the morning. I like it," I say, then lean down to kiss him softly. I have to meet the girls out front in a few minutes, so I don't want to kiss him any deeper, afraid I won't be able to pull myself away for another hour if I do.

"You'll find that I can talk dirty and dish out spankings any time of the day, baby." His voice is rough and gritty from sleep, but being as I feel his hard cock pushing into my stomach, I assume his tone is also that way because he's in need.

"Well, as much as I'd love to see that play out, I have to get going. The girls are probably already waiting for me," I say, a little sad and disappointed I made these plans now, but there's no way I'll tell him that. He'd probably order me to stay or tell the girls I can't go. As much as I want to stay here with him and have buckets of rough sex with lots of dirty talk, I want to go with the girls more.

Groaning and closing his eyes before throwing his arm over his face, he nods his head. "Guess I'm destined for a cold shower this morning, huh?"

Kissing his lips, I say, "I'll be back before you know it. Just think of this as a form of foreplay."

Lifting his arm a little, he cracks open one eye and asks, "How so?"

"Well, think about how hot you'll be for me if you keep thinking about all the things you want to do to my body for the next few hours," I say in a sultry voice, grinding my covered pussy against the bulge underneath me.

He sucks in a harsh breath through gritted teeth and squeezes his eyes shut like he's in pain. I almost feel bad for him, but I'll be in pain too. My pussy is throbbing and aching to be filled.

Before I lose every ounce of willpower, I have to leave. I remove myself from on top of him and sway my hips as I make my way to the door, grabbing my purse from the chair on the way. "See you soon, stud." With those parting words, I make my way out to the bar, excited for when I return. I wonder what he'll have in store for me?

"Hey girl. You ready to go?" Harlow asks as I walk up to the table where they're sitting with what looks like a hot cup of coffee. Mmm, coffee. That's exactly what I need right about now, but them? I don't think they should be drinking that.

"Um, I hate to be a Debbie Downer, but should you all really be drinking coffee?" I hope they don't get upset with me, but I'm a nurse—it's to be expected.

"Don't worry, Nurse Rose. It's decaffeinated green tea. But we did brew a pot just for you," Sara says, making me smile with their thoughtfulness.

Squeezing her shoulder, I say, "You are a life saver."

Once I have my coffee in hand, we make our way toward the door when we notice that someone is following us. Dani's the first to turn around and see a man I've only seen a few times but have never talked to. I think Michael said he was one of the prospects or something like that. He's not a full member, but he wants to be. He's in the "try-out" phase, I guess, where he can try the club on for size, but really, it's for the club to test him. They want to make sure he's good for the club and loyal. Those things are very important, I've gathered.

"And what do you think you're doing, Prospect?" Dani asks with attitude. I've learned that this is her way with a lot of people, mostly when she doesn't know you well or if she's testing you.

The prospect stops abruptly and looks like he's staring down a lioness who is preparing to pounce on her prey. "Uh, I'm supposed to escort you, ma'am."

"What the fuck? Ma'am? Do I look old enough to be referred to as such?" she growls back. It's kind of funny to watch her go up against a man that is twice her size and see this man wither under her glare. Although, from the stories I've heard about Dani, I know she can pack a pretty big punch, so the attitude she puts off…she can back it up one hundred percent. Shit, I'm kind of scared of this girl right now.

"No, ma'—I'm mea—no, Miss." This man has no idea what to do right now. I feel bad for him.

"Oh, now I'm a miss? Jesus Christ, do you realize who you're talking to? I could kill you right now and it wouldn't make me lose any sleep at night," Dani says, but I can hear a little bit of amusement in her tone now. She's loving every second of this.

This time, instead of answering with words, he just nods, but he keeps eye contact with her. He's got some balls, that's for sure.

"Good. As long as you know that," she says, then crosses her arms and asks, "Now, who told you we needed an escort?"

The prospect looks like he doesn't want to answer, but he knows he doesn't have a choice. Opening his mouth to respond, he gets interrupted by a loud, booming voice from behind him. "We did."

Looking past him, I see four large men who look ready to do battle. Michael is in the middle, and he's flanked by Toby, Louie, and Blaze. Looks like we're all getting ganged up on.

"Oh come on! Really?" Dani yells, hands on her hips now. She looks ready to breathe fire.

Not wanting to upset anyone and knowing the men only want to make sure we're okay, I decide to defuse the situation.

"Dani, maybe it wouldn't be a bad idea for him to follow us. It's not like he'll be breathing down our backs, right?" I ask pointedly, looking at the prospect, then directing my gaze to Michael.

"No, he'll keep his distance," Michael answers and the prospect nods.

"There you go. No harm done," I say. "This way, he'll be able to hold all of our bags while we continue to shop till we drop!" I add in with more enthusiasm than I feel. I don't really like shopping, but today, I'll do my best to have fun with the girls. Who knows, maybe my perspective will change.

"Fine, but he's carrying all of our bags and he better not bitch about it," Dani says in defeat, but still with attitude.

She turns around to go outside and the other girls follow. I turn to look back at Michael and he gives me a big smile, like he's proud of me for something. I just don't know what. I only said what I did so there wouldn't be a fight. I've learned there are some things you just don't need to argue about, and this isn't one of them. Plus, it won't hurt, especially since there's still a fear inside me that my brother will turn up.

Shit, maybe this isn't such a good idea. And with having the girls with me, what if one of them gets hurt?

Michael must see the war I'm waging from my face because he makes his way up to me and gathers me in his arms. "What's wrong, baby?"

I don't want to tell him why I'm scared. He doesn't need to know, but then again, what if it will help? Fuck, I don't know what to do.

"Do you think we'll run into any problems? Is that why you're sending someone with us?" I ask, figuring if he thinks there's something to be concerned about, he'd tell me. At least, I think he would.

"No, baby. It's just as a precaution we always follow when the girls go out. It makes the guys feel better and I know I'd feel better as well knowing that you girls will be safe. The prospect can handle anything that comes at him, and we won't be that far away if he needs back up. But don't worry, baby, nothing is going to happen." He kisses my head and pulls back to look me in the eyes with a smile on his face.

"Now go. Have fun. I'll see you soon." With that, he shoos me away and I feel a little bit better. Maybe I should have told him, but he's right. Nothing is going to happen and we have the prospect if it does. I really don't think my brother would be dumb enough to try something when we are surrounded by a lot of people. We'll be at the mall most of the time, so we'll be fine.

***

The ride to the mall is full with playful banter and talk about the upcoming babies. Dani is excited for her twins to have a baby brother and says they are probably more excited than she and Blaze are. I find that so cute that the twins are happy about having a brother. Most little kids love and hate the prospect of having another sibling in the house, afraid that they will no longer get the attention they're used to. But on another note, they're thrilled to have another brother or sister to play with.

Harlow talks about her worries about having twins, but I know she'll be fine. With Dani there to help her through it, and Sara as another strong friend, she'll be just fine. Plus, she has all the guys around too.

Sara is thrilled to be having a baby. She said she never really thought about having kids, but she's so excited that she and Toby will be starting their family together. They got married a few years ago and things have been great with them. I'm so happy for them. All of them.

I stay quiet for the most part since I don't have much to contribute to the already close trio. Plus, I'm not pregnant, so there's nothing to add there. But I do give my support and answer any medical questions they may have. It's still a nice conversation, even if I'm not active for the most part. It's nice having this time with them and hearing their thoughts and concerns. Even their wishes.

Dani has talked about hiring another tattoo artist or two for her shop so she can spend more time at home with the kids. And since Louie works with her too, she thinks it would give him more time to spend with Harlow and the twins, and of course the club. I think that's a great idea, but she's worried what Michael with think.

He's the one that brought her into the trade and gave her a job. And he's the one who handed down the shop to her. She's just unsure how he'd feel about her stepping back a bit. She'd still own the place and come in a few times a week for a few hours, but she'd have more family time. I told her I think Michael would have no problem with that. Heck, I think he'd actually be thrilled that she'd want to do that.

She seemed a little unsure at first when I put in my two cents, but then she smiled and thanked me, and said she thinks I'm right. She's going to talk with Blaze and Louie soon and then sit down to talk to Michael.

We pull into the parking lot of the mall a few minutes later. We all get out and ignore the fact that the prospect parked a few spaces away and is following us at a leisurely pace. He doesn't even seem upset that he got the job of babysitting us. But then again, he's probably willing to do anything the club says to win their loyalty and respect. He'd probably even clean toilets, if he hasn't already.

The girls want to stop at a few stores to look at baby clothes and furniture first. It'll probably be better to get all the regular shopping out of the way before we start getting stuff for the party, which is planned for next month sometime. We haven't hashed out all of the details and the date, but they agree with me and want it to be well before the babies are born, that way they can get things situated and get anything else they need or want. That's the way I'd want it if it were me.

Moving in and out of stores, they buy everything from baby clothes, diapers, and set up delivery times for the furniture they picked out. I asked at one time if they should wait to ask the men what they think, but they all laughed and said that the guys would just say something like, "Get whatever you want."

Next, they wanted to do a little shopping for themselves, so I decided to take advantage of that and do a little shopping of my own. I'd like to pick out more jeans and shorts since I am no longer working at the hospital. Though, eventually I'm going to have to find a new job, but I want to wear normal clothes more, even when I do get a new job.

I find a few pairs of jeans, a couple shorts, some shirts, and even a dress or two that I want to try on. I'm not sure that I'll get everything because it's a lot of money and I'm going to have to be careful with my spending, but I want to at least get one outfit.

"I'm going to go try these on," I tell the girls as they look through a few racks with some sexy lingerie. I didn't even know this store carried shit like that.

"All right, hon. Let us know if you need anything or want us to grab different sizes for you," Sara says.

"Yeah, and make sure to come out and model for us," Dani says, wagging her eyebrows at me just like Michael does.

I laugh and shake my head as I make my way toward the dressing rooms.

I'm talking to one of the associates, waiting for her to find a room for me when I feel like I have eyes on me, watching my every move.

Turning around, I scan the store, but don't see anything or anyone out of place. Dani, Sara, and Harlow are still where I left them. There are a few women shopping here and there, and there are three employees walking around, restocking and checking on customers. I don't see anyone else, not even the prospect.

Shaking my head, I let it go as paranoia. I've always been this way, but the past couple months more so than usual. Whenever my brother pops into my life like he did that night at the hospital with that note, it always spikes it up though. But I'm safe and he doesn't even know where I am. Shit, for all he knows, I'm out of the fuckin' country...and I'd like to keep it that way.

After trying on all the clothes, I look for the girls but they are nowhere in sight. Where they hell did they go?

"Um, excuse me. Did you happen to see where the three women I came in here with went?" I ask one of the sales ladies.

She smiles. "Oh, sure. They left rather quickly with a man that came in."

Starting to panic now, afraid that my brother did come here after all and took them, I drop all the clothes and run out of the shop. I'm sure I'm getting a bunch of weird looks from everyone inside the store, but I just don't give a fuck. I have to save them. I'll offer myself up on a silver fucking platter if that's what I have to do, but they don't deserve to pay for my sins of having an evil brother.

I'm almost out the door when I run into what feels like a wall of brick, but is really a hard mass of muscles covered by an MC cut. At first, I think it's my brother and start to fight him, getting ready to scream, but then I notice the patches; Forsaken Sinners. Looking up, it's the prospect.

"Hey, what's the matter? Did something happen?" he asks, seeming to get worried, but looking around the store with a hard glare, willing to throw down with anyone if necessary.

"The girls. They're gone. I don't know where they went, but I think—" I start to say, but the prospect interrupts me.

"Hey, it's okay. They're down at the food court waiting for you. They got hungry and told me to come and get you," he says, and instantly my body relaxes and I feel so fucking stupid. I really need to get a handle on this shit.

"Thank god. I was really worried there for a minute," I say stupidly, trying to explain my panic to him, but in the end, I don't care if he thinks I'm a freak. As long as the girls are safe and my brother didn't take them.

Stepping away from him, I make my way toward the food court when the prospect asks, "Did you want to get anything here?"

Looking back, I see the sales clerk picking up the pile of clothes I threw down in my haste to get to Dani, Sara, and Harlow. "Oh, um, no. I can come back and get the few things I found. The girls are probably waiting for me and I don't want to keep them." That was a dumb excuse, but honestly, I don't care much about the forgotten clothes now. I feel drained and just want to go back to the clubhouse and curl up in a ball and maybe have a good cry.

"Are those the clothes that you were going to get?" he asks, pointing to where I was just looking.

"Yes," I say, already turning away.

"Okay then. You go on ahead and I'll be along shortly," he tells me, but I don't even reply. I'm just ready for this day to be over.

After finding the girls, I sit down while they eat. I don't get anything because I'm not sure if my stomach could handle food right now.

"Aren't you going to eat?" Sara asks, looking at me with concern.

"No. I'm actually not feeling the best all of a sudden," I tell them.

"Yeah, you do look a little pale." This comes from Harlow.

"We can take the rest of the food to go," Dani says, already standing and helping me out of my seat. It's not needed, but it's much appreciated. "Let's get you home, honey."

CHAPTER THIRTEEN

Mack

Things have been different for the past few days. Off is probably a better term.

The day Rose went shopping with Dani, Sara, and Harlow, she came back feeling sick. Looking at her, it was like she'd seen a ghost or something. But every time I asked her if she was okay or what was wrong, she'd brush me off and just say she wasn't feeling well.

All she does all day is lie in bed, either sleeping or staring at the wall. She doesn't talk and she says she doesn't want to see anyone. Sometimes it's like she doesn't even want me there. I fucking hate it and I don't know what to do. I feel like I'm losing her.

After waking up this morning, I asked Rose if she wanted any coffee, to which she replied that she wasn't thirsty. I asked if she was hungry and maybe wanted to go out for breakfast, to which she freaked out. She practically ripped my fucking head off.

Deciding to give her some time alone—or more time alone—I left the room and went outside to the garage. There was one girl I knew would want my company. My bike.

The past few days, Blaze and I have been coming out here and working on me riding again. Even though I haven't done more than maybe a few laps around the garage, I'm still riding. And it feels great. I can't wait until I can take her out on the open road again.

Taking the cover off of her, I checked all her fluids and started to gather everything I would need to change the oil. I know it was done right before I got shot and was in the hospital, and I think Blaze mentioned he did it again before I got home, but I needed to keep my hands and mind busy. Otherwise, I'd march back into that room and make Rose tell me what's going on with her.

I go through the motions of grabbing all the tools, making sure I have all the supplies, and then sit down on one of the stools out here, just staring at my bike. It was the only thing I cared about after my old man died. Then, the club came and I started to add more and more people to that list. I had a family again, a mission, a duty. I started my tattoo shop and things were great. I never thought they could get better.

Then Dani came into my life. She may think I helped her, but that's not true. She did all that herself. But something else she doesn't know is that she saved me. I never knew what I was missing until her. She gave me something more to protect, to love, and it was different than my club. She became my daughter and reason for living.

Sure, I had the club and I wouldn't go down without a fight, but with Dani, I had more fire and more of a will to not go down before I was ready.

Next came Sara, the twins, and then Harlow. And again, I thought I was complete, that I didn't need anything else in my life. But I was wrong again. I needed Rose.

A few minutes later, Blaze comes strolling in. "Hey, brother."

Nodding my greeting, I get back to the task at hand. Blaze doesn't make any further comment and lets me do my work in peace.

By the time I'm done, he's taken a seat on the work bench watching me with a crazy look on his face.

"What do you say we take her out for a spin?" he asks, nodding toward my bike.

Laughing, I stand up, not feeling any pain or weakness. "Fuck ya, brother."

Saddling up, I strap on my helmet. I wish I had Rose behind me when I take my bike out for the first time since being in the hospital, but I'd probably get another earful if I asked. Guess I'll just have to wait until she's feeling better to do that.

Starting the bike, I feel her rumble underneath me and it makes me smile. God, I've missed this. The feeling of being free with nothing but open road ahead of me.

I walk the bike out of the garage but as soon as I hit the dirt, I'm revving her up full throttle and taking off down the road. The wind on my face and nothing but dust behind me, I know everything is going to be okay. Even if Rose doesn't tell me what's wrong, even if we don't figure out what the Street Kings want, I know everything will be okay. Because if I can get through being shot, if I can walk again when no one thought I would, I can make Rose see I'm the man for her and I can figure out a plan to take care of all our problems with the MC. It may take a lot of work, but I'll figure it all out.

***

We get back to the clubhouse an hour later and I feel better than I have in a long time. Not in the sense that my legs aren't hurting or the way that Rose makes me feel. No, I mean I feel like I've been revived and refreshed from all things old and bad, and now I'm a new man. The road will do that to you after so much time away.

"You good, brother?" Blaze asks as we walk our bikes backwards into our spots in front of the clubhouse. Stepping back, it's a damn good sight to see my bike in its rightful spot.

"Yeah, man. I'm good."

When we make our way into the clubhouse, I see it's a full house today. Everyone is here, including most of the hang arounds and club whores. I don't know what the occasion is, but I don't care. The only thing I want to do is see my girl and get her to tell me what's going on. I need her to get out of this funk or whatever it is that's going on with her. I have a feeling it's not that she's ill, but something else entirely and I'm going to find out what.

On my way through the bar, heading toward my room, I'm stopped by a sight I haven't seen in months. It's a sight that used to make me smile and long for the feel of release, but now, I feel nothing at all.

"KitKat, how are you, darlin'?" I ask the woman standing in front of me. She's staring me down like I'm her last meal.

"I good now that I'm with you, Macky," she says, and even though she's not the woman I want to see, her voice isn't annoying. Kat is kind of like the house mama. She keeps all the whores in line and keeps things running smoothly when it comes to the pussy. This place would be a wreck without her; no man getting the pussy he wants or needs and all the whores thinking they're worth more than they are.

Now, I'm not some degrading asshole, but these bitches need to know their place. They will never be an old lady and they need to know not to try. I've never seen a brother turn a whore into a house wife and I probably never will. They're only good for one thing and that's taking the guys' minds off of the hard shit by sucking or fucking them.

Kat and I used to have a mutual understanding. She liked having me and I liked having someone I could get a release from when the moment rose. I really don't want to be a jackass and point it out to her, but I will if I have to. I just hope it doesn't come down to her leaving the clubhouse for good.

"Listen, darlin'. I missed seeing your beautiful

face around here, but what we were before is not possible now," I tell her, hoping she gets it.

She looks hurt at first and then a look of understanding crosses her face. She may be in her late forties, but she's still one beautiful woman. "I was wondering when the right woman would come along to sweep you off your feet, honey." Smiling, she closes the distance between us to give me a hug.

After a few seconds of embracing me, she whispers in my ear, "I know it would never happen—you taking me as your old lady—but that doesn't mean I didn't hope for it."

I pull back and grab a hold of her face. "I'm sorry, darlin'. You are an amazing woman, and if any of you girls would be old lady material, it would be you," I tell her with a sad smile.

"Just not for you," she finishes for me, and I nod. I do feel sorry that she's getting the shit end of the stick, but this is our life. It's the way things are. But I know she understands that, maybe even better than anyone else.

"It's okay, honey. I'm just glad you found someone. I hope she's good to you," Kat says before kissing me briefly on the lips before making her way to the bar. I'm not sad to see her leave though because I know what waits for me in my bedroom.

That thought has a smile breaking out all over my face. Desperate to get to my girl, I turn around, but stop in my tracks when I see a very pissed off Rose.

My smile drops marginally, only because I'm not sure why she's upset, but I continue on. "Hey, baby.

I was just coming in to get you," I tell her, but she just glares at me.

"Are you feeling better?" I ask, trying a different tactic to get her to talk, but nothing. Now I'm starting to get pissed. Why the fuck is she acting like this?

Rose looks me up and down, almost in disgust, then shakes her head in anger before turning on her heels and taking off down the hall. Not going to let her get away without telling me what the fuck her problem is, I go after her and grab her by the arm.

"What the hell is the matter with you?" I yell as I whip her around to face me.

"Don't fucking touch me!" she yells back as she tries yanking her arm from my grasp, but I don't let go.

"Baby, stop," I try to calm my voice, but I'm not sure if it's working.

"Let me go," she growls, staring pointedly at my hand.

"No. Not until you tell me what's going on."

"You want to know what's going on? Why I'm mad?" she seethes, getting angrier as each word leaves her lips. "You're a fucking pig. That's what the problem is."

"What the hell did I do?" I ask. I've been trying to get her to talk to me for the past three fucking days, only to be ignored or bitched at. I've done nothing but give her space when she wanted it and been nice.

"Really? You really have to ask me that?" she asks, though I don't think she wants an answer, but I'm going to give her one.

"Yes, I really have to ask. I have no idea what you're going on about."

Is she mad because I left her alone after it didn't seem like she wanted me around? If so, then she's fucked up in the head, because the only reason I did that is because she told me to or wouldn't say more than two fucking words to me.

"You and that whore!" she yells, and then rips her arm out of my hold and takes off down the hallway. It finally makes sense. She's jealous. She saw me with Kat and thought it was more than it was, but she's wrong.

Taking off after her again, I can tell by one look into my room that she's in there tearing shit apart. She's in the closet throwing every piece of clothing out; hers and mine.

"What are you doing?"

She doesn't answer me, but continues to throw shit around the room, cursing up a storm to herself, though I can still hear her. She's calling me every name in the book and even making up a few I've never heard of.

"Rose. Baby, you need to stop. What you saw wasn't what it looked like," I start, but when she looks up at me with a look of hatred, I stop in my tracks. I hate that look on her and when it's directed at me, I feel like my world is crashing down all around me. Like the floor was whipped out from under me and now I'm freefalling to my death.

How did everything go to such shit?

"Just let me explain, please." When she doesn't make a move to stop me, I continue on. "Kat and I are friends. Yes, she's a club whore, but she's not

208

like the rest. This club is all she has. She's not in it to become an old lady or to manipulate anyone. She doesn't even care about having sex with any of the single brothers. She's just a nice woman. I like to talk to her," I tell her, knowing I need to tell her the rest, but dreading it. I know she's not going to understand.

"And yeah, before I met you, there were a few times that it went beyond friendship, but it was only sexual. That's it. What you saw just now was a friend talking to a friend. I told her about you and that I care about you a lot. She said she's happy for me—happy for us. She knows you're special to me, baby. Please, just stop being mad so we can talk about this," I plead, not even caring if I sound like a pathetic fool. Rose is too important to me to lose over my foolish pride or my ego. I'll lay it all out on the line and bare my soul for her if that's what it takes for her to see that she's it for me.

"Yeah? Well, that's not what it looked like from where I was standing," she whispers. I'm not sure if the words were meant for me, but I'm going to reply.

"It was a hug and peck on the lips from a friend...that's it. There was nothing sexual about it, I swear." She's got to see it like it is. She just has to. I can't lose her, not over something so fucking stupid.

She doesn't answer me, but now instead of throwing shit around the room, she's found her bag she brought all her stuff here with and is now throwing all her clothes into it. I panic.

"Come on, baby. You have to believe me.

Please, Rose," I beg.

Stopping what she's doing, she looks up at me and her face is void of all emotion for a few seconds before I see the saddest look I've ever seen on anyone's face. "I'm sorry, I just can't," she says. She falls down to the floor, then sits there with her face in her hands and cries.

I want to go to her, comfort her, but I don't know how or even if it will help. It fuckin' destroys me that she doesn't believe in me—in us. I could deal with her being angry and even yelling and throwin' shit around, but the fact that she doesn't trust me? It's devastating.

"I'm sorry, Michael. I wish I could believe what you say is true, and maybe I do in a way, but this just isn't going to work. Shit, maybe we were doomed from the very beginning. But this—what we had—is no more. I can't do this with you. We're not a good fit for each other. I'm sorry," she says. I hate that those words are coming out of her mouth. We are a good fit for each other, I know it. I can fuckin' feel it. Why can't she see that?

"I'm leaving. Going to go home and try to get my head straight. Maybe when things settle down and the fog in my head is gone I'll see things differently, but please, just give me space, okay?"

No, it's not fucking okay, but what the hell can I do? She's already made up her mind. Shit, maybe she had her mind made up before she saw me and Kat…who the fuck knows? What I do know is that she's leaving, possibly for good, and she's taking a piece of me with her. I feel dead inside, numb.

"You're making a mistake," is all I say. They're

the only words I can come up with.

Sighing, she stands up with her bag over her shoulder. "Maybe. But it's my mistake to make," she says, then walks toward me and stops in front of me. "I'm sorry, Mack." Then she's out the door.

When it closes softly behind her, it's like the door to my whole world has slammed in my face. Everything I had, everything I wanted or needed, just walked out on me. What the hell am I supposed to do now?

I don't know how long I stand in that one spot in my room, feeling numb and desolate, but I finally get feeling into my body. Throwing open the door, I rush out into the bar to see if I can stop Rose, but she's already gone.

Maybe she was right and she needs some time away from everything to get her head around what we are and what she wants, but I need to know she's all right.

"Prospect!" I yell, waiting for him to come running.

"Yes, Prez?" he asks, rushing up to me, eager to do whatever it is I tell him.

"Rose left. I need you to catch up to her and follow her wherever she goes. Update me on anything that goes on or if she leaves anywhere, but do not engage her. I don't want her to know you're there," I order in a commanding voice.

"Yes, sir," the prospect replies and he scurries on his way.

There's really nothing else I can do but wait; wait to hear from her or wait to hear from the prospect. Either way, I fear that Rose leaving is more final than I originally thought. It may just kill me in the end.

***

I've been sitting at the bar nursing a bottle of beer when Jax comes up and sits beside me. "Everything okay, Prez?"

I nod my head, then shake it no. He's probably thinking I'm insane, but right now, I pretty much am. I'm insane with worry, I'm insane with anger, and I'm insane with feeling the loss of Rose.

"Not really, brother," I tell him. I hate how I'm feeling but don't have a clue as to what I'm supposed to do about it. I tried talking to Rose and calming her worries, but she didn't want to hear it. She didn't want to see what is plainly in front her, and that's me. I'm broken and surrendering to her because that's what she does to me; she brings me to my knees with everything she makes me feel for her. I think I may actually love her. But it's pretty fucking obvious she doesn't feel the same way.

"Rose left. Thought I was running around with Kat behind her back," I explain because maybe he can shed some light on what I should do now. I'm pissed that she left me and didn't believe me, but I'm pissed at myself more because I wasn't enough for her. I wasn't worthy of her trust, her love.

"You love her?" he asks, picking the words right out of my mind. Do I love her?

"I can't be sure, but I think I do. She makes me want to be a better man; for her and for the club. She makes me happy. I feel more alive with her

212

than I think I have ever felt in my whole life." There's so much more I could say about Rose and the way she makes me feel, but I can't put them into words. She's simply everything to me.

Jax is quiet for a moment. I'm not sure if he's thinking about what I said, or something else. I've never been one to really ask for advice, because I haven't really had anything important enough to ask for. Until Rose.

I'm not trying to sound like I'm a know it all, but I've never been in a situation where I needed it. I'm usually the one people look to be the voice of reason or give advice. So if Jax has anything to add or has any idea of what I should do, I'm open to suggestions.

"I've been around you guys for a while and I've seen a lot in that time. I've kept my mouth shut about a few things because my input wasn't needed, and I thought you'd all figure it out," Jax says, but waits until I look at him to continue. "And I don't mean any disrespect to you, Prez, but you ain't figured it out yet."

I can't help but get angry. "You don't think I fuckin' know that, Jax?" I yell.

Sighing, he's the one to look away now. "I think there's something going on with her, or she's afraid of something. It was weird, but when I picked her up from her apartment that night she came here, she wanted me to go up with her to help carry stuff down. I didn't think anything of it, but she was kind of skittish. Once we got up to her apartment, she seemed relieved to not find anyone there or whatever she was scared of," he says, then looks at me finally. "While she went into her room to pack her stuff, I did a search around her house. I didn't find anything, and I mean anything. No little knickknacks that chicks usually like to have around. No pictures of family or friends. Of course that could just mean she either doesn't have any family, or maybe she's just too busy being a nurse to decorate, I don't know, but I found it odd. Then when she came back out, packed and ready to go, she only had the one bag. Not the amount she said she'd needed me for. It's like she wanted protection from something."

It makes me upset that he's just now telling me this, but I'm sure he had his reasons. Did Rose tell him not to say anything? Did she tell him what she's scared of?

"Why are you telling me this now and not when it happened?"

"I wasn't one hundred percent certain, ya know? So I watched her, and she seemed better once she got here. I didn't see any trace of her being scared, so I let it go. Maybe I shouldn't have or maybe I should have just told you, but I didn't know what to do, brother." I can't fault him for not telling me because I didn't even notice what was going on. But now that he mentions it, I can see that maybe that's why she's been so off the last few days. Did something happen while she and the girls were at the mall?

"It's okay, brother. I get it. You did the right thing," I tell him, trying to ease his guilt for not saying anything.

Smiling a little, he nods. "Well, I do have to say

one more thing."

Laughing, I say, "Of course you do."

"You may not know that you love her, Prez, but I do. I see the way you are around her, the way you look at her, and even the way you talk about her. You love her. And I'm not sure what happened or why she left, but if I were you, I'd go after her."

I think about what he said. Do I love her? I love being around her and I love the way she makes me feel. And I know I didn't want her to leave…that much is for certain. Then it hits me; Jax is right. I do love her.

"What if she doesn't feel the same way?" I ask, afraid that if I do go after her, she'll get angry and I'll lose her all over again.

"She does. She looks at you the same way, Mack. She follows you with her eyes and smiles to herself when she thinks no one is looking. And I think maybe the reason I saw the change in her since she got here is because of you. She feels safe and protected with you. She loves you, just as sure as Dani loves Blaze, Sara loves Toby, and Harlow loves Louie."

With a new drive of determination, I get up to go after my girl. My phone rings, so I grab it off the bar and talk as I make my way to the door, but the words stop me dead in my tracks.

It's the prospect and he doesn't sound good. "Prez," he says, in pain. "It's Rose. She's in trouble. It's the Kin—" There's a loud gunshot and then there's nothing but silence.

CHAPTER FOURTEEN

Rose

After leaving the clubhouse, I'm a wreck. I hated to see the look of defeat and pain on Michael's face. I lied when I said I don't trust him, but I had to do something. What we're doing isn't going to work, mainly because I can't be honest with him. He's the one that shouldn't trust me.

I was on my way to look for Michael, to tell him I was leaving, that we weren't a good match. I put him through hell the past few days with the way I've been acting, but I didn't know what else to do. At the mall, it became too real that the life I live isn't something that lets me have a normal life. I can't love someone and bring them into the danger zone with me, because that's what it would be. Anthony is still out there and eventually he will find me. And then what I thought happened at the mall will *actually* happen. And I won't risk that. I won't risk the people who have come to mean so much to me.

So when I saw him with that woman, yeah, I was jealous, but I knew he wasn't going behind my back to be with her. And when he explained what was going on, I believed him. But it helped me in my case that we weren't good for one another and that I was leaving. It gave me the perfect excuse so I wouldn't have to tell him the truth. I know that makes me the worst person in the world, but when you're desperate, you'll do just about anything.

I'm not proud of what I did, but it's done now and there's nothing I can do to change it. The only thing I can do now is go home, pack my things, and leave for good. Get as far away from here as I possibly can and never look back. I should have done it when I planned to do it, instead of taking on the job of caring for Michael, but I'm glad I didn't. It gave me that time with him and his family, and I'll treasure it for the rest of my life. That's all I'll have to sustain me—memories.

It seems to take forever to get back to my apartment, but I finally pull into my parking space. It's getting dark, but I don't mind. It fits my mood perfectly. Actually, I think every day for the rest of eternity should be dark, rainy, and gloomy. Maybe it would make me feel better about my situation and who I left behind. Well, probably not, but I deserve to be unhappy and remember that I lied and left them.

Getting out of my car, I don't even bother to grab my bag because I'll be coming right back out with the rest of my stuff. I didn't even really need to come back, but I want to do another look around and grab a few things. I won't be back so I don't want to leave anything behind that is either embarrassing or that I'd miss. It's probably not much though.

I'm fishing out my keys and am almost to the door that leads to my apartment when I hear a sound behind me. It's a bike. Did Michael come after me or did he send someone to come and get me? I don't think Michael can ride his bike yet, so if I had to guess, it's one of his brothers, or maybe the prospect.

I hear the bike come to a screeching halt behind me, so I turn around, exasperated that I was followed, but when I finally turn around, I'm met with chilling eyes that are terrifying, yet familiar.

Gasping in shock, I try to turn around and run away, but I'm rooted to the spot. I can't move. My muscles are frozen and they're not allowing me the escape I so desperately need right now.

"Well, hello, sister dearest," my brother, Anthony, says in a mockingly sweet voice. I know it's just a mirage. He's anything but sweet.

"A-Anthony. W-What are you d-doing here?" I ask, my eyes jumping around, trying to find an exit or help, but they come up empty.

"Well, my dear sister, I've come to retrieve you. See, I've made a deal and it's time to pay up," he says. The façade he only moments ago was using with a sweet voice is starting to fade and my real brother is coming out now. This is Brutus, a member of the Street Kings MC.

Not really sure what he's talking about, but

218

knowing I won't like it, I try to stall him by keeping him talking. I don't want to know what it is he's done and what deal he's made—or what's more, what the payment is and what it has to do with me—but if it will give me more time to figure out what I'm going to do or how I'm going to get away, I'll do it.

"What deal?" I ask, this time a little more smoothly, but still scared out of my mind. I know this man in front of me is dangerous. It doesn't matter if I'm his sister or not—he'd kill me if it benefited him.

"I've been promoted to Vice President. But in order to do that, I had to give my president something. And there was only one thing he wanted. You," he says, stepping closer.

Finally, my muscles allow me to retreat, but it's not fast enough. He reaches out and wraps his large hand around my bicep. It's painful, and even though I know crying out will do nothing to stop him, I do it anyway. I can't help it, the pain in my arm is almost as bad as when I broke my leg when I was ten. Well, actually, I didn't break my leg. He did. My brother.

We were at the park playing, and he thought it would be funny to push me off of the monkey bars. I was so frail from barely eating at home that when I landed on my leg wrong, it snapped right in two. I was lucky the bone didn't protrude out of the skin and that there was a nice family close by that called the ambulance right away.

Anthony went with me, saying he was concerned about his little sister, but it was all a farce. He really just wanted to make sure I kept my mouth shut, which I of course did. I was too scared not to. I just told the doctors that I fell and that my brother tried to save me, but it all had happened too fast. They of course believed me and I was sent home after they set my leg and put me in a cast.

"Gutter has had a thing for you for years. He's even followed you around and placed cameras in your apartment. Sick bastard probably even sniffed your panties," he says, laughing like it's the funniest thing in the world.

I feel sick to my stomach and scared to death. I've been stalked and spied on for years? By some pervert who has been in my home! I can't believe this. And now, my own flesh and blood has auctioned me off to this guy for a promotion? I can't fucking believe this.

"Anyway, he came to me a few months ago and said he'd give me the title of vice president and make sure I take control of the club when he's gone if I brought you to him. I, of course, had no quarrels about that, sis, but I do want to thank you for your help in my promotion. Guess it was a good thing I didn't kill you all those times when we were little, because you've turned out to be very useful to me."

He laughs like not killing me all those years ago is the funniest thing he's ever heard. If I didn't know it before, I do now; my brother is a soulless monster.

"And as it turned out, you're even more important now than you were when I first made the deal."

I don't see how that's possible, though. What is

different now than before? But then it dawns on me. Michael.

"Ah, I see you've connected the dots. I guess you are smarter than I thought—just not smart enough," he says, then starts dragging me toward his bike and away from my freedom.

Knowing that I'm going to play a part in hurting Michael and his club, I fight. I can't let him do this to the people I have grown to love. "I will not go with you, Anthony! You can't do this," I yell and pull with all my strength to get him to stop, but it's no use.

Anthony stops and backhands me, making me drop to the ground. I forgot how much his hits hurt, but I'll suffer hundreds of his heated blows if it means Michael and his family will be safe.

"What are you going to do to them?" I need to know what he has planned. Maybe I can talk him out of it.

"Ah, I'm so glad you asked, sis. You see, we've been looking for a way to hurt the Sinners ever since they killed our brother, Titus. But not only that, we want them gone, extinct. Their time to rule this state is over. It's time for The Street Kings to take their rightful place on the throne."

I don't know what he's talking about with this Titus guy, but if he's right and the Sinners did kill him, he probably deserved it. They wouldn't kill someone for the fun of it or because they wanted to make a point. No, they would only do it if he was an evil man, which seeing what club he belonged to, he had to have been evil.

"Leave them alone," I say weakly, unable to put

much venom behind the words. My face hurts along with my heart.

Anthony grins devilishly. "And if we don't? What are you going to do about it?"

I may not be able to physically save Michael and his club, but I can do something. "I'll give myself to your president willingly. I'll do anything he wants. I won't fight him and I won't try to run. I'll be his. I promise. Just don't hurt them," I plead.

Suddenly, I hear another motorcycle, and I fear it's more men from my brother's gang. But if I'm going to save the ones I care about, I better get used to them. It doesn't matter what happens to me as long as they are okay. Shit is going to get worse than it is now. My brother's president, Gutter, is most likely pure evil. He's got to be if he keeps company with my brother. Plus, I've seen a few of them in action and heard all the rumors. These men are bad fuckin' news and I'd bet money on it that Gutter is probably the worst of them all.

"Hey! Get your fuckin' hands off of her," I hear, and I instantly know who it is. It's the prospect from the Forsaken Sinners. Michael sent someone for me after all. I almost smile, but know this isn't over yet. My brother is not a man to mess with and I fear the prospect will suffer for trying to save me. I need him to leave before that happens. It's too late for me, but not for him.

My brother starts to laugh as he steps toward the prospect. My god, I don't even know his name, but here he is, trying to save me.

My brother's chilling voice brings me back to what's happening. "Who the hell are you?" He's a few feet away from the prospect but still close enough to hurt him.

"Leave him alone, Anthony. I said I'd go with you, just don't hurt him or anyone else in the club," I demand with steel in my voice.

But of course my luck is shit. Anthony doesn't pay me any attention and he continues staring down the prospect.

"Leave him alone. It's me you want," I try again to get my brother's attention, but it's no use. He doesn't see me as a threat.

Looking around, I try to find anything I can use to distract him or hurt him, but I'm not finding anything. There are no rocks, or anything else I could use. But then I remember the keys I'm still holding.

Tightening my grip on them for a second, I look down and place the biggest key between my pointer and middle finger while holding the rest tightly in my fist. It probably won't do a lot of damage but hopefully it will be enough for the prospect to get away. I can only hope that the rest of them stay away so no one else gets hurt because of me. I know it will be hard for Michael, but he's got to know this is the best option.

Charging forward, I scream, "Ahhh!" and as soon as Anthony looks at what I'm yelling about, I punch him right in the face with my key weapon fist.

"Fuck," he roars, holding his cheek while staring daggers at me. When he removes his hand, I see a long gash on his right cheek and it's bleeding bad. Shit, this worked better than I expected.

Anthony starts to come after me, but before he can reach me, the prospect is moving to my rescue. "No!" I yell, trying to get him to save himself, but he either doesn't hear me or he just doesn't care.

He jumps on my brother's back and they begin to fight. I have a hard time keeping up with them and I don't have any idea who's winning until my brother lands a solid blow to the prospect's face and he's down on the ground.

He's not dead or even unconscious, but he's hurt, that much I can tell. I don't know if the wind was knocked out of him or if a bone was broken, but he's not breathing right and he's in a lot of pain. I'm not sure if there's any blood because it's too dark, but I know if I don't do something soon, he's going to die.

Looking back to my brother, I see him pull something out of his cut. It's a gun and he's now aiming it right at the prospect.

Not even thinking, I rush forward and grab a hold of the arm that the gun is in, which causes a shot to ring out. I just hope it didn't hit its intended target, but I can't stop to look because I'm too busy grappling with my brother. Or more like being tossed around like a rag doll.

"I won't let you hurt him," I yell, trying everything I can to keep Anthony from getting his hands on me but also to keep him away from the prospect, who may or may not still be alive.

I hear a low moan and then the prospect talking, but I'm not sure who he's talking to. I can't make out the words. The only thing I know for a fact is I heard my name.

Turning around, I try to see what he's doing or what he's saying, but that was a mistake. As soon as my attention is diverted, my brother punches me in the face, which causes me to fall down to the ground.

My head hurts like a bitch and everything seems fuzzy, but I try like hell to keep my eyes open. If I don't pass out or die from a brain bleed, maybe I can still keep my brother's attention on me long enough for the prospect to get away. I just hope he takes the chance this time and not try to save me again. I'm already doomed for a fate worse than death, but the prospect doesn't have to suffer with me.

I see my brother look from me to the prospect, who seems to be on the ground mumbling. Maybe he's trying to check if I'm okay or maybe he's taunting my brother. I don't know.

Anthony turns his back on me and starts to walk toward the prospect again. I try to call out to him and get his attention back on me, but the words won't come out. Or maybe they do, they just don't make sense. Everything is garbled in my mind and my vision is going black.

I open my mouth to try again when a shot rings out. It's deafening and final. I feel tears well up in my eyes as I am now looking at a motionless prospect. There's no way my brother missed, so I know he's dead. He died trying to save my life and it was all for nothing.

Unable to keep my eyes open any longer, I finally surrender to the blackness. I just pray I'm dead so I don't have to endure the hell my brother is taking me to…and so I don't have to live in a world where someone died for me.

***

Hearing voices, I open my eyes but don't see anyone. I have no idea where I am, but I probably don't want to know.

I still remember hearing the shot ring out that ended the life of the prospect who was only following orders to go after me, and died in the process of trying to protect me. I hate that he was killed because of me and I'll never forgive myself. I may not have asked for him to try and save me, but he did. Whether out of feelings of obligation to the club or to Michael, or if it was just from the goodness of his heart…it doesn't really matter now because he died regardless, doesn't matter what his motives were.

Looking around the room I'm in, there is nothing here except the bed I'm sitting on. My hands are tied behind my back. I'm leaning against the wall and my ass is asleep. I don't know how long I've been here, but going off of that fact alone, I'd say it's been awhile.

I still hear voices outside the closed door but I can't make out what they're saying and I don't recognize the voice. Not like that means anything. The only person I really know here is my brother, and it's not like I try to remember what his voice sounds like. So it could be anyone. Maybe that Gutter guy is coming for me. Did my brother tell him I'd willingly be his if he left the Sinners alone?

Hearing the doorknob turn, I look toward it, dreading who will come through. It opens slowly.

The man who comes in is huge. He's probably almost six feet five inches and he's got tattoos covering every visible part of his body besides his face. His face is actually quite handsome and when I look into his eyes, I expect to see raw evil, but I'm surprised when I see pain and concern. Maybe this guy doesn't like what these men do to women, but that's highly unlikely. He probably just likes to fool his victims into thinking he's going to help them, then crushes them with his iron fists or maybe his huge looking boots.

"Rose?" he questions in a deep voice but he seems to be trying to be quiet. Not sure why, but with my head still hurting from the blow to my head given not so kindly by my brother, it's a small victory I'm going to take.

"Who are you? Gutter?" I ask in disdain. I probably shouldn't piss this guy off, but I can't help it. I'm angry I'm here, and even though I've hated my brother for so long and knew he was an evil person, I'm still a little hurt I've been betrayed by my family. Someone who is supposed to protect me, love me, and always be there for me when I need them. Not someone who will hurt you and sell you off to the highest bidder. If my brother wasn't such a shitty person, I wouldn't be here and the Sinners wouldn't be in danger. The only thing I can hope is that Gutter accepts my offer.

The man comes closer, and I scurry as far as I can against the wall. It's probably not even an inch, but anything I can do to make it seem like I'm getting away, I'll do. This man could probably kill me with a single finger. I'm scared and uncertain, but I guess I better get used to those feelings. I'll be feeling them for the rest of my life, no matter how short it is.

"Hey, it's okay. My name is Tyke and I'm going to get you out of here," he says, inching closer to me but with caution and ease. It seems like he's trying not to scare me but it could all be a show. If I put my guard down and believe him, will he strike?

For some reason though, I want to believe him. And I swear I've heard that name before, but I can't put my finger on it. I know I've never seen him before, but he still seems familiar.

"Who are you?" I ask, relaxing my sore body a little bit. I guess if he lashes out at me, I'd rather it be him than my brother or this Gutter guy that wants me.

"I'm Tyke, a member of the Forsaken Sinners MC. I've been here undercover for a few months, but I know who you are. You're Mack's nurse."

As soon as he said he was a member of the Forsaken Sinners, I broke down. Here's another person putting themselves in danger for me. Sure, he was already here, but he's risking himself to make contact with me. And he shouldn't. I want to get rescued and be back in Michael's arms more than anything, but not at the risk of them being in danger. I won't do that to them if I can prevent it.

"No. You have to get out of here. Go back to the clubhouse and tell everyone not to come after me. My brother told me their plans to kill every single member of the Sinners and every person they care about. But I can stop them. Please, you have to leave." I can't help it when my voice rises with hysteria. What if another person dies because of me? Dear Lord, I won't be able to handle that.

"Shh, it's okay, sweetheart. Don't you worry about me. I'm a Marine. Ain't nothing going to happen to either of us, okay?" He still doesn't get it. He's going to die, along with everyone else if he doesn't leave me here.

"No, you don't understand," I say, but Tyke interrupts me.

"Look, we have to be fast—" he starts to say when the door opens and my brother and another man I don't know comes walking in.

Tyke looks behind him, but he doesn't seem worried. He actually looks void of all emotion, even the friendly look he had when talking to me. Was all of that just a nasty joke he was playing on me? Is he really a part of this gang and not the Forsaken Sinners? It's probably for the best if that was the case. Then they would know I'm serious about staying if it means saving the club.

"Hey, man. I was just checking on our little prisoner here," Tyke says, sneering at me over his shoulder for a split second before he looks back to the other men now in the room.

My brother closes the door behind him and stands guard while the other man steps past Tyke with a sick smile on his face.

"Finally, my angel has woken," he says, reaching out and touching my face, but I jerk away from his hand before I can stop myself. This must be Gutter. If I have any hope of saving Michael and everyone else, I need to get better at not reacting.

"You'll learn to love my touch. But until then, I guess I'll just have to have fun breaking you," he exclaims before slapping me hard across the face.

His hit hurt, but not as bad as the one my brother delivered. Or maybe I'm already getting used to it, which is a good thing because I know there will be many more to come.

My gaze falls on Tyke. I can literally see his jaw hardening, probably from grinding his teeth together. He had to have been telling the truth about who he is, but I wish it wasn't true. It hurts to know salvation is so close, yet so far away. Tyke would have to risk himself to save me, and even if he succeeded, what would the cost be? If I left, how long would it take before my brother and his club follow through with the plans they set out for the Sinners? A day? A week? I'd give almost anything to be back in Michael's arms and tell him that I love him, but the price is too high. I won't pay in their blood just so I can see him again.

I want to plead with my eyes for Tyke to play along. To let me be and to run as soon as he gets the chance, but I'm afraid if I do, the others will see. I can't risk it.

Gutter turns away from me and looks at Tyke. "I'm glad you're here, actually. There was something I wanted to ask you."

I can do nothing but watch and listen to the exchange and hope that whatever is going on isn't going to be bad. I can't handle any more violence.

Tyke just nods and folds his arms. He looks casual to the naked eye, but when looking closer, I can tell his body is stiff and ready for anything.

"I've been told that there's a traitor among us. Have any idea who it could be?" Gutter asks.

Tyke doesn't react the way I thought he would. I figured he'd play along, but instead, he drops his arms and looks at Gutter with a look of pure malice.

Quicker than I thought possible, Tyke strikes Gutter with a solid left hook and then follows it up with a right uppercut. It all happens so fast, I can barely follow the moves. Neither Gutter nor Anthony saw it coming, but my brother is quick to respond.

Jumping onto Tyke's back, he tries to put some sort of hold on him but Tyke is easily able to evade and dislodge him.

Gutter hasn't made a move from where he's kneeling on the floor. Blood pours out of his nose and covers his face. I'm surprised those blows didn't knock him out. If he was unconscious right now, the fight that still ensues between my brother and Tyke might be fair then. I'm not sure if Tyke can win two against one, Marine or not. Tyke is big and I have no doubt he's a good fighter just by what I've seen so far, but who knows how dirty the other two fight. And it's already not fair because he's outnumbered.

Right now, it looks like Tyke has the upper hand against my brother, but then out of the corner of my eye, I see Gutter stand and pull something out of his sleeve. It's a crowbar.

I scream to get Tyke's attention, but it's too late. Gutter swings out with the crowbar and hits Tyke in the middle of his back. He surprises me by not going down, but Gutter is quick to hit him again. This time, it's in the back of his head.

Tyke drops to his knees, stunned from the blow. His back is facing me and I can see blood running down his neck and soaking into his black shirt, so it now looks wet and glossy.

"Stop!" I yell, though I know they won't listen. It didn't help last time I tried to stop my brother, so why would it now?

I'm full out sobbing now and don't want to look anymore, but I can't look away. It's like watching a horror flick and knowing the scariest part is coming and you'll have nightmares if you watch, but you just can't close your eyes to the horror. It's probably my punishment. Another man is going to die tonight because of me, so I should have to watch it. That way I'll always see it when I close my eyes. Tyke and the prospect will haunt me till the day I die.

I watch as my brother delivers blow after blow to Tyke's face until he's a mass of blood on the floor. But Tyke still hasn't given up. He may be down, but he's not out.

Gutter kicks him in the stomach as Tyke tries to get up, effectively dropping him back down. He tries once more to get back up, but he's kicked again, and this time, Gutter doesn't stop. He kicks him over and over and over again until he's still.

"Please, stop," I cry again but even I can't make out my words. I'm a blubbering mess and can barely see.

Gutter looks at me and actually smiles. "Don't cry, love. I'm doing this for you," he tells me. It only makes me cry harder. He's killing this man

232

because of me and I hate myself for it. "He's a traitor and tried to take you away from me. He has to die."

"No," I say. "Don't kill him. I swear, I'll stay with you. Just please don't hurt him anymore." But my words go unheard. Gutter starts to hit Tyke everywhere on his body with the crowbar. The sound of steel hitting flesh and bone is sickening. It's a noise I will never forget. It sounds wet, and you can literally hear bones breaking and the skin being broken open.

Not able to hold it in any longer, I puke up what little I had left in my stomach and continue to dry heave even after my stomach is empty. I can't bring myself to look away from the mess of unrecognizable flesh on the floor in front of me. What was once a handsome, brave man minutes before is now covered in blood, his skin torn open and swollen to the point I can't even see anything that resembles the man I had just met.

I don't know how long I sit there and cry as I stare at the second man who died tonight because of me, and I have no idea if my brother or Gutter are still in the room with me, but soon my eyes grow heavy and I can no longer hold them open.

Lord, please forgive me for what I've caused. I'm sorry. I'm so sorry, I say to myself before I allow myself to fall into darkness.

CHAPTER FIFTEEN

Mack

I stand there, with my phone attached to my ear long after I heard the shot ring out and knew the prospect was dead. *Tyler*. He'd been prospecting for only a few months and had barely begun. How is it that he's already been killed? He died trying to look after my girl, and when he knew that his life was over, he called me to make sure I knew what was going on. For that, I'll be forever in his debt.

Tyler hadn't been able to finish his sentence before he was killed, but I got enough to know who has Rose. *The Street Kings*. I don't know who or why they took her, but I'm going to get her back. I don't care if it takes my life in the process, I will do whatever it takes to make sure she's safe.

"Get the brothers here. Now!" I yell out as I put my phone back in my pocket and head into the chapel. As much as I want to go off half-cocked and find my girl, I know if I have any chance of doing this without any casualties on our side, I have to think this through. If I go off on my own, I could risk losing Rose, or worse, hurting her. And that is not a fuckin' option.

It's only a matter of minutes before all of my brothers come barreling into the chapel with mixed looks that range from confusion, anger, and determination. They have no idea what's going on, but they know me well enough to know that if I'm calling an emergency meeting, that shit is important and they know it's most likely something they won't like.

Plus, I'm sure Jax filled them in a little bit from what he heard from my conversation. My face probably told it all.

Once everyone is seated, I start out with, "Prospect Tyler is dead." I figure I need to get that out of the way now so we can focus on Rose and what we're going to do to get her back.

The room turns into an uproar of brothers asking what happened and just angry yells about losing a brother. Because that's what he is now. He may not have been fully patched in when he was alive, but dying for the club, that's an honorable way to go. He'll be buried with full patch status. I'll make sure of it.

"Settle the fuck down. There's more," I yell out so they shut the hell up so I can finish. I know they're all upset and confused, and they deserve to be this way, but right now, we have more important things to do. There will be a time for getting angry and grieving, but now isn't the time. I need everyone's heads in the game.

"I don't know much, but here's what I do know;

I sent the prospect out after Rose. We got into it and she left. I told him to find her and keep his distance, but to keep me posted on what she was doing or where she was going. And hour later, I was getting ready to go out myself to get Rose when my phone rang. I knew it was the prospect right away and I could also tell he was in bad shape. He was able to tell me that Rose was taken and who took her before he was shot." Of course I can't be sure that he's dead because I wasn't there, but with what I know about the Kings, they wouldn't leave him alive.

"Who did he say took her?" Blaze asks on my left.

Looking to him, I say, "He only managed to get three letters out, but it was enough." I now look all around the table, at each of my brothers who I know will follow me wherever I ask them to go. "The Kings have Rose," I say, and let that sink in for a moment.

Everyone is quiet for a few seconds, either not knowing what to say or waiting for me to tell them the plan.

"Now, I don't know why they took her and I don't care. They ain't keepin' her. So we need to figure out where they would have taken her and how we're gettin' her," I tell the boys, and then leave the table open to suggestions, but this shit better happen quick, otherwise I'll say the heck with it and we'll be going in blind.

"I say we call Tyke and see what he knows first. Then, we can do a little digging into some of the guys and see if there is anything we can find that would be useful," Toby says.

Nodding in agreement, I set it in motion. "Toby, call Tyke. See what he knows and if he can spot where Rose might be. Tell him not to make a move until we get there. I don't need them catching on if they haven't already from Tyler calling me." Toby nods and leaves the room to make the call. "Jax, I want you to do the digging. I want info on all the guys we know about." Jax gets up and leaves the room as well.

"Now, for the rest of you. I want somebody to go back and listen in on the bug we have. See if you hear any chatter about Rose or where they might be holding her. I want the rest of go out and scope their clubhouse and other places of business. Go in quiet, so no bikes. Keep me in the loop, but do not make a move without my say so unless Rose is in immediate danger. Got it?" I ask, looking at all my brothers around the table.

They all nod or say, "Yes, sir," and then they leave the room. All except Blaze.

"You think they took her as payback for us killin' Titus?" Blaze asks, but I'm not sure how to answer. There are plenty of reasons they could take her.

"I have no idea, brother. If we learned anything from when Harlow was taken, it's that not everything is as simple as it seems. They could have taken her as payback or they could have taken her for a bargaining chip. Or fuck, maybe she knows one of the fuckers, I don't know," I say, already feeling the heat and exhaustion of what's taken place.

Being the president of a club, everything lands

on your shoulders; the lives of your brethren and everyone else who knows you. If someone can be used against you, they will be. It makes me long for the times I used to hear stories about the wild west. You had a beef with someone, you'd go out into the streets at high noon and duke it out. But now, they don't take you head on or come at you directly. They take your loved ones or anything that means something to you. It's a cowardly thing to do, but they don't seem to give a shit and honor.

"What I do know is that no one outside of here knows she's my woman. The only thing someone would know is that she was hired to be my nurse and was seen with the girls. So either someone has some inside details about what goes on here, or she was an easy target and they're just hoping she means something to us." I don't want to make the call and be wrong though. Her life is in the balance and if I'm wrong about this, it could mean death for her. The safest way to play this is do our research and have a plan. I hate it, but it's the best way to go about getting her back.

Blaze stands and places his hand on my shoulder. "We'll get her back, Prez." Then he leaves the room to hopefully keep everyone on their toes and doing what they need to do.

I should be the one out there leading everyone, but I need this time to gather my thoughts and try to come up with plans based on different scenarios that could come up. I'm good at planning and giving orders, even leading everyone into battle. But all the busybody work? That shit ain't for me. I leave that to the men I trust and who can do a better job at it than me.

Ten minutes later, Blaze, Toby, Slayer, and Louie come walking back into the room. I can't tell from their facial expressions if they found anything out or if they have useful information, so I just wait until the door is closed and they take a seat.

Toby's the first to say anything. "I tried calling Tyke, but he's not picking up. I sent him a text message in code that it's important, but he hasn't gotten back to me. I have no idea what's going on, but something doesn't feel right."

Nodding in agreement, I say, "I agree, brother. Tyke knows the importance of keeping in touch and would have contacted you back with at least something if things hadn't gone to shit. So either he's been made or it's worse there than we thought. I hope it's just him working behind the scenes and getting Rose out of harm's way, but we need to plan that it's gone south."

Everyone nods and is quiet for a moment. God, I hope Tyke is okay. We don't need another funeral to plan.

"I've got everyone split into groups; we'll have brothers on the clubhouse, at their warehouses, and sites of known businesses. They know what to do once they get there," Blaze says, giving me a rundown of what's going on from that end.

"Good. That's good. Thanks, brother," I tell him.

Looking around the table, I wait to see if anyone else has anything to add.

"And we've also sent prospects out to get the other girls and bring them here. I think it's a good idea for them to be here so we have one less thing to

239

worry about. Who knows what those fuckers are going to do, but they've got one of our girls, we don't need them to get anymore." This comes from Louie. I'm glad they had the foresight to think about the bigger picture. We need to make sure Dani, Sara, Harlow, and the twins are safe.

"Good. Thank you, brother."

I can't believe I didn't think of that before, but I know my brothers understand. They've got shit locked down for their women while I figure shit out on how to rescue mine.

"Do you have an idea of how you want to do this, Prez?" Slayer asks just as Jax comes into the room, not even bothering to close the door behind him.

Throwing a folder down on the table in front of me, at least a dozen pictures slide out.

"What's this?" I ask as I pick one of the pictures up. At first, I don't know what I'm looking at, but then I look closer. It's a picture of a family; there's a woman and a man standing in front of a building and standing in front of them are two children. They look to be in their early teens. The boy isn't smiling and looks pissed off at the world. The girl looks tiny and scared to death.

The little girl looks just like Rose. Lifting my head, I ask, "Is this who I think it is?"

Nodding, he says, "It's Rose as a little girl."

Looking back down at the picture, I try to figure out what this means and how this helps us, but I'm not seeing it. I can't get past the look on her face and how frail she seems in this picture.

"Do you know who the boy is?"

Moving my eyes from Rose's young, scared face, I look at the boy. There are parts that look familiar but I don't recognize him.

"Who is he?" I ask, not wanting to waste any time guessing. If this brings us closer to how to find Rose and bring her home safely, then I want to get the show on the road.

Reaching out, Jax pulls out another picture and places it down in front of me. It's a mugshot of someone name Anthony Chambers. Picking it up and holding the two photos side by side, I now see the connection. "Is this the same man?"

"Anthony Chambers, born August 7th, 1979. Son of Robert and Greta Chambers. Brother to a Tiny Chambers," Jax says, then grabs a paper from the stack. "And this is a court paper for a request for a name change. One Tiny Chambers to be changed to Tiny Rose Chamberlain."

This just doesn't make any sense. First of all, why would Rose change her name? Did she get married? No, that doesn't seem right. But nothing else makes sense either.

Looking back at the mugshot, I figure this has to be the clue we need. Reading the information at the body, I finally see it. "Anthony Chambers, aka Brutus—member of the Street Kings MC," I read aloud so everyone can hear.

"You have got to be shittin' me," Louie says, as the rest of the brothers sit in silent shock.

But it still doesn't make sense. Why would she change her name when she turned nineteen and why would her brother kidnap her?

"Do we have any club info on Brutus?" I ask,

trying to get a better understanding of who her brother is and what to expect from him. The mugshot says that he's a felon and has a list as long as my arm of charges that range from drugs, guns, theft, suspected murder, rape, and assault. Shit, no wonder Rose didn't want to be associated with her brother. He's bad fuckin' news.

"He's the newly appointed VP and is as ruthless as they come. He's been in the club since he was in his twenties," Jax says. He must have done more research on him after finding out who he is to Rose or he'd been digging into all of the Kings.

Grabbing the folder, I sort through everything else that's inside. There are more pictures, police records, court documents, and medical records. Those are what concern me the most. All of the medical records are for Rose and shows the hell she went through growing up with someone like Brutus. She's had several broken bones and fractures, cuts that needed stitches, and bruised ribs. All from supposedly falling or getting into car accidents. Now I'm not saying they couldn't be true, because there are people out there with that bad of luck. But I highly doubt this is the case for Rose, considering who her brother is. If I had to guess, he's the one who beat her and played it off as accidental.

Knowing all of this just enrages me more. He's done way more than just kidnap her, he's tortured her since the very beginning. And right here, right now, I swear to be the one to end his life.

Over the next hour, we figure out what our best options are as far as attacking different locations where we think they could be holding Rose. I think our best bet is at the clubhouse but I don't think they'd be so stupid to take her there, but who the fuck knows with these clowns.

I had sent Slayer forty minutes ago to talk to one of his contacts in the city clerk's office to get blueprints on the clubhouse and a few of their bigger businesses—all the logical or probable places they could be holding Rose. They could be keeping her at one of the warehouses like Titus did Harlow, but if they are, we won't need blueprints because they are most likely an open layout.

He had gotten back about ten minutes ago, so we're all pouring over the blueprints like they're treasure maps when Toby's phone rings.

"Yeah," he answers, and we all quiet down, listening in on what he's saying.

"Okay. You sure?" we hear him ask, and then he nods to himself before saying, "Got it. Thanks, brother."

He hangs up the phone and glances at me with a look of disappointment. "Sorry, Prez. That was Bones. He's scoped out all of their business locations and there is no movement there. He was even able to get close enough to each to confirm that there is no one there. They aren't holding her there, brother."

I release the breath I was holding and nod. "Thanks, brother."

Not even three minutes later, his phone rings again and it's the same as the last phone call. Rose isn't at any of the warehouses. But I guess that doesn't mean all bad news. That only leaves one location—the clubhouse. I just hope they don't have a location we don't know about, because if they do, then we're fucked.

Toby calls our brothers located outside of the Kings' clubhouse and fills them in. Then he calls everyone else and tells them to meet us there. We leave the prospects with the girls and the kids at our clubhouse, then we take off on our bikes.

We make great time and pull in a few blocks away from their clubhouse, then we walk the rest of the way to where the rest of the brothers are hiding and waiting.

"So what do we have here?" I ask Tom Tom and Bic, since they are the ones who were sitting on the clubhouse the longest.

"We haven't gotten eyes on Rose, but we think she's in there. They had the whole damn club here for a while, but most of them left ten minutes ago. If our count was right, there are only four more left inside, probably guarding your girl," Tom Tom says.

"Why did they leave?" Blaze asks, just as confused as I am. If Rose is in there, why leave her there, even with a few guards?

"Not sure, brother. We spotted four members carrying something big out, looked like a box. They loaded it into a van and they all rode off together," Bic answers.

"How many left?" Louie asks, trying to get specifics on how many men we are dealing with in total. We know there are at least four inside, but how many left?

"I counted seven." This comes from Bic as well.

"Was Tyke one of them?" Toby asks, but the

only answer we get is a shake of the head from both Bic and Bones.

Where the hell is he? Hopefully he's there taking care of the men inside so we can just storm in, grab Rose, and get the hell outta Dodge.

"All right, Blaze and Toby, tell us what we're doing," I order, leaving the details to them. They're the ones most skilled in areas of search and rescue, so I'm going to let them take point on this mission.

We spend the next few minutes listening to Toby give us directions and then Blaze adding anything last minute. Once we have our plan together and no one has questions, we all move forward to where we're supposed to be.

Blaze takes Jax and Slayer to the back of the clubhouse. Tom Tom and Bones take the left side of the clubhouse, and Louie and Bic take the right side while me and Toby have the front. We are fewer numbered than we'd like, but with the prospects with the other girls, Tyler dead, and Tyke out of contact, we're limited. But once this is all said and done, we need to do some serious recruiting, that's for fuckin' sure.

As soon as we're sure everyone is where they should be, we send a mass text that we're going in in ten seconds. We all silently countdown, and as soon as we hit one, you can hear doors being kicked down, glass breaking, and feet pounding.

I spot two guys sitting at the bar, which is the first room our door leads into. Blaze and I are able to take them both out simultaneously with a single shot each. Once they're down, we move further into the room, looking to see if there's anyone else in

245

here hiding, but we find none.

We hear a few shots ring out coming from the back, so we rush that way, making sure to keep our eyes open for anyone else.

Toward the back door, we find Blaze standing over top of one guy with a bullet hole in his head and Jax standing over one with two holes in his chest.

"You good?" I ask them, to which they answer with a nod.

Turning back around, we meet the rest of the brothers in the middle of the clubhouse.

"Are there any more besides the four we took out?" Toby asks everyone.

"None on my end," Tom Tom says.

"I had one on my end, but he was sleeping. Was able to take him out quietly," Louie says with a grin. Sick bastard loves this shit. I probably would too if we weren't here for Rose.

"Anyone see Tyke at all?" I ask, but everyone shakes their head. Where the fuck is he?

"All right, everyone split up. Look in every room, every crevice, and every fucking hole in this place. We have to find Rose and get the fuck outta here before the rest come back," I order. Everyone takes off in search of my girl.

Toby stays with me, insisting he's got my back. We check the rooms in the back and come up empty. She's not here. Moving down the hallway, we start re-checking those rooms to make sure no one missed anything when we hear a blood curdling scream come from the opposite side of the clubhouse.

Taking off at full speed down the hall, not feeling any pain from my once-numb legs, I make it to where Slayer is fighting off Rose. She's scared and probably doesn't know what's going on or that we're here to save her. Shit, she probably doesn't even know who we are. Lord knows what she's fuckin' been through while being held here, but I swear on all that is holy, I will make sure they pay. All of them.

Rushing toward her, I take her in my arms. "Rose! Baby, it's me. Calm down," I soothe until she finally stops fighting and finally sees me.

"Michael!" she yells, sobbing and trying to put her arms around me but she can't because they are tied behind her back.

Pulling out my buck knife, I tell her to hold still so I can cut her free. She obeys and quietly cries into my chest as I work on her bindings.

As I cut through the final rope holding her here, I start to massage some feeling back into her arms, but she shrugs me off and wraps both arms tightly around my neck. Her hold is so tight, I worry she's going to suffocate me, but I don't fuckin' care. She's here and she's safe in my arms where no one will hurt her again.

"I got you, baby," I whisper in her ear.

Toby comes up behind me and places his hand on my shoulder. "We need to get out of here, Prez."

Nodding, I start to pick Rose up, but she jumps out of my arms. "No! You have to leave me here. Get out of here before they come back," she cries.

I try to step toward her to calm her down, but she holds her arms out for me to stop. Fuck, we don't have time for this shit!

"Rose, baby. We need to go," I try to soothe her so she'll calm down enough that I can get her out of here, but if I have to, I'll pick her up kickin' and screamin' if that's what it takes to get her out of here.

"Michael, you don't understand! They are going to kill all of you and everyone you love! They already have it planned out. I can't let them do that. The only thing Gutter wanted was me. Please, you have to leave me here. I have to save you," she says. I want to kiss her and slap some sense into her at the same time. This woman is stupid beyond all reason, but her heart is in the right place. The fact that she would sacrifice herself for me and my club means more than her telling me she loves me.

"Baby, I'm not going to let anything happen to you or my club. But if you don't shut up and come with me right now, I'm going to hogtie you and carry your ass out of here. Either way, you're coming home with me, where you belong."

I don't give her time to think about what I said. Instead, I take the few steps that separate us and pick her up into my arms. Thankfully, she doesn't fight me anymore.

We make it just outside of the room she was being held in when she says, "You have to find Tyke! They beat him so bad because he tried to save me."

Her words make me falter. "Is he here?" I ask, my anger spiking.

"No. He was in my room when they beat him. Oh God, Michael, it was so bad. He wasn't moving," she cries. "But then I passed out and I'm not sure where they took him."

Looking back to my brothers, they each shake their head. He's not here. If he was, we would have found him already.

"We'll find him, baby. I swear to you, we'll find him," I promise.

I'm raging mad, but I'm also scared as fuck for my brother. For all of my brothers and all the people I care about. We just got thrown into a war. But I swear on everything I have that I will not stop until I see the last member of The Street Kings dead at my feet.

CHAPTER SIXTEEN

Rose

I can't believe Michael came for me. Even though he's risking a lot, I trust him fully. I know he'll do everything in his power to make sure no harm comes to me or his club and family.

At first when I heard the commotion outside the room I was being held in, I thought they were coming back to kill me. It wasn't until Michael took me in his arms that I felt the first thread of relief hit me. But it didn't last long because I knew what my brother and his club had planned.

I tried to get Michael to leave me, to save himself and his family, but he wouldn't. A part of me is happy about that. I know Michael would do everything in his power to make sure no harm comes to me or his club and family. He's risking a lot, but I trust him fully. I just hope I'm not making a huge mistake. That we're both not.

After we exited the building, we run down the street to where I see motorcycles parked.

250

Michael doesn't even slow as we approach his bike. He must have done this a few times before because he makes it look so easy; running and getting on his bike without falling over.

Pulling me on behind him, he starts up the bike and signals his brothers with a circular motion of his finger. Everyone else starts their bikes and we're taking off down the street like a bat outta hell.

I tighten my hold around Michael's waist so I don't fall off. It's a little scary going this fast, but I know there's an urgency in the air to get the hell out of here.

We drive for a few minutes and then stop in an abandoned parking lot. The rest of the guys pull up alongside us.

"You doing okay, Prez?" Blaze asks Michael, and it's then that I remember his legs.

"Oh my god, Michael! Should you even be doing any of this?" I ask frantically. Did he hurt himself even more coming after me? And what about riding this bike? I don't think he should be doing that just yet.

"I'm fine," he growls, then points toward Toby. "Call the clubhouse. No one comes in unless it's us and no one leaves without my say so. I want it on lockdown." Toby nods and lifts his phone to his ear.

"Blaze, call our contacts at the DPD. I want them looking for Tyke," Michael orders again and Blaze doesn't hesitate to do his bidding.

"Michael, are you sure you're okay?" I whisper in his ear. I'm so worried he's going to hurt himself with saving me and then all of his hard work will have been for nothing.

"Baby, I'm fine. Better than fine. Don't worry about me, okay?" he says in a soft voice, but I can hear the undertone of demand. I need to drop it.

A few moments later, everyone has done their task and we are ready to hit the road again.

"You ever ridden before, baby?" Michael asks me, and it causes me to flush out of embarrassment.

"No. This is my first time."

"Well, as happy as that fuckin' makes me, I'm sorry that your first ride is under this circumstance. But I promise, I'll make it up to you. Now hold on tight," he says before revving the engine and taking off again.

This time when we take off down the road, I allow myself to relax and really feel the vibrations all the way through my body. It's kind of thrilling being on top of such a beast like this. But I don't have much time to think about the thrill. I just wish we were going on a leisurely ride and not racing back to the clubhouse to prepare for a war.

It seems like only minutes later we're pulling into Dixon, and a few minutes after that, we arrive at the Forsaken Sinners' clubhouse.

Michael gets off his bike, then lifts me up and carries me in his arms toward the door. I struggle a little, worried that I'll hurt him, but he stops me cold with a look. "Hold still," he growls, but it's not a mean sound.

"I could walk, ya know," I say, a little irritated at him but loving it all the same. I love being in his arms. And every time I'm there, I feel safe and wanted. Loved even.

As soon as the door opens and we walk through,

Dani, Harlow, and Sara rush up to us. "Oh my God, Rose, are you okay?" Harlow asks.

"We were so worried about you," Sara says.

"Glad to have you home, babe," Dani adds on with a smile.

I smile and hug each one of them, but Michael soon pulls me away. "All right. She's back home where she belongs, but shit still needs to get done," he says, then he turns to face his men.

"Toby, I want you to call in our nearby support chapters. Tell them we need them here like yesterday." Toby nods and makes his way into what they call the chapel.

"Louie and Blaze, call our contacts and see if they have any news about Tyke. We need to find him and get him medical attention," Michael orders, and I just pray it's not too late for Tyke. From the few moments I had with him, he seemed like a good man. Please don't let him die because of me and end up like the prospect. Which reminds me, I need to ask Michael what his name was.

"The rest of you, get all of our weapons together and take them into the chapel. We need to know what we have so we can come up with a plan to take care of the rest of the Kings."

When the rest of the guys leave, it's only the girls remaining. "Where are the twins?" Michael asks Dani.

"They're in Zane's old room napping," she replies.

"Okay, good," he says, then addresses them all. "Could you all go into the kitchen and see what we have for supplies? We're on lockdown as of right now and nobody leaves without my say so, do you hear me?"

Sara and Harlow nod and take off toward the kitchen. Dani stays behind, but I'm not sure why, until she says, "Mack, is there anything I can do?"

Michael looks at her, then smiles softly. "No, honey. I just need you to keep the kids safe and help the girls in the kitchen. We're going to have more guys here soon and we need all the food and supplies we can get with this lockdown in effect until further notice."

Dani seems pissed, but she keeps a handle on it. When she speaks, you can barely even register her anger. "Mack, you know I can do more than that. Let me help."

"I said no, Dani. I need you safe and to help the other girls. That's what you can do to help, and that's final. Now go," he demands in a hard voice, but I know he's not trying to be mean. He's just trying to keep everyone safe, especially his girls and grandkids.

Dani huffs out a breath, but nods and takes off down the hall, probably to check on the kids.

"And you...my room, now." He doesn't give me any time to reply, he just takes my hand and leads me down the hall to his room.

Once there, he sits me down on the bed before pulling up a chair and sitting in front of me. "Tell me everything."

God, I don't even know where to start, but I guess I'll just start at the beginning.

"Do you remember when I told you at the hospital that when I first met you, that I didn't want to like you?" I ask, and wait for him to acknowledge that he does remember. "That's because I swore to myself I would never be a part of or associate with anyone in a motorcycle club. You see, my brother—he's a member of the Street Kings MC. He's not a good man, never has been. Since I could remember, he was always a bully and hurting people, me included. I don't know how many times I went to the hospital from a wound he had inflicted on me," I say, remembering all those times in full detail. I can still feel the pain of those injuries like they're still there.

"When I was nineteen, I tried to get away, but he would always find me and bring me back. I don't know why because he hated me, but it was like he wouldn't let me go, either. I even went so far as to change my name so he wouldn't find me, but it didn't work. I finally learned it's because he needs me from time to time. Like when he's short on money or needs me to get one of the doctors to write a prescription for a 'friend.' He'd come barreling into my life and ruin everything. One time, he even broke into my apartment, took everything of value, and trashed the place." I hate that I have to tell him about who I'm related to, feeling like he'll think of me differently, but he needs to know. I just hope it doesn't change anything.

"Anyway, I would just try to stay quiet and forget about him until the next time he'd show up, praying that what he'd want or need was something I could give him so he'd leave me alone. But then one night after I was leaving the hospital right before you were released, I got down to my car and found a note from him. It said he had a surprise for me. I knew it wasn't going to be anything good, and most likely worse than anything he's ever done in the past, so I went home and came up with a plan that I would leave. I was going to pack all my shit and leave town for good, get as far away from here as I could and hopefully he wouldn't find me." Thinking back on it now, I can see that it never would have worked anyway. Anthony had always found me before and I'm starting to wonder if it's because of Gutter.

Anthony told me his president had a thing for me, even went as far as putting a camera in my apartment and following me around. He probably had a tracker or something on my car and that's how they always knew when I was running and where I would be. I'm so fucking stupid. I never even knew someone was following me, let alone watching me inside my personal space.

But back to telling Michael the truth. "The next day, I got to the hospital late because I overslept. I'd been up all night, waiting for my brother to show. I was going to talk to my superior when Dr. Yorkshire told me he needed me to sign off on your release papers. I didn't want to go back into your room for fear that if I saw you again I would chicken out and not leave. And I was right, except for a whole other reason. You see, before I stopped by your room, I had looked at my bank account and knew I wouldn't have enough money to live off of when I left here. So when you offered me the job of being your in-home nurse, I knew I had to take it."

I feel horrible making it seem like I was using him, but it was so much more than that. Hopefully he'd give me the chance to tell him.

"I took the job with you, planning on just staying until you were better, and then leaving with the money you'd pay me. But during that time, I fell for you, Michael. I fell hard and never wanted to leave."

Michael looks at me with a blank expression, and I don't know if he's mad or hurt.

"So what changed?" he asks in a monotone voice.

Blowing out a deep breath, I tell him about the mall and how I was afraid when I couldn't find the girls that my brother had taken them. He hadn't, but that didn't stop me from worrying that if I stayed here, that he eventually would.

"And that's why I left. I'm so sorry I didn't tell you all this before, but please know that I did believe you about that woman. I know you'd never do that to me, but I couldn't stay and I thought that was the easiest way for you to let me go. And you did, or so I thought, but when I got to my apartment, my brother was waiting for me. And then that prospect showed up and tried to save me, but Anthony shot him. Right in front of me. I passed out after that and woke up in the room you found me in."

He's quiet for a few minutes, thinking about all the information I just unloaded onto him. Then, looking back up at me, he asks, "Did your brother ever tell you what he wanted with you?"

A shiver runs through me, remembering what it

was he needed me for.

"He wanted a promotion and his president only wanted one thing," I say, leaving the sentence hanging because I'm pretty sure Michael could figure it out.

His face pinches in pain and then he growls, "You." I nod and more tears slip free.

"But when they found out I was with you, they said it was a better deal. They want you all dead. Said they were going to kill all your loved ones in front of you and make you beg for them to kill you. But I couldn't let them do that, so I told Gutter I'd stay with him if he left you all alone."

This seems to anger him more than what I told him about what they were going to do to his family. "Like hell you're staying with him," he growls.

"I'm so sorry, Michael. I didn't know what else to do. He was going to kill Dani and the kids. Sara and Harlow. And make you all watch! I couldn't let him do that, so I was going to sacrifice myself so you would all be safe," I tell him, needing him to understand.

Blowing out a long sigh, he looks at me. "I know why you did it, but it was still stupid. Baby, I wouldn't let anyone hurt my family and that includes you. Just trust me, please. No one is going to hurt Dani or the others and no one is going to take you away from me."

Nodding, I start to sob again.

"I'm so sorry, Michael. I should have told you all this right from the start. I just didn't want you to know who my brother was. And now the prospect and possibly Tyke are dead."

I can't stop the tears that are flowing fast and hard.

"Baby, it's not your fault," Michael says as he grabs my face and wipes the tears away.

"Shit was going to go down with The Street Kings eventually. I can't tell you everything, baby, but it's not your fault. It's theirs, and I swear to you and everyone else they've hurt, I will make them pay."

Looking into his eyes, I see he means it. He'll protect me and make sure nobody else gets hurt. I don't condone murder, but my brother is always the exception.

Nodding, I kiss his lips. "Make them pay, Michael. For me, for the prospect, and for Tyke," I tell him.

"I will, baby. I promise you that."

Standing up, he puts me on my feet. "Why don't you clean up a bit and then go sit with the girls out in the bar? I've got to go talk with the guys and figure out what we're going to do." He makes his way toward the door, but I can't let it go another minute without telling him something.

"Michael," I call out, waiting until he stops and turns around to face me before I say, "I love you."

Smiling, he winks. "I fucking love you too, baby." Then he's out the door.

***

After Michael leaves the room, I do exactly as he said. I take a shower and change into some comfy clothes, which is the only outfit I left behind when I left here only hours before. Shit, so much has happened it feels like longer than that, but that's all it's been—five hours.

When I'm dressed and my hair is pulled back into a messy bun, I make my way out into the main room to find Dani, Harlow, and Sara sitting around a table drinking what is most likely green tea.

"Got any of that for me?" I ask as I walk up to the table.

"Of course, honey. Or I can make you some coffee if you'd like," Sara says, already standing and pulling out a chair for me beside her and Dani.

"Oh no, that's okay. I don't think I need the caffeine." I'll probably be up for days after everything that went down anyway. I may have to get some sleeping pills in order to get some rest. I just pray that when I finally do lie down to sleep and close my eyes that I don't see the face of the prospect right before he died. Or Tyke's limp body as Gutter and my brother beat him.

Sara comes back a few minutes later with a cup of hot tea for me in one hand and a canister of sugar. "I wasn't sure how you take you tea so I thought I'd bring some sugar," she explains.

"Thank you, sweetie." I only put a few shakes of sugar in my tea and then stir it up before bringing it to my lips.

Mmm, it tastes like heaven. This is exactly what I needed.

We sit there for a few minutes in silence, each in our own thoughts and enjoying our tea when Dani finally asks me what happened. I really don't feel like explaining this all again, but I want to at least give her something. I mean, I am the reason this is all happening right now, no matter what Michael says.

"Long story short; my brother is the new VP of the Street Kings. He took me because he used me as a bargaining chip with his president to get the promotion. I guess the guy's had a thing for me for a while and I was the only thing he wanted, so my brother agreed," I explain.

There are mixed looks of shock, sadness, and anger on the girls' faces.

"I'm so sorry that happened, honey," Harlow says.

I laugh even when it's not funny, although it kind of is. They don't know my brother or the way things are with us.

"It's okay. Nothing any of you need to be sorry for, that's for sure. I learned a long time ago that my brother is a bad man, so what he did doesn't surprise me. Plus, I'm starting to get that this was all set in motion a long time ago

"Well, still, I'm sorry you had to go through this all. I guess it's just something we all have to go through." I don't know what she means, but I nod anyway. Maybe I'll get to hear her meaning later, but for now, I'm content to just sit here in the knowledge that for now, we are all okay.

We sit there for a few more minutes silently. "Did you girls already go through the kitchen? I could help make a list of everything," I offer, needing to keep busy. I can't just sit around and wait for the guys to decide what they're going to do. It's not in my nature to sit idle, no matter what the reason is behind it. That's one of the reasons I wanted to be a nurse, because I'm always on the go and busy.

"Yeah, we've already been through it all while you were in the shower," Dani answers, but she too stands up like she can't sit anymore.

"Well, is there something else I can do? Dishes, maybe?" I ask.

Laughing, Dani replies, "Sorry, babe. I beat you to that one too."

I look around the bar to find something out of place or get an idea of something else that could be done, but there's nothing. For being a biker clubhouse and bar, it's sure fucking clean, though I think that's all thanks to these three women. Though none of the guys really seem like the messy type either, so maybe it's everyone.

"Look, the best thing for us to do—" Dani starts to say but cuts herself off when she sees something behind me. Turning around, I look for what she saw when I see a small screen television on top of one of the coolers behind the bar. It looks like it's surveillance feed.

"Who's that?" I ask when I notice what she did. Lots of bikes pulling up to the clubhouse.

"I don't know. It's too soon for them to be our support chapters," Dani says, then turns to Sara. "Go tell the guys something's up. And hurry." She pulls out a gun from behind her back. What the fuck? Where did that come from?

"Here," she says, thrusting the gun into my hands. "Take this. If anyone comes through those doors that ain't Forsaken, you shoot. Do you understand me?" she asks in a hard voice.

"Whoa, what?" I ask, panicking. We don't even know who they are yet, why is she giving this to me?

"Just do it, okay?" she yells. Then the doors to the chapel burst open and the guys start rushing into the bar just seconds before total chaos breaks out.

CHAPTER SEVENTEEN

Mack

As soon as Sara came and told us someone was here, I knew right away they weren't friendly. We had just gotten off the phone with our sister chapters, so it couldn't be them.

When we made it out front, we were just in time to see the first bullet fly. "Everybody get down!" I yell, looking all around for the girls.

Harlow and Sara are closer to me than Dani and Rose, so I grab them and get them behind the bar. It's built out of wood, but what most people don't know is that there's bulletproof glass on the inside. After our first clubhouse got blown up, we decided to take a few extra measures to make sure something bad didn't happened again. So if I can get all the girls behind there, I know they'll be okay. Then I can worry about everything else and kill these fuckers.

I misjudge them. I thought after they came back to their clubhouse and found their brothers dead and Rose gone that they'd regroup for at least a little while before trying to hit us again. I thought we'd have time to plan but I was sorely wrong. I just hope I don't have to pay for that mistake with someone's life.

"Stay here. Don't fuckin' move," I yell to Sara and Harlow as soon as I get them safely behind the bar. They're both crying, but they nod. Good, now I just have to get to Dani and Rose.

"Toby, Louie, cover me!" I yell to my brothers who are currently laying down fire from behind the bar. I don't know if they saw that Dani and Rose are out in the middle of the bar, no protection except the few tables and chairs, but it doesn't matter. I'm going to get my girls.

As soon as I hear Toby and Louie laying down some cover fire, I take off like the devil himself is chasing me down. Shit, he might be.

"Get down," I tell the girls when their heads pop up to see what's going on.

Thank God they listen because just as their heads go down, a bullet flies right above them. That could have been one of their heads! I'm seeing nothing but red but I can't do anything about the fuckers outside shooting up my family until I know the girls are safe. I need my family out of harm's way before anything else happens.

"Mack, the twins!" Dani yells at me and I practically stop dead in my tracks. Fuck! I forgot they were here.

Looking behind me, I don't see Blaze anywhere.

I'm caught between a rock and a hard place. I need my girls to be safe but I need to get my grandbabies too. Fuck!

"Mack! You need to go get them!" Dani yells again, and it kills me to see her tear-soaked face with fear written all over it.

I look to Rose and she locks eyes with me. "Get her behind the bar!" I yell above the sounds of bullets flying everything.

A look of determination and strength passes over Rose's face and I know she'll be fine. She's strong and knows what to do. They'll be fine, at least for a minute while I get the twins.

Turning on my heels, I run down the hallway and make it to Blaze's old room in seconds. Throwing open the door, I don't see the twins anywhere. Panic sets in as I rush into the room and start throwing the pillows and blankets off the bed. They're not here!

"EJ! Harley!" I yell, afraid that someone came in and took them.

I think I hear a whimper from somewhere close, but I can't be sure with the sounds of war going on all around us. Thankfully, I don't see any bullet holes in this room, but that doesn't mean one won't come flying in any minute now.

"EJ, Harley, it's Papa! Where are you, babies?" I try again, praying to any god they will hear me that they're okay.

Then suddenly, like an angel was looking down on me, I hear a small voice say, "Under here, Papa."

Not even wasting time to get down on my knees, I lift the whole bed up and see my grandbabies lying on the floor, crying and scared out of their minds.

Again, I see red. My fucking family is here; my brothers, my daughters, the woman I love, and my fucking grandkids. And those fuckers come rolling up and start shooting? Hell fuck no! I will end them. Every last fuckin' one of them. I don't care if it takes me years, I will eradicate every single one of them from the world.

Bending down, I grab the twins and hold them close. I need to get them out of here. I don't dare take them out into the bar, even with a bulletproof shield. They don't need to witness what's going on. And then I remember the panic room Dani asked me to put in when we built the new clubhouse. When she and Sara were here and that crazy bitch Trixie and that piece of shit ex of Sara's came in and took them, she said that if anything like that happens again, then we need a panic room. One that only a few people knew about or knew how to get into. That's where I need to take EJ and Harley.

Grabbing one of the blankets they were covering up with, I cover them both up and they sit cradled in my arms, clinging to my neck. "It's okay. Papa's here. I won't let anything happen to you, I promise," I tell them, then make my way out the door and carefully down to my office. I didn't know where to put the damn panic room so I just put it in my office. I figured that's where the girls are half the time and it would be easy for people to get to if needed. Now I almost wish I would have put it in the back room so I wouldn't have to take my grandkids closer to the danger and not away from it.

A few long seconds later, we're in my office. I try to set them down so I can move the desk to open the door to the panic room, but the twins won't let go of my neck. "Hey, it's okay. I just need to put you down so I can open the door to a special room. It's going to be fine. I promise. You gotta trust Papa," I tell them, ready to pry them off me if that's what I have to do to get them to let go, but EJ lifts his little head and looks me dead in the eye. His face turns from scared to brave. Such a young boy like him shouldn't have to be brave, not yet, but he's having to step up, and that pisses me off, but makes me proud of him all at the same time.

"Okay, Papa." Then he lets go of my neck and reaches up to his sister's hands. "Let go, Har-har. I'll protect you." His words melt my heart but harden my resolve at the same time. These fuckers must die.

When Harley lets go of me, I quickly push my desk out of the way and put in the passcode to open the door to the little room underneath. Once opened, I pick them both up and jump down inside with them. There's a little switch that will light the room so it won't be pitch dark but it's not enough that will be seen through the door. Not like anyone could anyway with the seal we have around that fucker.

"Okay, Papa has go back out front to help your uncles. Nothing is going to happen to you. I promise. But you need to stay quiet and you need to stay in here," I say, motioning to the little room that's big enough to fit five adults.

I hand them the blanket and see that Harley is hanging on to her brother's hand for dear life. I look at EJ and place my hands on his shoulders. "I need you to look after your sister for me, okay?" I tell him.

"I will, Papa. I won't let anyone hurt her. I promise," he says and I know that even at his young age, he would do just that.

Kissing them both on the head, I climb out of the panic room. Just as I'm getting ready to close the door, I hear someone scream from the front room. It sounded like it was one of the girls.

"Papa, what was that?" Harley asks, concern and fear on her beautiful face.

Getting down on my knees, I tell her, "I don't know, baby, but Papa will go and find out. Stay here." I close the door, looking at Harley's tear-soaked face and EJ's brave one. As soon as it closed and I hear the clock engage, I move the desk back and rush out of the room, not even caring that bullets are flying everywhere and one could hit me. I need to know what happened and which one of the girls screamed and why.

I skid to a stop in shock and fear when the first thing I see is Rose and Dani on the floor close to the bar. They're both covered in blood, so it's hard to tell if either of them were hit or both. I see Blaze, Toby, and Louie trying to get them but every time they make a pass to leave the protection of the bar, bullets come flying right at their heads, like those fuckers know exactly where we are and when they're trying to come out.

Rage like nothing I've ever felt before takes over my whole body. I feel invincible and strong, like nothing and nobody can stop me. I'd like to see them fucking try.

I rush over to where their bodies are lying still on the floor, dodging bullets like I'm in the Matrix. I don't even know how I'm doing it and didn't know my body could move that way, but it can and I am.

Sliding up next to them, I pull Rose's body off of Dani. She fights me for only a moment until she sees that it's me. "Are you hit?" I yell, searching her body for injury.

She's crying and shaking her head from side to side and looking down at Dani with fear. Following her eyes, I look down to Dani's limp body. The first thing that registers in my brain is the puddle of blood underneath her. Then a spot on her shirt, just below her ribcage on her side, a massive amount of blood. Her shirt is torn and it looks bad. Really fucking bad.

"What happened?" I ask Rose as my hands fall down to Dani's stomach, trying to stop the bleeding. I don't know exactly where she was hit but if the amount of blood soaking through my fingers is any indication, I'd say I found the right spot.

"We were trying to get to the bar, but every time we stood up, bullets were flying everywhere. We were so close I thought we could make it. I'm so sorry, Michael! She got hit just before we could get behind the bar!" Rose sobs, losing control, but I can't let that happen.

"Listen to me," I say, but when she doesn't respond or look at me, I yell, "Goddamn it, look at me, Rose!" This time, she obeys. "It's not your fault, baby, but I need you to help her. You're the only one here that can save her and the baby. Do you hear me? You need to get your shit together and be the fucking nurse I know you can be," I tell her, tears filling my eyes. I can't let myself believe this is the end.

Dani has been through too fucking much to die now. Not when things are going so damn well for her and her family. I won't fucking let that happen, not to my girl. No, Rose is going to save her. She has to.

Rose finally stops sobbing, but the tears don't stop…but that's okay. At least she seems more under control now and the take charge nurse I know her to be.

"Okay. Okay, I can do this," she says, but I think she's talking to herself, not me.

"Yes, you can, baby, and you will." I pick Dani up and somehow make it behind the bar without jarring her or getting shot myself. Rose follows me with a look of determination.

Once they're behind the bar, I look at her and nod my head in encouragement.

"I need towels and lots of them," she yells to no one in particular.

Sara and Harlow were both sitting behind the bar crying, but now that Rose and Dani are there, and Rose needs help, they jump into action. They scurry to a cupboard and grab all the hand towels they can fit in their arms.

Knowing that everyone else is accounted for, my grandkids are safe, and that my woman will do everything she can to save my daughter, it's time to focus on killing the assholes outside.

***

271

Rose

I can't believe what I have to do right now. I have to keep Michael's daughter from dying. I can't believe any of this shit is happening right now. This place is being riddled with bullets and there's nothing any of us can do but take cover.

Sure, the guys are putting off some shots too, but that's mainly for cover. This shit is insane. I don't know how any of us are going to get out of here alive.

And poor Dani. She's been shot. And in the stomach. I don't know if she's going to make it or if the baby was hit. All I know is that Michael is counting on me. Dani needs me and so does her unborn son. I'm a fucking nurse and its time I quit crying like a little bitch and pull up my big girl panties. I got this shit.

Harlow and Sara hand me the towels and I start to pull Dani's shirt up so I can see what I'm dealing with. I'm not sure if the bullet entered through the front or the back, but at this point, it doesn't matter. The only thing that does is that I find out if the bullet is still inside or if it went through and through. Then, I need to dig around to see what kind of damage was done. Thank fuck she's passed out right now because otherwise she'd be screaming in pain.

I'm only able to get her shirt up her stomach halfway, but it's still in my way. "I need a scissors or a knife," I yell out to no one in particular.

Seconds later, I have a buck knife thrust into my hand and I'm able to cut the shirt away from her.

Once that's taken care of, I make fast work getting the material completely off of her so I don't have to worry about it getting in the way or inside the wound. While I have her tilted onto her side to get the shirt out from under her, I take a look at her back to see if there's anything back there. Nothing. That means the bullet entered through the front and is still lodged inside her somewhere.

Laying her back down, I take one of the towels and sop up as much blood as I can.

Looking over at Sara, I ask, "Can you get me a bottle of water and a bottle of whiskey?" After she goes to do my bidding, I look at Harlow. "Find me a lighter," I order. I'm not trying to be a bitch, but this is just the way it is sometimes during an emergency. Hopefully after all is said and done they'll forgive me.

They both make it back to me in under a minute, but now I need to figure out what I'm going to do next. I'm not a fucking doctor, for Christ's sake, but I'm all she has right now.

Dumping the water over the wound, I wipe the blood off again so I can get a better look at the bullet hole. It looks to be a clean shot and not too ugly looking. If all goes well, and there's no internal damage, a few sticks and she'll be fine. But that's not my main worry. It's the baby.

I'm fairly positive that in her stage of pregnancy, that the baby shouldn't be this far up, so he shouldn't have been hit, but that doesn't mean that anything else the baby needs wasn't. But without the proper equipment, I won't be able to know for sure.

Taking the bottle of whiskey, I do my best to sterilize my hands, then start probing around the wound. I can't tell if I feel anything swollen or not because of the baby. It worries me that she's not awake right now. Did she hit her head when she fell? I can't fucking remember if I saw her hit her head or not.

I wish I knew how deep the bullet went and to do that, I'm going to have to insert my finger to find out. Taking a deep breath, I stick my finger into the open wound. I try not to wiggle it around too much, but I can't feel the bullet. That's not a good sign. That means it's lodged deep inside her or possibly in an organ. Fuck, I need to get her to the hospital now. She may need surgery.

I look up to try and find Michael so I can tell him we need to get her out of here when I hear Dani start to wheeze. She's struggling to breathe, which could mean one of two things, possibly both; her lung collapsed, or it's filling up with fluid. My guess would be the latter.

Going with that theory, I yell, "Someone get me a pen. Hurry!"

I hold my hand out and wait for someone to drop what I need into my palm, not even caring who it is that does it.

Once I have the pen, I stick it in my mouth to pull the cap off so I can pull the insides of the pen out. I need the outside of it to act as a tube so I can drain the fluid. Fuck, I hope I'm right about this.

Taking the knife back into my hand, I dump some whiskey on it. Then I pour it over her chest where I need to make the incision. Counting her ribs so I know where I need to cut, I take a deep breath before pressing the knife into the side of her chest cavity.

After I've done that, I take the pen tube thingy out of my mouth and dump whiskey on that too. It's not the best thing to use, but it's all I have and better than doing nothing. Blowing out a breath, I slowly insert my finger into the hole I cut and feel for where I need to put the tube. Finding it, I slip the tube in and feel a waterfall of relief wash over me when I see blood start to drain and Dani's breathing start going back to normal. Or as normal as could be in her situation.

Looking up from what I'm doing, I see Sara, Harlow, and a few guys I can't remember their names right now just staring at me, waiting for their next order. But there's nothing more I can do.

Turning my head, I see Mack and the rest of the guys sitting behind some tables close to the door.

"Michael," I yell but he doesn't hear me. Trying again, I yell louder, "Mack!"

That got his attention so I yell, "She needs a hospital. *Now!*" I hope he understands there is nothing more I can do. She needs medical attention, possibly surgery. I've kept her away from immediate danger but if her heart fails or something else happens, I won't be able to do anything except watch her die.

A mixture of emotions washes over Michael's face, but the most prominent is fear. He knows what's a risk and what needs to happen. For us to get Dani out of here, he has to take care of the guys outside.

***

Mack

When Rose yelled to me that Dani needs a hospital and now, I don't know what to think. Does that mean she's in bad shape or she just needs to go in? I don't know, but I'm going to get her there if it's the last thing I do.

"We need to end this. Now," I growl the last part, but Blaze isn't looking at me. He's looking at his woman lying bleeding and unconscious on the floor.

"Hey!" I yell, slapping his face to get his attention. "I need you now, brother. In order to get Dani to the hospital, we have to go through these fuckers first."

His eyes are vacant for only a moment, but then determination and rage takes over. Good. He'll need that to get through the next couple of minutes.

"All right, this is what we're going to do," I start to say, but I hear one of the prospects yell over the chaos.

"Prez, we got more company!"

Looking up to where he's pointing, I see on the security camera that dozens of bikes are pulling up around the back. Squinting, I try to make out if they are friendly, but I'm too far away to tell.

"Pork Chop, they friendly?" I ask, needing verification. They could be more Kings trying to take us by surprise from behind or it could be our sister chapters. I don't know how much time has passed since we made the call, but it'd be fuckin' perfect if it was them.

"Friendlies, Prez," he yells with a smile on his face. Thank fuckin' Christ. We may all make it outta here in one piece after all.

"Go meet 'em in the back. Give them a rundown of what we got going on," I yell back, but Rose calling my name stops me.

"Michael. She's getting worse." There's panic barely concealed in her voice and that means we're out of time.

Grabbing Blaze, I look to Louie and Toby and relay with my eyes that we need some massive cover fire. They nod they understand and stand up, kick open the door, and those crazy sonsabitches start shooting like they're in the fuckin' mafia.

Pushing Blaze in front of me, we make our way to where Rose is crouched by Dani.

"What's going on?" I ask as Blaze takes Dani's hand and starts to whisper something in her ear.

"The bullet is lodged inside but I can't locate it. It needs to be removed but I'm not sure how deep it is." She starts listing off her injuries. "She had fluid building up in her lungs. I was able to drain some of it but the tube is starting to clot over. If that happens, she'll drown in her own blood."

Nodding like I know what she's talking about, I open my mouth to ask what we need to do when Blaze beats me to it.

"What about the baby?"

Rose looks at him and shakes her head. "I don't know. I don't have equipment to check on him. I'm sorry," Rose says. Looking back to me, she urges, "We need to get her to a doctor now, Michael. I'm not sure how much longer she can wait."

I hear the gunfire wane for a second, but then it picks up tenfold, but I'm not sure who's doing the shooting. More glass is breaking and people are yelling but I can't focus on any of that right now.

Just then, Pork Chop comes running in, dodging bullets like he's in the Matrix with members of our support chapter right on his tail.

Knowing that they came in from the back, I come up with a plan to get Dani and the rest of the girls out of here.

I spot our sister chapter's president, Rocker, and motion him over. "Hey, brother. Thanks for coming," I say as he approaches.

"Not a problem, brother. Looks like you could use the help."

Nodding, I look down to Dani. "We need to get her out of here. She's pregnant and has been shot. We have three more women, two of them pregnant also. My two grandkids are in the panic room, but we need to get them somewhere safer as well," I say, hoping he's catching my drift.

"Yeah, man. We can do that," he replies without me having to say it outright.

"Did you run into any problems on the way in?" I ask, wanting to make sure the back door is clear before I send my family out that way.

"They had a few guys back there but we left our bikes right after we pulled onto the road. We were able to ambush them, so it's clear now. But I'll send a guy out first to make sure the fuckers didn't send anyone else back," he says, then motions to one of his guys to do exactly that.

"I'm going with. Prez, I'm sorry, but they need me," Blaze pleads, but there's no need. I need him there with them as well.

"No, you go. We'll be fine here. Make sure our girl is okay and the others are safe." I look to Rose.

"I want you to go with them. Help keep her stable until you get to the nearest hospital. But I want you to be there when they treat her. You understand me?"

Rose nods her head in understanding and raises her chin. "I'll move Heaven and Hell, Michael, I promise. I'll take care of our girl." I don't know if she realizes it, but she just referred to Dani as ours, and I love it. But that's for another day to discuss.

Kissing Rose hard on the lips, I go to get back to where I'm needed, but Rose stops me. "You be careful, Michael. And when you come face to face with my brother, you kill him. You understand? You kill him for me," she says with hatred.

I have no problem agreeing to that, she doesn't even have to ask. "I'll do it with pleasure, baby." I kiss her once more, then we wait a few seconds for our brother to come back in to give the all systems go sign. I watch as Blaze picks Dani up and Rose hurries after them. Thankfully the bullets have slowed down some so they can make their escape. Maybe they're running out of ammo. Who the fuck knows?

Other members of our sister chapter help the rest of the girls out from behind the bar and they shield them with their own bodies. I don't worry about them getting the twins out. Blaze will know what to do or Sara and Harlow know how to get in there, they can tell one of the brothers. My family is safe and now there's nothing left to do but take these motherfuckers out.

"What do you want to do, Prez?" I don't know who asks the question, but the answer remains the same.

"We kill them all."

CHAPTER EIGHTEEN

"How do you want to do this, Prez?" Toby asks, and for the first time in a long time, I'm going to lead the charge.

Turning around to face the president of our sister chapter, I ask, "Did you bring any bigger or louder weapons?" I ask with a smile, really hoping that he did.

Smiling back at me, he turns toward one of his brothers and grabs a bag. "I thought you'd never ask, brother."

We all kneel down and look through the goodies that they brought. I don't know who they get their shit from, but it's military grade and high firepower, that's for sure. They've got everything from flashbangs to grenades. M-4s to AK-47s. They even have a few of those saw guns the military use; a M-249 that shoots over 500 rounds. I may have to get us a few of these. They may come in handy.

We probably won't even use most of this, but it's

nice to know we have it.

"All right, the back is clear, so I want Jax and Louie to stay here with Bulldog and a few others from the support chapter. The rest of us will split into two groups and go out the back. Flank both sides. The guys inside will keep them distracted while we get set up, then we'll take them from the sides," I say, setting the plan up.

Everyone nods in agreement.

Looking back to Rocker, I ask, "Before you came in, were you able to get a good look at their set up out front at all or how many are left?" It would be good information to have before we move forward with this plan, but if not, we'll move ahead anyway.

Rocker replies, "I was able to count at least ten. They're all spread out, but most of them are in the middle, so my guess is the higher ranks are there."

Nodding, I put the plan into action. "All right, brothers. Let's do this."

Those of us that are going out back take most of the M-4s and hand guns. I grab a few grenades too just in case, but we left the AK-47s and M-249 saw guns, which will shoot off more rounds. It's perfect for what they need and will maybe lay a few fuckers out in the process.

Everyone except those staying inside head toward the back door. We're only going to have one shot at this, so we need to make sure we do it right.

I can hear the boys inside yelling and making a bunch of noise and shooting like crazy, trying to make it seem like we are all still inside. Good. Hopefully it works and allows us to get outside where we need to be.

Listening to it all, it's almost comical, but this isn't a laughing matter. Maybe one day after all the dust settles we can look back on this and have a good laugh, but not today. Today, we need to be machines, killing everyone that comes in our path. We need to get this done so we can get to Dani and the rest of the girls. They need us now more than ever.

A text message goes off on my phone from the guys inside to start the countdown once we are set up. I nod to Toby so he can send a message back that we are all set.

Once we hit the end of the countdown, the guys inside use the saw guns to lay down heavy fire. I just hope that they don't kill Brutus or Gutter in the process. Those fuckers are mine.

Twenty seconds later, the heavy fire ceases. I nod to my brothers outside with me. It's our turn now.

I try to see if I can spot the fuckers that I want the privilege of killing but everything is too chaotic. Bullets flying, men shouting, and adrenaline spiking.

It only takes a few seconds before everything goes quiet. Most of the men in front of us are dead, bleeding out on the ground. I can see a few men in the middle hunkered down, but I can't tell who they are or if they are injured.

The door to the clubhouse opens and I know my brothers are coming out to join us.

Suddenly, one of the men starts shooting at us, but one of mine quickly puts an end to him. Now,

SHELLY MORGAN

we see two sets of hands fly up in surrender. Fucking pussies. But I'm thankful because that means we can get this over with and get to the hospital.

We all make our way toward the middle and kick all the weapons away on the trek out there just in case someone is still alive and decides to get a hero complex.

Bodies of at least ten men are scattered around and blood and guts are everywhere. They all look dead, but I can't be sure. I think most of these men were hit from the cover fire. It was meant as a distraction, but it turned into something so much sweeter.

So far, I haven't laid eyes on Brutus or Gutter, so I pray that they are the two pussies surrendering a few feet away. I still can't see their faces because they have their heads down. In shame or fear, I'm not sure, but they should feel both.

When we get to the middle of the parking lot and am standing in front of the men, I yell, "Stand up."

They don't hesitate, maybe hoping that if they follow our demands we will let them live. *Not a fucking chance*.

When their faces raise, I'm thrilled to see that one of the men is Rose's brother, Brutus. The other man isn't looking at me, so I can't be sure, but I'm pretty positive that he's Gutter. The president of the club that tried to take down mine. And the man that tried to take Rose away from me.

"Well, well, well, look what we got here. My woman's piece of shit fuckin' brother and the dickwad president who thought he could take her

284

away from me and keep her as his own," I snarl at the two pussies who aren't so fucking tough now that they're surrounded.

"You want them both, Prez, or you want us to take PussyGutter?" Rocker asks, but I just smile my answer.

"Ah, you want to have all the fun," Rocker mock complains, but I know he's got no problem with me finishing my business.

"Line 'em up," I yell and I watch as Louie and Toby grab them and force them down on their knees.

The both struggle a bit on their way down, but they know it's futile. They're done for and there's nothing they can do to stop it.

Starting with Gutter, I stand right in front of him. "Your first mistake was thinking you could take my club and still live to breathe another day. But your biggest mistake was thinking you could take my woman and make her yours. You're fucked in the head, but lucky for you, I have a solution for that," I growl before putting a bullet in his skull. I wish I could make it last longer so he could feel the pain I want to inflict on his body, but there's not time.

Before his body even hits the floor, I move on to her brother, Brutus. "And you," I say, holding the gun right to his fucking head. "You beat her, broke her bones, and probably did a number of other things to my woman, and for what? To feel like you're a man? To feel powerful?" I ask, but I don't expect an answer in return, and he doesn't waste his breath giving me one. "I'd love to take my time on you and break every single one of your bones to

285

make up for the pain you caused Rose, but my daughter and my woman are waiting for me. And frankly, you're not worth it. Not to me, and not to her." Cocking the gun, I say one last thing before I end his life. "This is for Rose, you piece of fuckin' shit." With that, I end his life in one shot, but it's not enough. Once he hits the ground, I empty out the rest of my clip into his lifeless body.

It still doesn't make me feel better, but at least I know Rose will be safe for the rest of her life and she'll never have to worry about her brother finding her or taking her again.

Now, I just need to make sure my daughter and grandson make it through the night.

***

Rose

One of the guys had a van in the back so we were able to load Dani in there. While I was getting her situated, Blaze made sure that the other girls had the twins and directed the man he tasked with protecting them where to go before he jumps into the van with me to help with Dani.

I don't know if they left before us or if it was the other way around, but I didn't have time to think about it. We had to get Dani to the hospital. She's stable, or as stable as she can get right now, but it won't last long. She needs a doctor and medical supplies I don't have. And possibly surgery.

The driver and passenger I suspect is with the other club because I've never seen them before. I

286

don't question them or worry about who they are though. Blaze is with us and I know Michael wouldn't send us off with them if he didn't trust them.

On our way down the road heading into town, I noticed a lump of something that looks sort of like a body. I ask the guys to stop, but Blaze looks at me like I'm out of my mind.

As we get closer though, I know exactly who it is and yell, "Stop the fucking van. We have to stop. That's Tyke and he's hurt!"

The van skids to a stop and the two guys in the front jump out with me following close behind. When we make it to the body, I can see right away that I was right. This is Tyke, but I knew it was. There's no way I'll ever be able to get what he looked like after they beat him out of my head. Checking for a pulse, I feel one but it's very faint.

"Get him in the van. We need to get him to the hospital fast," I say, honestly not sure at this point who is worse; Dani or Tyke.

We make it to the hospital in Dixon within five minutes, which is perfect because the tube I put in Dani's chest is almost completely clogged and I fear she'll suffocate if they don't do something about the fluid build-up soon.

And Tyke, I have no idea what his injuries are because I was afraid to touch him too much without having equipment around to save his life if he flat-lined on me.

I have the guys pull into the emergency entrance and as soon as we stop, I have one of them run in to grab two stretchers, not even bother to get a nurse or doctor. I can get that shit figured out when I get in there.

Once the stretcher is outside the van, Blaze helps me load Dani on it just as personnel start to run outside to see what we're doing. As soon as Dani's on the stretcher, I turn to help the guys put Tyke on one.

"I'm Nurse Rose Chamberlain, formally from St. Matthews hospital in Gibson. The patient has a GSW to the abdomen and she's about five months pregnant. Her lung filled with blood about twenty minutes ago so I inserted a makeshift tube to last until we got here, but it's clogging up fast. The bullet is still lodged inside though. I'm not sure where." I give them all the information I have and help them wheel her inside.

"What's her name?" one of the doctors asks.

"Danielle DeChenne," Blaze answers before I do, which I'm glad, because I didn't know her last name. How is that possible? I feel like I've known this woman for years instead of months, but I don't know her last name? *That's pathetic, Rose.*

"The second patient was beaten with a crowbar and left for dead. I don't know what his injuries are, but they are extensive," I tell them.

We're almost to the doors were it says **'Personnel Only'** and the other nurses try to stop me from moving forward with Dani. "I'm sorry, ma'am, but you'll have to wait out here."

Knowing I can't very well go with them both, I decide to keep my word when it comes to Dani.

"I understand, but this woman and man are my patients. I can't go with both, but I will be going with Danielle. You can check my credentials if you need to, but she doesn't have time for that. But I can assure you I have more time in than you've probably been alive," I say with pride and a little bit of attitude, but who fucking cares? This is Michael's daughter and I promised him I wouldn't let her out of my sight, and I don't plan to.

"Let her come, Denise. She's fine," the doctor orders and I almost want to stick my tongue out at this Nurse Denise, but I'm adult enough not to actually do it. Doesn't mean I didn't think it though.

One doctor takes control of Tyke's care and the other doctor takes care of Dani. He checks her vitals before checking for signs of life from the baby she's carrying. "Baby's heartbeat is strong," he says to no one in particular, and then continues on with his assessment.

Even though I told Michael I wouldn't let her out of my sight, I let the doctors and nurses do their thing without interfering. I'm here if they need me, but otherwise, I'm just here for Dani. Unless I see them doing something wrong, then all bets are off and these assholes are going to hear about it.

"Her lung is collapsing from the fluid and we need to get the bullet out. Call up to surgery and tell them to get prepped," he calls out to the nurses, then turns to me. "I understand she's your patient, but I'm going to have to ask you to wait outside during surgery. I'll allow you to spectate, but you can't be in the OR."

Because surgery was never my strong suit and I'd just be in the way, I concede to his orders.

They rush Dani off to prep, but I hold back for a

moment, needing to check on Tyke.

"What's going on? Is he okay?" I ask the doctor working on him.

"He's been badly beaten. I have to take him in for surgery to fix the damage done and stop the internal bleeding," the doctor tells me.

"Will he be in the operating room next to the girl he came in here with?" I ask, hoping that's how this hospital works, that way I can keep an eye on both of them.

"Yes, ma'am," is all he says before he takes off to prep Tyke.

One of the nurses is kind enough to follow me up to the sixth floor and show me where the spectating room is.

It seems like a long wait before I finally see them wheel Dani and Tyke into their separate rooms. It's even more grueling to stand there and wait as they perform the surgeries.

I pace the spectating room and bite every single nail I have. I wish I could pull out my phone to call Michael and tell him what I know about Dani and that we found Tyke, but for one, you aren't allowed to use cellphones in here, otherwise it would mess with the machines used to help keep Dani alive and two, I don't even have my phone with me. I don't know if it's still in my car or lost somewhere, but that's not a concern right now. Hopefully one of the men waiting downstairs will tell him at least about Tyke.

Two and a half hours later, my nerves are shot and I'm in desperate need of a coffee, but the surgery is over. I can't be one hundred percent sure, but from where I was standing, everything went off without a hitch.

When I see the doctor that worked on Dani leave the room and a nurse starts to clean Dani up, I make my way outside to talk with him.

He takes his sweet ass fucking time removing his gloves and face mask, but as soon as he faces me, I demand to know what happened.

"How is she? What did you find? Is the baby okay?" I can't help it, I ask one question after the other. My medical training is lost to me and I can't be patient. This is personal and I need to know now.

"She's going to be fine. The bullet entered through the front, but missed all vital organs. It was lodged in one of her ribs. We removed it and were able to find all the pieces of bone that were floating around," he tells me.

"Was that the cause of the fluid and her collapsed lung?" I ask, finally getting a little bit of control now that I know she's going to be just fine.

"Yes. When the bullet hit her ribs, it shattered her first and second rib and sent debris into her lungs. We were able to repair all the damage to her lung, so there shouldn't be any lasting side effects."

That's a fucking relief. Things would become difficult and cumbersome if she'd have to deal with that.

"We fixed her ribs as much as we could, but unfortunately, the rest of the healing process for that, as you probably know, they'll have to heal on their own. There's not much more we can do for that," he adds on.

That I do know. It sucks, but that is life. At least

she's alive and the baby is well. At least, last I knew he was.

"And the baby?" I ask, needing to know for sure.

"The baby is just fine. He's perfect actually. Nothing hit him or any of the organs needed to sustain him," he confirms with a smile.

"That's fantastic news, thank you, Doctor," I tell him as I shake his hand. "So what is the treatment or orders moving forward?"

"Well, she'll be in the hospital for a few weeks so we can monitor her lungs and make sure her ribs don't cause any further damage. After that, we'd suggest her being on bedrest so not to aggravate her injuries and so the pregnancy will go on without any problems. But other than that, there's nothing. She'll have a scar, but there's no helping that unless she wants to talk to a plastic surgeon. She can discuss that with her family."

Nodding, I thank him again and wait for the doctor who worked on Tyke to come out, which isn't long.

"How is he?" I ask, worn from all the adrenalin and worry from everything that's happened.

"He's going to be just fine. He has a few fractured bones in his legs, one broken arm, he's severely dehydrated, but those we can treat and he'll heal. What has us worried is the fluid in his brain. We've placed a drainage tube to help relieve the pressure and we'll do another MRI in a few days. We've set the bones and are going to keep an eye on his head, but other than that, he's going to be just fine."

It concerns me that his head has fluid in it but I

know that they're doing everything they can. The rest is up to Tyke, but if he can survive a beating like that and make his way to the road where someone could find him, I know he'll be just fine.

"Thank you, Doctor," I say and shake his hand.

Heading down to the waiting area, I'm surprised to see all of the men there waiting not so patiently.

Blaze is burning a hole in the carpet with his pacing and Michael isn't much better.

When they see me coming, they rush out of the room, but I pull them back in and close the door.

"How is she? Is the baby okay? What took so fucking long?" Blaze questions and I have to laugh inside because this is probably exactly what I looked like a few minutes ago.

But I don't make him wait. I tell them what the doctor told me and what will happen now. They are all relieved that she and the baby are fine and that there will be no lasting side effects.

Blaze takes off to see her in the recovery room and Michael looks at me like he's waiting for more.

"I heard you found Tyke. How's he doing?" he asks.

I tell him everything the doctor did and what the concerns are now, but that I think he'll make a full recovery. I may be counting my ducks before they hatch, but I have a good feeling I'm right.

Michael hugs me close and then takes me by the hand to lead me outside.

"Where are we going?" I ask, wanting to stay close to check in on Dani after she wakes up.

"Not far. I just want to talk to you in private," is all he says as he pulls me outside to an area where

293

there aren't a lot of people. Actually, there aren't a lot of people out here anyway, but I guess he wants to be sure we have our privacy. I just don't know what for.

Finally, he feels we've gone far enough and he stops. Pulling me into his arms, he hugs me like his life depends on it. I hug him back though, not wanting to let him go. Everything that happened tonight was scary, but I'm so happy we made it out the other side.

"I finished it. You don't have to worry about your brother or that scumbag president ever again," he says without letting me go.

I stiffen at first at the mention of my brother and Gutter, but then his words sink in and it doesn't matter to me that he means they're dead. I'm actually glad they are. The world will be a better place without them.

"Thank you, Michael. For everything. You came after me and saved me when you didn't have to. After everything I did, led you to believe, you still saved me. And not once, but over and over again. Not just from my brother, but from myself too. I was destined to live a life alone and on the run, but then you came along," I say, tears filling my eyes. "I never thought that destiny would have a new hand in store for me, but she did. And it's the best fucking hand anyone could ask for. You're my ace of hearts, Michael, and I love you so much."

Pulling back, he looks at me with a smile. "Baby, I learned a long time ago that our life isn't up to destiny or anyone else but ourselves and the people we keep in our lives. When my father was killed by a biker, I hated them." I gasp in shock at this tidbit of information because this must be the story he told me he'd tell me. "See, I told you. I was once like you," he says with a smile and then kisses me on the forehead.

"Anyway, when my father was killed, I hated all bikers, thinking them all the same. But then I met a man who was the exact opposite. He was actually a police officer who was also the president of a motorcycle club. He taught me that all bikers aren't bad and that in order to change the way people think, you have to own up to what you fear or hate and be the exact opposite. So instead of steering clear of all bikers, I became one. I know I may be considered a bad guy because I've done some pretty bad things to some really bad people, but I am what I am, and in my heart, I know I'm not like the man that killed my father. I took what destiny gave me and I owned that shit. I didn't let it stop me or sway me. So I guess what I'm trying to say is that you saved yourself when you got away from you brother. It wasn't your fault he kept coming back. You just didn't have a way to get rid of the bad in your life. Until you met me."

I can't take any more of his words without kissing this man. He is everything I always wanted and everything I never thought I'd need. He's rough and sweet and a biker. He's my biker.

But he's right about one thing. When life throws you lemons and you don't know if you should make lemonade or drink tequila, you do both. 'Cause like Michael says, "Life is like riding a bike...take it by the handlebars and own that shit."

EPILOGUE

Rose

Two and a Half Months Later

It's been almost two months since everything went down at the clubhouse with my brother, and everyone is doing great. Dani was released from the hospital three weeks after she was shot—which she was not happy about—but she's healing perfectly. The baby is growing just as he should, and even though she's technically supposed to be on bedrest, she still goes to work for a few hours a week, but just lounges around mostly while everyone else works.

She hired two other artists and a new receptionist for when Sara and Harlow take their leave, which is scheduled for a week from now.

Blaze was a mess for a while after Dani was shot, but could you really blame him? What happened was horrible and could have turned out so much worse. But after Dani had had enough of his brooding and extreme over-protectiveness, she gave him a piece of her mind and since then, I think he's been fine. If you ask me, I think he just needed some good sexy, which I have no doubt Dani gave to him freely.

Harlow and Sara didn't get hurt, but they suffered for a few weeks after Dani was shot. They were really scared and worried about Dani and the baby. But after Dani was allowed to come home, they got better too.

Everyone else was just glad that Dani and the baby were okay and life continued on, but things were different. The clubhouse had to be re-done—again, from what I gather—but Michael took that opportunity to add a few new additions. Some for me and him and some for the new babies that were due in a matter of weeks.

Sara's pregnancy has gone well with no problems. Harlow, I wouldn't say there were problems, but when carrying twins, things are always more complicated. She was put on semi-bed rest and is only allowed to work twelve hours a week, but Dani pretty much stopped scheduling her due to Louie always complaining, though Harlow didn't mind. I think she likes spending more time at home with her man and getting the nursery ready for the boys.

Tyke made a full recovery. The swelling went down in his brain almost right away and the tube was removed a few days after the surgery. It was a slow process for his bones to heal, but looking at him now, you'd never know he was beaten almost to death mere months ago.

I didn't know him, only having had met him once, but from what Michael says, he's different now. He's quieter and seems to be on edge. I want to talk to him so badly, to thank him for what he tried to do for me, but I can't seem to find the words. I mean, what do you say to someone who almost died trying to save your life? Michael said he wasn't there for me specifically, but I have to wonder if this wouldn't have happened if he hadn't tried to free me.

Regardless, I still feel responsible and probably will no matter what anyone has to say. I just hope he finds some level of peace and normalcy. I just want him to be all right.

And me? I filled my time with spending every moment I could with Michael. I also had him take me to a place to get a big memorial stone made for the prospect whose name I found out was Tyler. His body was flown back to his family in Tennessee, but Michael had the memorial placed behind the clubhouse. He said it was for everyone, but I think he mainly did it for me.

And then I started planning the baby shower for the girls. Since everything went down, we weren't able to do it when we originally planned, but I think now that things are settled down, it's the perfect time.

I've spent the whole day getting ready for the guests to start arriving so I've barely seen Michael. When he walks in with a bouquet of flowers, a smile is instantly cemented on my face and I couldn't get rid of it if I was paid to.

"Are those for me?" I ask, though I think I know

the answer.

"Oh these?" he asks, motioning to the flowers. "No, baby, they're for my woman I keep on the side. She'll be here soon so you can meet her if you want," he says, but I don't let it phase me. Michael has a demented sense of humor that takes some time to get used to.

"Oh yeah? Well, I hope you or the girls don't mind a bloodbath when she arrives," I say, stepping toward him to take the flowers out of his hands.

"Nah, it'll just add to the thrill of the party."

Kissing his lips, I then slap him lightly on the cheek. "You're too funny," I say, then kiss him again. "Thank you for the flowers. I love them."

"Anything for you, baby."

It's not long after that people start showing up. Usually at a baby or bridal shower, it's just us women, but I thought that since the girls aren't regular women, and neither are their men, that we didn't have to follow those rules. So everyone was invited, men included.

They played around that they were upset that they had to attend, but you could tell they were thrilled they didn't have to spend the day away from their girls. Michael included. I don't think we've spent more than an hour apart since that night. Not that you'll hear me complaining.

The party was a huge hit and the girls were surprised even. I tried my best to keep it all a secret, but I honestly thought they caught on to what I was doing.

When they came in, they all had tears in their eyes and each hugged me tightly. That was probably the highlight of the party for me.

I had the guys grill out so we had everything from burgers and chicken, to steaks. I made a potato salad and I asked Sara for her brownie recipe a few weeks ago, claiming Michael was wanting some, so I made those as well. Louie especially loved those.

After everyone ate, we moved on to the games. I had a hard time finding games I thought everyone would enjoy playing, but I think I did a good job.

We played a drinking game for the men; they had to drink a Jack and Coke out of a baby bottle and whoever finished first won a full bottle of Jack Daniels. I was actually surprised when Michael took the win on that one.

Then we had the guys play a game where they put a balloon under their shirt and they had to untie and tie their shoes. I don't think any of them won that game because they all just slipped their boots off and on, said they don't tie their boots. Everyone got a kick out of it though.

Now, we're on the last game. It's the diaper smelling game. I put a bunch of different foods in diapers and everyone has to be blindfolded and see if they can guess what's in the diaper. We're only on the second diaper and the guys are naming shit that I've never even heard of before, but the girls are getting a kick out of it.

But then suddenly, Harlow lets out a squeal. Louie of course is the first to rush over to her but when he gets there, I think he gets the surprise of a lifetime. "I think my water just broke," she pants.

Louie's quiet for a moment, then he runs around like his head's chopped off. "Shit. Shit! Her fucking water just broke. Her water just broke!" he yells as he's trying to find his truck keys when Michael holds them up for him.

"I think someone else should drive," Harlow says, which earns her a look from Louie, but Sara got a kick out of it.

In fact, she starts laughing so hard, she yells, "I think I just peed my pants." But then she gets a serious look on her face. Toby rushes up to her and takes her hand.

"You okay, Doll?" he asks her.

"Um, you're not going to believe this, but I think my water just broke too."

Now we've got two bikers running around, not sure what the hell to do. This has Blaze laughing so hard he's got tears rolling down his face, calling his brothers morons and jackasses.

Dani elbows him in the chest—hard. "Shut the fuck up and go get the truck. Unless you want to deliver three babies?" she asks with a straight face.

That has him jumping into action and Michael takes off to make sure they don't run each other over.

I hurry over to the girls to check on them. "How are you girls doing? Do you have any contractions yet?" I can't help it. It's the nurse in me. It's unbelievable that both of their waters broke at the same time. Usually that rarely happens until after you get to the hospital. But leave it to this group to do the unimaginable.

"Mine are coming pretty fucking quick and strong," Harlow pants and she looks like she's about ready to have the babies right now.

"Mine are there, but I think we have some time yet," Sara says.

Nodding, I look over to Dani, who is just standing there rubbing her stomach. "Are you in labor too?"

"I'm good, Mama. Help the other two," Dani says, speaking softly. She's taken to calling me Mama and I let her. I kind of like it. Michael loves it.

Michael directs someone to take the twins and that he'll call when it's okay to bring them to the hospital.

A few seconds later, the guys pull up one after the other outside the new clubhouse. I help Harlow in the truck and tell Michael that I'm going with her. She may actually deliver before we get the hospital. So once we get her situated, I tell Louie to go and not worry about traffic laws. Not like he probably would anyway.

I know the men will get Sara and Dani there okay, so I just keep Harlow distracted and make sure she doesn't deliver.

Once we make it to the hospital, Harlow is already dilated to eight centimeters and the doctor says it won't be long now.

The other girls show up a few minutes later and they get taken up to a room. I wish I was up there with them right now, but with all the nurses and doctors, it's probably best I stay out of the way. But it's driving me insane to not be there for them.

***

Mack

As soon as we get to the hospital, Dani starts feeling pain in her stomach, so one of the doctors take her into a room to check her out. They are concerned since she was shot a few months ago and with her being close to her due date, they want to make sure everything is going okay. Turns out, she's going into labor too.

They immediately set her up in one of the birthing rooms. Blaze is a mess, but when Dani holds out her hand with tears in her eyes, he instantly becomes her rock, telling her everything is going to be okay and that soon they'll get to meet their son.

I have no idea who is going to deliver first. I'm in shock that all three of my girls are in labor at the same time. They wheel Harlow into surgery right away since she's having twins and one of them is breech, so a c-section is the best way to go.

Sara is progressing fast but she's going to have a normal delivery. There have been no problems with her pregnancy, so hopefully it stays that way.

About thirty minutes after arriving at the hospital, Louie comes walking out in his scrubs with a big smile on his face. "They're here! Healthy, beautiful little boys."

Me and my brothers all slap him on the back and congratulate him while Rose gives him a big hug.

"Momma is doing fine too. They're cleaning her up now, then they'll bring her back into one of the recovery rooms," Louie informs us of Harlow.

"So what are their names?" I ask after everyone

has given him either a hug or back slap. They wanted to keep that part a secret and it's killing me not to know what to call my grandsons.

"Maxwell Michael and Matthew Henry," he tells us with tears in his eyes. I feel taken aback from their choice of names. I know Matthew was Harlow's brother's middle name, so that makes sense why they named one of their sons after him. But naming the other after me?

The room falls into cheers and everyone congratulates him one more time before he makes his way back to Harlow and his boys.

Louie makes his way over to me, pulling me into a hug. "My father's name was Mike, and he was an amazing dad while he was alive. But after his death, you were the one to pick up the pieces and help me become the man I am today. You've been like a second dad to me, so not only is my son named after my first dad, he's named after my second dad too."

I feel my eyes well up with tears but I don't do anything to stop them from falling. Louie's words hit me right in the heart, but in a good way. When I came across him all those years ago, I only wanted to help him. Maybe I saw a little of myself in his eyes, I don't know, but he called out to me unknowingly and I knew I had to be there for him. And I'm so fucking happy I did.

I couldn't be more fuckin' happier or prouder of him. My boy becoming a father. It's amazing to remember the boy he was when I first found him and the man he is today.

About an hour later, Toby comes into the room with a smile that just about splits his face in two.

"Nevaeh Danielle has arrived. She's six pounds, seven ounces, and as healthy as a horse," he tells us and I can't help but hoot and holler. She's gonna give her daddy a run for his money, just like little Harley did Blaze.

Everyone else yells their congratulations and hugs Toby before he too takes off, back to his girls.

Now, we just wait to hear about Dani and her baby boy. But when an hour passes, I start to get worried. Blaze hasn't been by to update. Did something go wrong? Did they have to take her back after all for a c-section?

Just as I'm getting ready to rain hell down on this hospital until I know what's going on, Blaze comes walking into the room. Unlike the other two men, his face is completely void of all emotions.

Rose gasps and holds her hand over her mouth, fearing the same thing I am.

"Are Dani and the baby okay?" I ask, needing to know what's going on. Dani will be devastated if something happened to the baby. She still has a few hiccups when it comes to how EJ and Harley came into this world.

Blaze is quiet for longer than I'd like and I'm about ready to slap him upside his head when finally I see a smile break out across his ugly mug. "Dani is doing just fine. A little tired, but she's doing great. And little man, he's perfect. Weighing in at eight pounds even."

Now the sad vibe in the room lifts and everyone is smiling again.

"What's his name?" Rose asks.

This time, Blaze doesn't hesitate. "His name is

Wyatt Xavier."

AUTHOR'S NOTE

What's next?

I'm aware that I didn't end this the way I usually do, but I promise, I have good reason. I do plan on writing at least one more book, and even though it's still going to be in this series and about the Forsaken Sinners MC, it's going to be a little different.

The next book is going to be Tyke's story. The Nomad.

I know most of you want Jax's story, but Tyke has been a loud voice in my head since I brought him into the fold. His story is demanding to be told. Who am I to deny him?

Tyke's story is called Claiming Destiny and I'm going to try to release it before the end of the year.

I hope you all are looking forward to getting to know him more and are as excited to read it as I am to write it.

Follow me on Facebook or check out my website for updates on this book.

http://www.facebook.com/AuthorShellyMorgan
www.AuthorShellyMorgan.com

ACKNOWLEDGEMENTS

First of all, I want to thank my family and friends. They've been the ones who have dealt with all the late nights and all the times I was too busy trying to write this book to hang out or take the kids to the park or pool. I know it was long and grueling for you, but thank you for never turning your back on me and always understanding when I had to write. Writing is important to me, but never more important than you all. But knowing that you all stand behind me and support me, it means more than I can ever say.

To my Aunt Tiny Rose. I don't get to see her much, but when she found out I was writing books, she became an instant fan, buying everything I wrote. She kept telling me I needed to write her into one of them soon, and I thought what better book than Mack's? Even though she wanted her character to be "the Wicked Witch of the West" I hope I've made her proud with her character. She's strong and blunt, just like her. I love you, Auntie Rose! Xoxo

To my good friend Blue Remy who was my go-to girl when I needed to make sure my information was correct about the MC life. You never made me feel like I was asking stupid questions and you always explained things so I could understand. Thank you for everything, girl!

I want to thank my publishing company, Limitless Publishing, for continuing to have faith in me and wanting my books. It's a dream come true.

To Toni, who edited this beauty for me. Thank you so much for the time you spent to polish this baby up. I know I've probably driven you crazy with writing gibberish at times or leaving sentences hanging. Sometimes I don't even know what I mean myself, but for you to take my raw words and make them shine is truly amazing. *You* are amazing. Thank you for everything!

To everyone else at Limitless; the team that made this awesome cover to the amazing woman who wrote the back cover blurb. To the marketing department that helps get the word about my books out there and for making kickass graphics to use to promote. You all are rock stars and I thank each and every one of you.

And finally, to my mom and dad. Thank you for being you and supporting my dream with open minds and open arms. I wouldn't be here without you. I love you both! Xoxo

ABOUT THE AUTHOR

I grew up in a small town in Iowa. I have 2 older sisters and amazing parents. Growing up, I was always a daddy's girl, hanging out with him in the garage, fishing, and building stuff. I loved to play softball and swimming, but reading, telling stories, and writing were my passion, even at a young age. I took a break from writing for a while, but you could always find me with a book in my hand.

I have three children–two boys and a girl. They are my whole world. Even when I'm having the worst day ever, they brighten up my day and make me smile.

A few years ago, there was this story that would always play out in my head and no matter how many times I went through it, from beginning to end, it would never fade. So I decided to put it on paper. I didn't plan on publishing it, but when it was almost done, a friend asked to read it. She said it was a story that needed to be shared. And that's what started my writing career.

I love all genres of books, and even though I started with writing MC Romance, I have a whole book of ideas, so you can expect more from me than just MC, though romance is in my blood.

Even though I currently work two jobs, my ultimate dream is to become a full time author. I want to be able to spend my days filling pages with stories. I want to be the reason people find a reason to smile or laugh from lines on a page. Reading a book allows me to live in someone else's shoes, even if only for a few minutes. It's a way to leave my life and troubles behind and I want to be help others do that as well.

Facebook:
http://www.facebook.com/AuthorShellyMorgan

Twitter:
https://twitter.com/Shelly_Morgan34

Website:
http://www.authorshellymorgan.com/

Goodreads:
https://www.goodreads.com/author/show/10914599
.Shelly_Morgan

Join my fan group on Facebook:
https://www.facebook.com/groups/8667258767061
09/

DON'T FORGET...

If you haven't already, check out the first four books in the Forsaken Sinners MC Series.

Rewriting Destiny – Dani and Zane's story and prequel to the series

Fighting Destiny – Toby and Sara's story

Defying Destiny – Louie's story

Born Into Destiny – A Forsaken Sinners MC Series Novella

www.ingramcontent.com/pod-product-compliance
Lightning Source LLC
Chambersburg PA
CBHW052016240626
47153CB00006B/1838